Marsabit

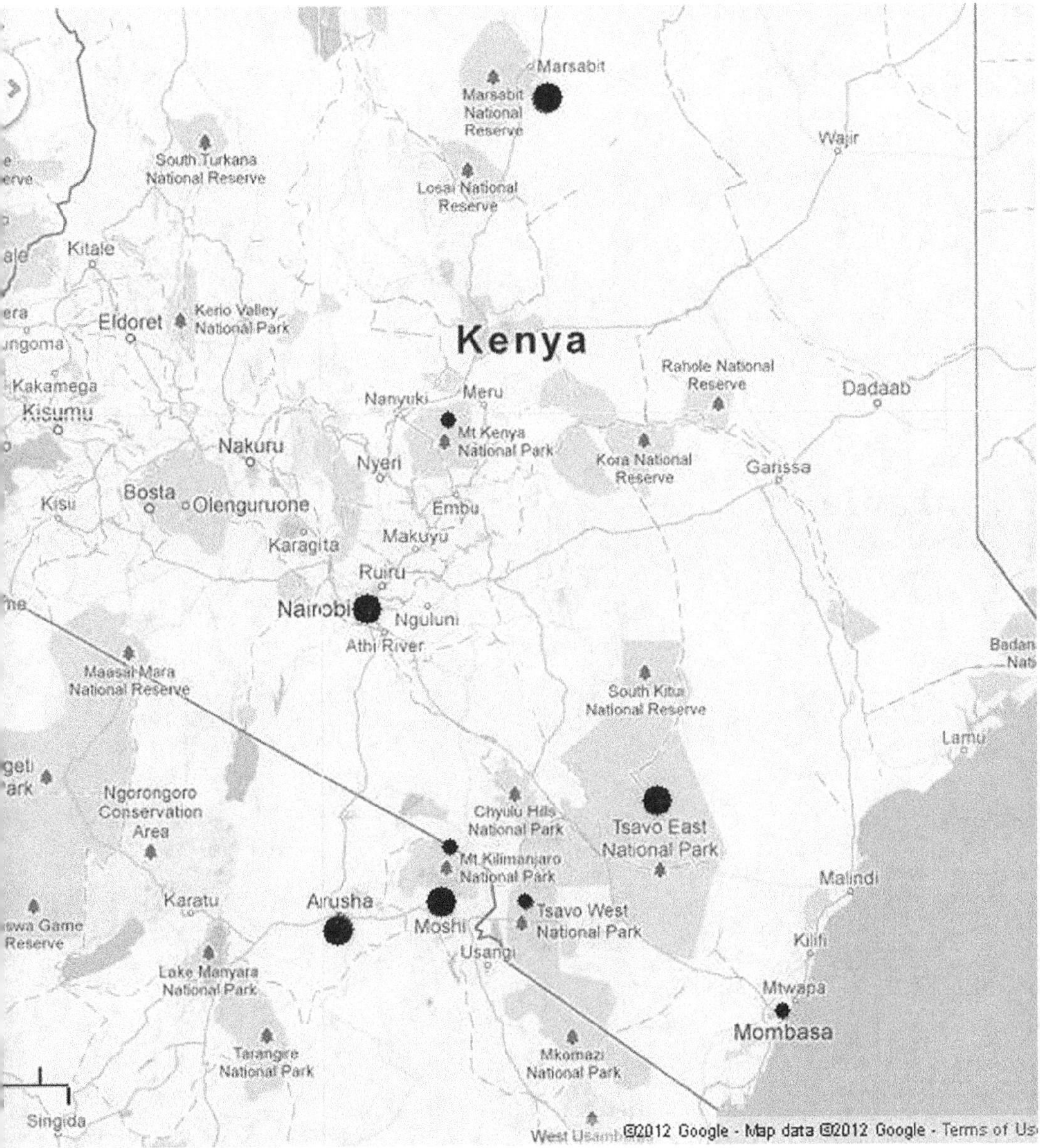

Marsabit
National
Reserve

South Turkana
National Reserve

Wajir

Losai National
Reserve

Kitale

ale

era

Eldoret

Kerio Valley
National Park

ungoma

Kenya

Rahole National
Reserve

Dadaab

Kakamega

Kisumu

Nanyuki

Meru

Nakuru

Nyeri

Mt Kenya
National Park

Kora National
Reserve

Garissa

Kisii

Bosta

Olenguruone

Embu

Karagita

Makuyu

Ruiru

Nairobi

Nguluni

Athi River

South Kitui
National Reserve

Badan
Nat

Lamu

Maasai Mara
National Reserve

geti
ark

Ngorongoro
Conservation
Area

Chyulu Hills
National Park

Tsavo East
National Park

Malindi

Karatu

Mt Kilimanjaro
National Park

Arusha

Moshi

Tsavo West
National Park

Kilifi

iswa Game
Reserve

Lake Manyara
National Park

Usangi

Mtwapa

Mombasa

Tarangire
National Park

Mkomazi
National Park

Singida

West Usamb

@2012 Google - Map data @2012 Google - Terms of Us

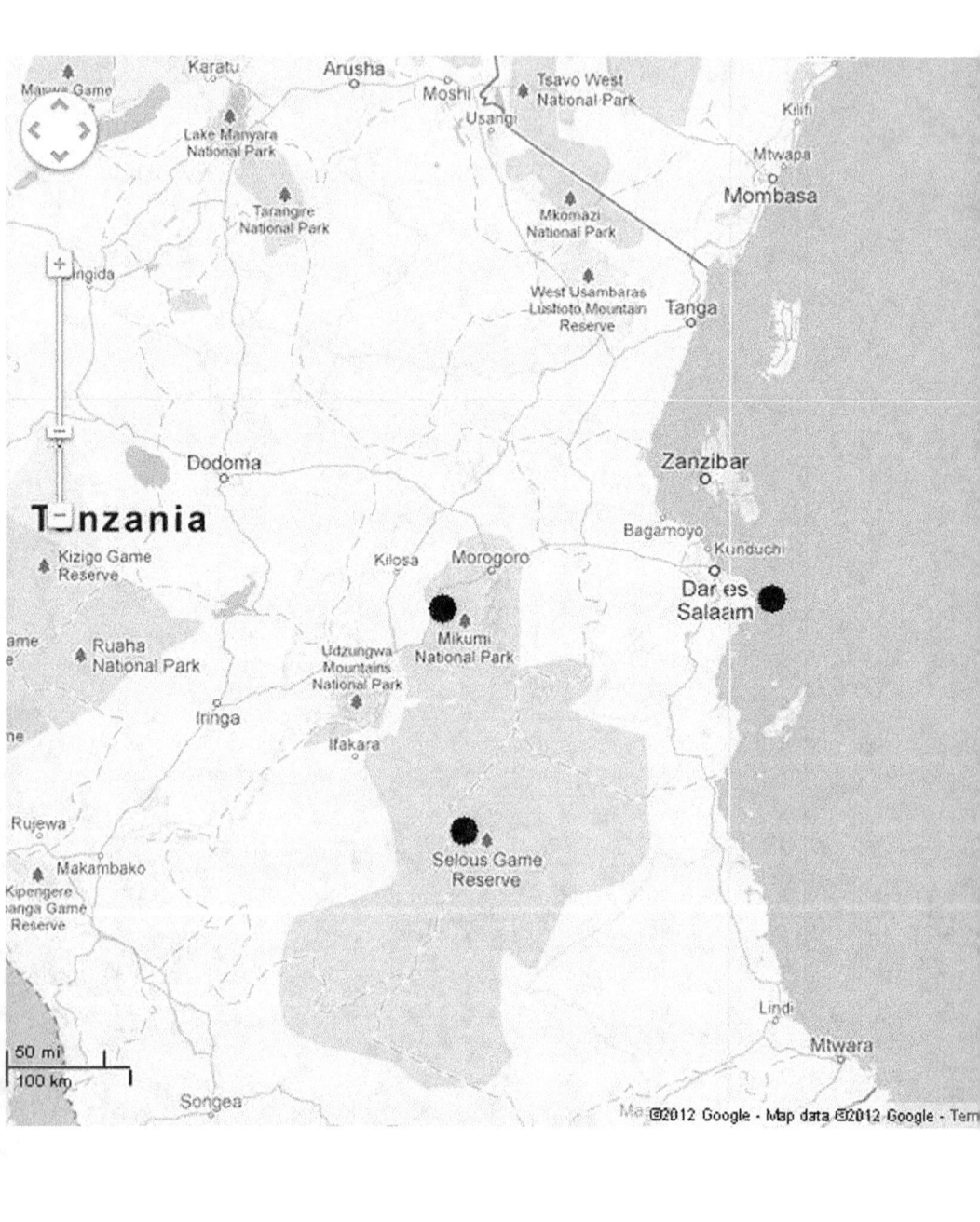

THE
GAMES END

WILLIAM LOUIS GARDNER

296 pp.
Bald Eagle Publishing Co.

This is a work of fiction. Names, characters, places, and incidents either are
the product of the author's imagination or are used fictitiously, and any
resemblance to actual persons, living or dead, business establishments, events, or
locales is entirely coincidental.

Published by Bald Eagle Publishing Co.
P.0. B0X 195
Palm Desert, CA.
92261

e-mail: Bill.elephantwalk.gardner6@gmail.com

ISBN: 0615456545
ISBN-13: 9780615456546

Congratulations on another page-turner.

"William Louis Gardner is a storyteller par excellence. I simply could NOT put his book down. Based on the ture story "Ahmed", a legendary African tusked elephant, recorded as one of the largest and most majestic of the species. The book deals with the illegal slaughter of countless elephants for their ivory tusks. Gardner has woven an exciting tale of intrigue, romance and the pervasive threat of cruelty and greed that plagues the Africa culture to this day.

Tightly written in short explosive chapters, this book allows the reader to experience the complexity and hardship of life for those seeking to protect these precious and unique animals. Based on existing conditions, one is transported to the very heart of the Kenyan society and their frustrating efforts to control this "invasion of destruction".

This struggle for survival and progress however, is joined by the protagonist, Astrid and follows her extraordinary efforts to gain the upper hand in this never-ending struggle.

"The Games End" is an entertaining read and enlightens as well. What a combintion! It has my hearty recommendation."

George B. Levine, PH.D.

Again, the detailed imagery makes the reader view the setting and action as if from through a camera lens. This goes beyond authenticity to a sense of immersion – like going to Africa, not as a tourist, but as a guest of a life-long resident.

The plot twists keep the pace brisk and suspenseful. The prison escape was particularly good.

Ellen Singer's most recent book is "Quicksand".

National treasure is a status that won't protect one from greed. "The Games End" is a novel about Ahmed, a massive tusk elephant in Kenya who captivated Hollywood throughout the 1950s through 1970s. Although he was ordered to be protected from hunters, the allure of this giant prize would not protect him from those who saw only dollars signs. "The Games End" is a riveting novel of adventure, highly recommended.

Reviewed by Small Press Bookwatch: May 2012
Widwest Book Review, James A Cox Editor-in-Chief

Also by William Louis Gardner "Confessions of a Hollywood Agent".

This book has been dedicated to all the people who have gone or want to visit East Africa. With wishes that it brings back again the experience they once had.

One

"Miss Astrid Dryden, the charge you face is that on March fourth nineteen hundred and seventy-four you forced Murani

Farasi into an animal trap and left him to be eaten by wild animals. How do you plead to this charge?" asked the magistrate.

"I'm guilty, sir," said the eighteen year old blonde Astrid, in a small soft voice, looking at the floor.

"In the eyes of the law you're not guilty until the prosecution proves you are," said the magistrate, looking over to the prosecution.

"Do you have any witnesses, Mr. Baku?" he asked.

"Yes, your honor. He cannot be here today. He's badly dehydrated and still in the hospital," answered Mr. Baku.

"Will he be able to attend these proceedings in two weeks?"

"Yes, sir. Trial is set two weeks from today. Bail is twenty thousand shillings. Is there someone in the court who will pay the bail?" he asked as he looked at Helmut Dryden.

Helmut, in his forties, knew his daughter had gone over the edge. He'd seen it coming for some time. Her love of wild animals had completely taken over her life and now it had become a nightmare. He got up and stood tall, and then walked to the court clerk. Pushing back the dark blonde straight hair from his high forehead, he wrote a check for the bail. Helmut was fearful Astrid

1

would be charged with attempted murder for what she had done, but the man was a known poacher, and the magistrate, Malcolm, had known Helmut and Astrid as old friends. Their fathers had served in the German East African army together, which brought Helmut's father from Germany to fight the English in the Kaiser's War in 1917.

Helmut saw Malcolm use his power to protect Astrid from being charged with a major crime for which she could have been sent to prison; or, if the poacher had died, even hanged.

The Magistrate looked to Mr. Baku.

"Next case."

The rear door opened and a guard led a chained *Liangulu* tribesman into the courtroom. He stood before the Magistrate in torn khaki shirt and shorts wearing sandals made with old tires for soles. The poacher was tall, had powerful biceps and the chest muscles of a bowman. His face had the look of hard dark granite. He looked down at the floor. The smell of his body had the odor of the wild animals he lived among filled the room.

"You're charged with killing an elephant in a National Park. How do you plead?" asked the magistrate. The guard, who was the interpreter, repeated the question in *Liangulu* dialect.

"Guilty, your honor," he said in *Luiangulu*. The guard repeated the answer to the magistrate.

"How was the elephant killed?"

"I killed him with bow and arrow from thirty paces," said the poacher.

Helmut sat back down in the courtroom and waited for Astrid to be released from the heavy iron shackles and chains while he listened to the testimony going on before him.

Helmut pictured the scene in his mind. He had often witnessed the bravery of these *Liangulu* tribesmen, knowing their poisons were more potent than any death sentence known to man. The ingredients were a guarded secret of the tribe. In Helmut's mind he saw the giant elephant coming toward the man. The great beast's ears moved back and forth, creating its own wind as it charged the brave hunter standing alone before it. Helmut could smell the creature's foul odor and breath as it got closer. The huntsman warrior with only a bow and arrow to protect him moved not a muscle as the mighty wild animal charged him. He saw the man as he drew back the long bow with all the power and strength of his muscled body, his arm letting the arrow fly forward to its precise target, stopping the elephant dead in its tracks.

The fatal arrow entered through the tough hide to the elephant's spleen. The stunned beast tried to loosen the poison shaft by frantically throwing its massive head back and forth, but in a few minutes the elephant would fall to the ground with an earth-moving thud, its massive body reeling, shuddering with spasms as the poison reached its heart.

Helmut's thoughts came back to the courtroom as the magistrate continued to question the poacher.

"Who were you going to sell the ivory to?"

"No one, sir, I need meat for family."

"You know it is illegal to kill game in a National Park?"

"But, Mister, family hungry".

"That's no excuse. You could have killed an impala for that. Killing an elephant tells me you were going to sell its ivory. You're to receive twenty lashes, and be flogged before the prisoners at the stockade, so they know of your crime and witness your punishment," said the magistrate as he wiped his wide black face.

Astrid stood up to leave. She looked dwarfed between the uniformed Tanzanian Park Rangers as they released her. Her china-blue eyes looked swollen and tear-filled as she left the courtroom with Helmut following her. The color came back to her high wide cheeks as she took a large white handkerchief from a pocket of her khaki shorts and wiped the tears away. She stepped outside the bright bougainvillea-covered courthouse in the small village of Moshi, Tanzania, to her father's Land Rover and got into the passenger side. Helmut sat next to her and drove on to the road to Kibo. A cool breeze came up after a light rain shower, and ahead they could see Mount Kilimanjaro as the clouds opened to reveal its glorious existence. Neither of them said anything as they gazed at the great snow-covered spectacle before them.

Helmut broke the silence.

"Why did you do what you did? You were lucky today. You could receive twenty lashes."

Two

"**D**ad. What do you think they'll do to me? I could go to prison couldn't I?"

"Malcolm protected you, but who knows what will happen when we go back to court when that poacher gets in front of the Magistrate to tell his story. You need a barrister. I have no idea who that will be. I never used one."

"I know someone in Nairobi."

"No, better a Tanzanian. I'll ask Malcolm, he should be able to help us. There's too much trouble between our countries right now. We can't keep our borders open. We'll find someone in Dar es Salaam." Helmut came to a fork in the road. A sign pointed to Arusha. He turned.

"Aren't we going back to the lodge?" asked Astrid.

"Ian is waiting for me at Ranger Headquarters. He has a job for me. We're taking a helicopter ride to Selous to check on an elephant herd."

"Selous, I've always wanted to see Selous. How exciting."

"I'm asking you again, why did you put that poacher in his trap?" Astrid took a deep breath.

"Dad, when you raise a motherless animal from birth, you get attached. I saw how poachers had killed sixty elephants when I went to see Mark at Tsavo Park. Bloated bodies in the hot sun, the smell, their tusks pulled. I'll never forget it. I've had nightmares because of it. Poachers are my enemy. I'll help anyone or any cause to stop their killing." Astrid looked over at her father as he drove along the two-lane road. She continued.

"Seeing Susie in that poacher trap, her carcass half eaten, her tiny tusks pulled. I wanted revenge, and took it. I have no remorse. I know it's terrible, but I can't help the way I feel."

"Astie, if your mother had lived she would have been proud of the way you grew up, but she wouldn't understand this streak of cruelty, nor do I. I'm lucky to have you, but I want to keep you. The idea of you going to prison or being stripped and flogged in public. I couldn't bear it."

"Don't worry, Dad. I'm a white woman. They don't do that to white women."

"Don't count on it. The Blacks have the power. Africanization is upon us. Look what they did to the East Indians, most lived their lives here; overnight they took their properties, their businesses, and made them refugees."

Helmut turned the Land Rover off the highway on to a red dirt road and parked in front of a one-story stucco building. The sign at the entrance said, "Ranger Headquarter, Arusha District." A few dirt-covered vehicles stood parked in the driveway. The *Tanzanian* flag flew open with the small breeze. Helmut got out of the car. Astrid could see a helicopter waiting on a pad, the name "GAME WARDEN" painted in big black letters.

"Wait here, I'll let them know I'm here," said Helmut as he entered the building.

Astrid remained seated. What a mess. Why does everything have to happen at the same time? She thought. Jim Fielding arriving in two days with his film crew. Dad off on safari with an American magazine publisher, and now I could go to jail. "Piss pot!" She murmured to herself.

Helmut came out of the headquarters building followed by Ian Parker, the head game warden, wearing a green uniform on his stocky frame. He looked no stranger to the outdoors with his creased face and sun-bleached sandy hair. Another middle-aged man followed, wearing glasses, khakis and a droopy khaki hat. Astrid left the Land Rover to join them.

"Ian, you know my daughter, Astrid. Astrid, this is Doctor Menzes. He's an ecologist under contract to the Tanzanian government."

"Hello, Ian." Astrid gave her hand to Ian and turned to Dr. Menzes.

"Nice to meet you." Astrid knew Ian and everyone in the area had heard about what she did to the poacher. No one said they thought she was right doing what she did, but underneath, she thought, they admired her for her courage.

"Let's get on with it," said Ian as he turned and walked toward the helicopter, the others following.

After a thirty-minute trip south from Arusha, the helicopter came upon an open dry-looking area of trampled trees and grass that cut a swath through what once was a thick forest. Up ahead a herd of about thirty elephants stood. The copter circled to have a look. Ian pointed.

"See, Helmut, even from the air the herd looks weak." The elephants moved around, looking confused, but not running off.

The helicopter landed not far from the herd. Astrid could see that most of them look sick. When Dr. Menzes got off the copter he bent down and picked up some dirt and let it fall from his hand.

"Ian, Look! This dirt can't support much more elephant grazing. The vegetation is turning to desert," said Dr. Menzes.

"You're saying you want us to cull the herd?" Asked Ian.

Astrid shot Helmut a do-you-want-this-to- happen? Look.

"Yes. Their numbers need to be reduced. My calculation would be between one hundred to one fifty head," said Menzes. Astrid was shocked by his answer.

Ian looked to Helmut.

"I need your help. My boys are too green for this job. I need an old pro. The government will give you a contract," said Ian.

Astrid pulled Helmut aside out of ear shot.

"You're not going to do it, Dad?"

Helmut pulled away and looked to Ian. "Can I bring a client? He's an American looking for a big tusker."

"If he's a good shot we can use him," replied Ian.

"Don't mention this around. There're animal lovers who don't think much of this plan but it has to be done to save the others," said Dr. Menzes.

"Dad, get out this business. You're not hunting anymore–you're slaughtering," said Astrid so no one but Helmut could hear.

"What will I do? I know of nothing else. It's my life's work." said Helmut.

"You can work on photo safaris. You're known in the film world. They don't kill. They shoot, but its film," Astrid said looking into Helmut's eyes.

Ian and Dr. Menzes had gotten back in the helicopter. Ian yelled to them. "Hey, you two. It will be dark soon. Let's go."

"We're coming," yelled Helmut "You and I will talk later." Helmut and Astrid boarded the copter. Ian lifted it off the ground and turned north.

The Land Rover turned off the main road. A sign up ahead read, "*MOUNT KILIMANJARO SAFARI LODGE & TENTED CAMP.* HELMUT & ASTRID DRYDEN PROPRIETORS. Helmut turned the Land Rover onto a gravel road and drove by large aviaries full of exotic birds, stockades filled with impalas, zebras, and two giraffes, who moved around their compounds waiting impatiently to be fed. Up ahead, a black rhino rubbed against a post behind a pole fence as they passed. A lion roared as they drove up to the front of a one-story African log lodge and stopped. Across from the lodge stood two rows of green canvas tents lined in a straight formation under a group of umbrella-shaped acacia trees.

Helmut parked the Land-Rover. They got out and walked up the steps to the lodge entrance when a chimpanzee ran to Astrid and jumped on her. The chimp wrapped its arms around Astrid's neck like a baby.

Helmut smiled.

"I've been thinking of what you said. The trip to Selous could be my last safari. See you at dinner." said Helmut as he walked off.

"You'd make me very happy, Dad." Astrid yelled after him. An African in a white gown came running after the chimp.

"*Molo*, take Ingrid." Astrid started sneezing. "I'm having an allergy attack. Find my medicine."

Molo had been Astrid and Helmut's African servant for many years, and had helped with the rearing of Astrid since she was a small child. He dressed in a white *kanus*, a long dress-like gown worn by many East Africans, and a red *fez*. He took the chimp and said, "The ostrich, he chase her around, Mama. She no let her be since you go."

"Catch her and put her in her cage."

"Yes, Mama. Is Mama go prison?" asked *Molo* with a concerned look.

"I hope not."

"*Bwana* Mark, he here. In Mama's cabin. He say tell no one."

"*Molo* go. Look for Mama's medicine."

Molo ran off with the chimp.

Astrid wondered about Mark. Usually he would have called to let her know about a visit. She went to the mirror by the door and looked at herself. Her eyes were still swollen. They reminded her of a Mexican *Chihuahua* dog she had once seen in *Nairobi*. She pulled back her straight bright blonde hair and fastened it with a barrette. She reached into the pocket of her khaki shorts and took out a lipstick and applied some. She pinched her cheeks to bring out the color, and took out a handkerchief and blew her nose. It was the best she could do, she thought, and left the lodge for her cabin next door.

The cabin had been built from logs that matched the main lodge. It had a screen porch to keep out the bugs and flies around the camp because of the animals. She opened the door. The room was dark. The curtains were pulled.

"Mark."

The door to her bedroom opened and Mark Livingston, stood six feet, on the threshold. His dark blonde hair, worn long, fell on his thin suntanned face where premature lines surrounded his blue-green eyes from all the time spent in the sun. He looked serious and apprehensive. As if he had lost his boyhood from the last time she had seen him.

"They're after me. I told you about the illegal poaching going on in *Tsavo* Park"

Astrid looked at him and nodded.

"They found out that I know who they are. They're going to kill me like they did Lucas, my friend. Can you hide me until I find a way out of East Africa? I wouldn't bloody well ask, but you're the only one I can trust."

Three

Astrid tried to calm Mark. He kept pacing, listening for any sound he didn't recognize.

"I can't stay here. It's the first bloody place they'll look for me. Do you have any ideas? Somewhere no one goes."

"The hotel has a hut on Kilimanjaro for guests who want to climb the mountain. You can stay there. It's comfortable. Nobody would find you." Astrid took Mark's soiled khaki shirt he had removed from his sweating lithe body. "I'll have *Molo* wash your shirt and get you some warm clothes. It's cold up on the mountain at night."

"Thank you, Astie. I have another favor to ask. Would you get word to Minister P.D. Mnazi in Nairobi that I have the information he needs? I've been working for him undercover. He's the only one in the bloody government who can stop the poaching in *Tsavo*. He's not afraid of the president's corrupt family and the *Kenyan* people like him. He wants to be our president and is willing to take action to stop the illegal ivory trade."

"Mark, you won't be able to come back to *Kenya*. Why do you want to get involved? Wouldn't it be easier to forget what you saw?"

"I'll come back when P.D. is president. Who knows? He could make me head game warden. You know what a bloody purist I am. I can't stand by and watch the elephants annihilated because some

11

greedy blokes in the President's family want to make a profit on their ivory." The phone rang. Astrid picked it up.

"Hello. Yes, Dad. I'll be right over." She hung up. "There's a call for me from London. Stay here. I'll bring you back some dinner. We'll leave the first thing in the morning."

Mark grabbed her as she was leaving the room. He took her in his arms and tried to kiss her on the mouth. Astrid felt his smooth youthful skin against hers, but decided not to let him. She moved her face to the side.

Mark looked disappointed.

"I'm still nowhere, huh? I hoped you'd change your mind about me. You know how much I love you. After our first time I always hoped it would be forever."

"Mark, I do like you, but I'm not ready to get serious. Please, try to understand. I want to see and do more in my life before I make a commitment. You know I have plans to go to England and get a degree in animal behavior."

"Why? You know more than most teachers."

"Nobody listens to you today unless you have a degree, and I need to get away. I've only seen Nairobi and Dar es Salaam and, besides, we're both in serious trouble. I haven't told you of what might be in store for me. This is no time to get involved in a love affair." Astrid looked up into Mark's clear blue-green eyes and saw the hurt. She gave him a kiss on the cheek and left the cabin.

Astrid ran into the lobby and off to a small office behind the front desk.

"*Ja*, she's here." Helmut handed her the telephone. Astrid hadn't met Jim Fielding, but she knew him through his reputation.

"Hello," said Astrid as she took the phone from Helmut.

"It's Jim Fielding. Are you ready for us?"

"Yes, Jim, everything's arranged. I'll be at the airport in Nairobi to meet you when you arrive. I talked to a ranger in Marsabit. He said the elephant, Ahmed, was seen in the area last week."

"Good news. Your dad told me some wonderful stories about you. We'll finally meet." Astrid smiled and looked at her father.

"I look forward to meeting you, too, Jim," said Astrid and hung up. "What's Jim Fielding like, Dad?" she asked, interested.

"American. He knows what he wants and he gets it. I liked his wife, too, but she wrote and told me they're divorced. She'd been a big help to him. Smart as they get. You be careful with Jim, he has a way with women."

"Dad, you never said anything like that before. Don't worry. I think I know what men are all about."

Four

Jim hung up the telephone in his hotel room at the London Governor House and looked out his window onto Hyde Park and saw the rain falling again. He liked London, but the rain always bothered him. This time of year he knew he couldn't escape it. His room felt cold. The radiator by the window gave only a small amount of heat. No one seemed to be bothered by the rain in London. If he lived here year-round, he thought he might adjust to it, but he looked forward to the climate in East Africa. Never a problem in Kenya, making a film there was uncomplicated. The light was the best and the sun always out. He finished unpacking one bag with the few clothes he could wear around London. He kept his other bag packed. The phone rang.

A director friend of Jim from Hollywood was in London also preparing for a film in Africa was on the phone.

"It's Tony. I'm glad I caught up with you. I need a guide for Tanzania. You must know someone I can call. I'm taking a 2nd unit film crew there." "When will you go?" asked Jim. "In three weeks" "My man is busy then. But call him. I just talked to him. His name is Helmut Dryden. Here's his number". Jim looks into his black phone book. "His number there is 255 306 7127.

"Where are you filming? Will I see you? Asked Tony.

"I doubt it. I'll be in Northern *Kenya.*

15

"Too bad. Well, good luck on your film, Buddy. I'll see you back in Hollywood. Jim hung up. The phone rang again when he put it down.

It was Graham Linley, Jim's English cameraman.

"Hello, lad, I'm picking you up at seven for dinner. I'm bringing a lady who wants to meet you. She says she's a fan. Her name is Lady Anne Conway, an absolutely delightful girl who's spent time in Kenya. You don't mind, do you?"

"Hell no. Graham. Sounds great. I'll meet you in the lobby. Bye." Jim looked at his watch. He'd have a couple of hours' rest before dinner. He went to the window, pulled the curtains, and lay down and covered himself with a blanket. He was experiencing jet lag. He wanted to sleep, but couldn't. Lorraine kept coming into his thoughts. It was the first film location he had been on without her. She'd made it easy in the past, handled everything. We were a good team, he thought. If it hadn't been my seven-year itch, I'd still be with her. I can't blame her. I was wrong.

His thoughts went back to how they met in film school at University of Southern California, in Los Angeles. They were in their first year. Lorraine had grown up in the Disney Studio atmosphere, a tight little group of dedicated cartoonists with Walt Disney as their leader and friend. Her father, an early animation man, worked for Walt. Jim had found out about Lorraine's background and had made a point to meet her. Lorraine, a pretty girl of eighteen, with long brown hair and soft brown eyes which made him feel warm, was easy to have a conversation with. He got her to talk shop about the movie business because he wanted to know everything, and Lorraine had first-hand information. Jim, a curious person, needed to know about any subject he didn't have knowledge of, except religion. Not that he didn't know about religion. He knew more than most people. He wasn't interested, but he did believe in God.

Lorraine fell hard when she met him. She loved his looks, his boyish manners, his thick dark hair which never seemed to have a part and his heavy beard, which always looked like he needed to shave. His quick, full smile and fast wit gave her a soft feeling of love and magic. Jim had a way with women. He put on a great show when he met a pretty girl. He impressed them with his bright mind and he knew how to get them to like him. He had been an only child. His mother and father divorced when he was five, and his mother married again to a wealthy oil-man who, like herself, spent a lot of time getting drunk. As a child, Jim was left alone to play by himself. He liked to read and spent most of his youth with his head stuck in a book. He hadn't known his father and he never liked his step-father. When he was in his early teens, his mother divorced and remarried Jim's real father again. Jim tried to get to know him, but he was cold and they had nothing in common. His father was a hunter. Jim hated hunting. His father kept horses. Jim tolerated horses. His father was opinionated. Jim was open to anything that he thought would interest him. He especially liked wild animals and secretly kept a few in his mother's basement. Until one night his pet alligator started bellowing, frightening his mother into hysteria. The basement was cleared out the next day.

Jim's mother adored her only child. She would stick up for him and took his side if his father became annoyed because Jim didn't share in his interests. She had a drinking problem. Not enough to make her not function, she slurred her words when she was drinking. This was something both Jim and his father had accepted. She was a sweet woman who never said anything to upset anyone. Besides Jim's interest in books and wild animals, he became fascinated with cameras. His mother bought him anything he wanted. Photography became second nature. He knew that someday film-making would become his life's work.

In their last year at school, Lorraine became pregnant. They got married in her third month. The wedding took place at Lorraine's parent's house in Hollywood. Even Walt Disney came.

Jim had to go to work, but couldn't find a job in the movie industry. They were difficult to get even if you had connections. Especially, if you had only school experience. To make money, he took a job as a landscaper. He went out on interviews when he got word of any opening. Lorraine promoted him with different people whom she knew through her family. One of her father's friends, who did documentary films, told them National Geographic had plans to start a television series formatted on their magazine. Jim had made a documentary on sea lions that lived on the Channel Islands off the California coast, while he was at USC for his senior film project. It was well received by his peers for he had put drama into the film about the life of a herd, which no one had done before. With that original concept, Jim got the job doing film assignments.

Lorraine gave birth to a little girl, but was left alone most of the time with Jim gone. On one of his films in Uruguay, Jim came back with a venereal disease. He told Lorraine while on location he had to relieve himself and when he crouched down and dropped his pants, a pampas spider stung him on the end of his penis. Lorraine loved him enough to never let on she knew he lied. Jim could tell a good story, and from then on Lorraine became Jim's film assistant. She, the baby, and the Mexican nanny traveled the world making documentary films.

The phone rang. He looked at the clock by his bed. It was seven as he answered.

"We're in the lobby," said Graham.

"I'll be right down."

Five

Jim walked off the elevator into the lobby. Graham Linley stood by the entrance to the bar talking to a beautiful tall brunette. Jim immediately knew he liked her.

"Jim, meet Lady Anne Conway." Anne put out her hand and Jim took it as he looked her over.

"Happy to meet you. Graham told me you lived in Kenya."

"Yes, I spent time in my youth. An uncle has a farm in the highlands near Nanyuki. Do you know the area?"

"Indeed. A wonderful climate."

"Why don't we sit in the bar and have a drink before we go on to the Clermont, said Graham. He directed them into the bar and over to a table. A waiter came and took their order.

"I've known Anne and her family for years. We'd lived in the same village in Yorkshire. We ran into one another last week and I told her what I was doing, about going with you to Kenya to shoot a film, and she immediately wanted to meet you because of her interest in mountain gorillas," said Graham.

"I hope you don't mind. I'm fascinated with your film on gorillas. They seemed to be so gentle when they get used to you. I had a chance to go to Rwanda to study them with Dian Fossey, but was never able to because of family commitments. I always felt I missed out on a great opportunity," she said.

"You don't seem like you'd be interested in roughing it. It's a difficult terrain to function in and it rains constantly. I felt like I was a rain forest plant and was starting to grow and bloom. Dian Fossey could be difficult. You wouldn't have got on with her. You seem too much of a lady."

"Is that a compliment? I'll take it as one. Are you always so direct with your observations, Mr. Fielding?"

"I'm honest. It saves time. Do you work?"

"Yes, I'm an interior decorator."

Graham interrupted them. "I have dinner reservations at the *Clermont,* and if we're not there on time they'll give our table away. Shall we go?" He got up from the table. Anne and Jim followed.

The cab dropped them off in front of the Clermont. The rain hadn't stopped. They ducked under the extended canopy as the doorman opened the door and they entered the lobby. At eight o' clock the club was crowded. Jim took off his raincoat and hat and gave them to the coat-room attendant. He helped Anne with hers. She wore an off-the-shoulder dress in deep blue which accentuated her violet-blue eyes, her long raven hair and the whiteness of her perfect English skin. Jim looked out of place in his clothes: a long-sleeved cotton jacket, a flowered tie and corduroy pants. He looked especially noticeable because of the way Anne and Graham and the other patrons of the club were dressed, the men in tailored suits and the women in designer gowns. The *Clermont* was a posh gambling club on Berkeley Square connected to the chic night club Annabelle's in Mayfair and had a reputation as being the gathering place for the fashionable crowd from all over the world. You could run into anyone of name value who visited London. The wagers ran big and the food was gourmet. Lady Anne loved to go there because of the atmosphere, and it was a good place to find clients for her decorating business. She knew the staff; and Rene, the maitre d' who she confided in, would let her know who was who in the room. The way he acted toward her you could tell he was impressed with her title.

They walked into the expansive foyer of black and white marble floors with a giant French crystal chandelier that hung from the plaster-molded ceiling that reflected blue-white light like melting drops from an icicle. A free-standing curlicue black wrought iron banister, with a gold railing, supported the staircase to the gambling room and lounge on the second floor.

Rene, the maitre d', greeted them at the entrance of the opulent dining room. Lady Anne gave him her hand. He bowed to her and escorted them to a table on the far end of the room.

"Anne comes here often," Graham told Jim. "Some of the patrons are her clients. They're mostly *nouveau riche*. They like the idea of someone titled decorating their homes. It makes them feel important when they tell their friends." Graham helped Anne with her chair.

Jim and Anne exchanged looks of mutual interest.

Rene handed out menus. "The *Filets de Poisson Gratines, Gratines, a la Parisienne* are very good today, your ladyship." said Rene.

"That sounds divine, Rene. That's for me, and a green salad with vinaigrette dressing," she said.

Jim asked. "What's that you're having?"

"It's fish filets poached in white wine with a cream and egg yolk sauce."

"It's too rich for me," said Jim. To Rene, "Do you have a steak?"

"*Oui, Monsieur.* The *Tornedos Rossini* is excellent and *bifteck saute` Bernaise* or *Filet Mignon* are always good, *Monsieur.*"

"I'll have a plain steak, nothing on it, charred well, with a baked potato. And you can bring me a green salad," said Jim.

Anne looked over at Graham who was still looking at the menu.

"Have you decided Graham?"

"I'll have the *Boeuf Bourguignon*," said Graham.

"Very good. Here's the wine list and I will be back." Rene took their menus and went off towards the kitchen.

"I had this thought in the cab that Anne could come with us to *Kenya*, Graham. I need a stand-in for my leading lady. She could do the doubling for her," said Jim.

Anne and Graham exchanged looks. "The money's good. All expenses. What do you say?"

"Are you asking me or Graham?" said Anne.

"You, of course, Anne."

"When do you have to have an answer?"

"In a few days."

"Can you tell me about the film?" asked Anne.

"It has a "*Moby Dick*" theme. The protagonist hunts down an old large tusked elephant in Kenya. The elephant charged as he was trying to shoot it. The hunter missed getting the animal in the heart so the elephant was able to continue the charge. It picked him up and threw him fifty feet. The fall crippled him. He recovered, but was maimed for life. He wanted revenge. He was obsessed about going back to even the score. Every day he thought about killing the elephant. His hate drove his family away. Only his wife faithfully stood by him, but he abuses her for it. He goes back to *Kenya* to hunt down the elephant, but in the end the elephant triumphs by killing him."

"It sounds like Hemingway could have written it," said Anne.

"I wrote it. I stole it from Melville. It's the Hollywood formula picture. After you've see a few, they seem the same. But Hollywood gives the money. They've been proven box-office draws."

Anne looked at Jim with new interest.

"I'd be a fool not to take you up on your invitation. I think I could get my affairs sorted out."

"Great. Let's have some champagne to celebrate," said Jim as he looked around for a waiter.

Anne looked over to the far side of the room and saw someone she knew. She got up from the table. Jim and Graham stood up. "One of my Arab clients is sitting over there," she continued. "He's been ignoring my statements. I'm going to asked him if he liked the job. Would you excuse me," she said as she left the table.

Jim and Graham sat back down. "Graham, what are you doing to me? She's beautiful. What is your relationship with her?"

"I told you we grew up together. Her family was our landlord. It's a sad story. Her father, the earl, lost all of the family money gambling. When the creditors took his property it killed him. It was in the family for hundreds of years. There were some rumors that he took his own life. Anne rebelled. She got into the sixties culture. Dope, Beatles, free love, flower child, you name it, she did it. She married an artist. She's out of that now. She had to go to work. She took a job with one of England's most revered interior designers and now she's on her own. I can't believe she said she'd go with us to *Kenya*. Something's going on between you two, isn't it?"

"You said she's out of her marriage. What do you mean?"

"She's still married, but her husband, Alex, is a nut. She doesn't live with him. They have some kind of open marriage. She never talks about it or him." answered Graham. They looked up.

Anne returned to the table and the waiter arrived with the champagne. She sat down and the waiter opened the bottle and poured their glasses full.

Anne picked up her glass and said. "First, I would like to drink to a very special new friend, to you Jim and to luck with your new film. And to our Kenyan adventure, a magical land of the born free."

They lifted their glasses for a toast. "To Kenya."

Anne thought, how am I going to get Alex to let me go?

Six

Clay Nobertson sat in his glass high-rise office building in downtown Manhattan. Hunting trophies from trips around the world hung, stood and sat everywhere. A large pair of elephant tusks framed the fireplace. An enormous grizzly bear skin lay on the floor in front of the fireplace hearth. In the corner of the room stood a polar bear looking in Clay's direction with a menacing expression. A wall of mounted animals' heads included a buffalo, a lion, a water buck, a wart hog and a *Bengal* tiger. On the other wall was a glass gun case with a collection of hunting rifles. An elephant's-foot wastebasket sat on the side of his French antique ormolu desk.

Clay had the phone at his ear talking to someone. He played with a long thin object that a taxidermist had made from a penis of a rhinoceros. He used it as a whip or a pointer. In his fifties, he was overweight, with thinning black hair, thick black eyebrows and black eyes that shifted back and forth when he talked. He wore his shirt open, exposing a tee shirt underneath and tufts of black hair that protruded from under the neckline. His voice and his body movements gave the impression of a man in charge.

"Nick, where's that ammo? I'm leaving for Africa in two days and you still haven't delivered. If you expect my magazine to do a story for you, you'd better get your ass over here. My editor from

"Guns & Targets" needs to test it first at the firing range. You know I'm not in the habit of asking twice." Clay slapped the whip down on his desk and hung up.

He reached over and punched the intercom.

"Miss Taylor, have my son Tim come to my office and see if you can find Helmut, my white hunter in *Tanzania*." He glanced at the international date clock on his desk. "Now is a good time to get him. It's about nine o' clock there." Clay moved his hand up to his neck holding it as he took his pulse. He got up and walked over to an oriental cabinet and opened the door to a concealed bar. He picked up a bottle of pills from a glass shelf and opened the bottle. He spilled out two pills and threw them into his mouth. He took a bottle of scotch whiskey, poured some in a glass, and gulped the pills.

There was a knock at the door.

"Come in."

Tim, Clay's youngest son, walked in. Tim was slight in his middle twenties, had short hair and was wearing steel-rimmed glasses and a business suit. Tim had always been intimidated by his father, but managed to conceal it.

"I had Nick on the phone. He's getting the ammo here today. Sit down." Clay said.

Tim sat in a straight-backed English chair that was covered in leopard skin.

Clay leaned back on his oversized ostrich leather chair, picked up the rhino whip and slid it through his left hand, stroking it out of habit.

"I don't have to tell you the circulation is off on "Guns & Targets". We need a special interest story for the January issue, hunting for the world's largest tusked elephant in Africa."

"That's a great idea, Dad. We'll put his picture on the front cover."

The intercom buzzed. Clay punched the button. "Yes."

"Mr. Norbertson, I have Helmut Dryden on line three from Tanzania," said Miss Taylor.

Clay put the phone on speaker for both to hear.

"Helmut, how goes it? I sent you my schedule."

"Yes, Mr. Nobertson. I'll be waiting at the airport in Dar-es-Salaam. You're in luck. I got us in on an event that has never to my knowledge happened before. The Tanzania Game Department has organized a hunt in the Selous. The elephant have overpopulated the reserve. They plan on culling the herd. You should be able to get a big trophy." Clay smiled at Tim.

"Helmut. I want the biggest elephant trophy that lives today. I'm spending a ton of money to find that animal and I am bringing my son, who's the editor of "*Guns* & *Targets*", to write a story on the hunt. You're sure that kind of elephant lives in or around Selous?"

"Mr. Norbertson."

"Call me Clay."

"Clay, Selous has the largest concentration of wild animals left in the world today. It is mammoth. Over twenty two thousand square miles. There are over a million wild animals living in and around Selous."

"I'm counting on you. I hear you're good. I consider myself the best big-game hunter in the world. We should be a good team. I'm bringing ammo no one has used before. I'm sure you'll arrange to have some good target practice. I'll splatter those critters. Do you get what I'm saying?" asked Clay.

There was a hesitance in Helmut's voice.

"I think I do," said Helmut.

"Good man. I'll see ya in Dar es *Salaam* on the seventh. Bye." Clay hung up.

"We're in for some fun. I can't wait to sight my rifle on that big one. I see his tusks already in my new game room. Report back to me after you used the ammo. And tell Miss Taylor to have Dorothy Marks of "*Teen Bop*" come to my office." Clay went back to looking at financial sheets on his desk as Tim left his office. This trip should put the scent of kill into that kid, Clay thought.

Seven

Astrid woke at six-thirty. She felt Marks's warm body next to her as she looked at his sleeping face. She argued with herself, why did I let him sleep with me? It makes me feel guilty when I tell him no, but I hate feeling guilty about sex. I know he loves me. So what's a little sex going to hurt?

Astrid eased herself out of bed, went into the bathroom and turned on the shower. At the equator the day starts at seven and ends at seven because the sun dictates. There's never any deviation; it's always the same. It would take at least a day to hike to the hut, she thought. She finished her shower and got into a pair of khaki shorts and a blue denim shirt. She took a pair of lace-up climbing boots and put them on. She opened the drawer of a storage chest and brought out a warm sweater and a pair of long pants that she would use later when they got up on the mountain. Putting them all into a backpack, she woke Mark.

"Mark. Are you to sleep all day?"

Mark sat up and looked at her. "You're dressed already."

"We have to leave soon. I'll get us some food from the kitchen and pick up Molo. He has warm clothes for you to wear. Meet me on the road near the entrance sign in twenty minutes. I'll be in the small lorry." She left the cabin.

Mark got up, took a fast shower and got into his clothes. He picked up his knapsack and took out the photos and film negatives. He examined them closely and put them back in his knapsack. He checked the room for anything he might have forgotten and left the cabin.

Mark passed the animal compound. The orphans had been fed their morning meal. The black rhino huffed at him and pawed the ground as he walked by. Mark followed the road that led to Kibo and stopped under a blooming yellow acacia tree filled with noisy starlings. They flew away in a black fluttering cloud as he approached. As he sat, he reflected on his life and the trouble he was in.

The rain had not fallen in *Tsavo* Park in three years. The elephant and the other wild animals were dying from a combination of starvation, poaching and lack of water at an alarming rate. How different it had been four years ago when the elephant herds were so large the Park Service was about to start a culling operation to thin them out. They were destroying scrub landscape, trees and ground cover, turning the park into a desert. He knew East Africa was subject to terrible droughts and famine, but this was the first time Mark could remember a season as bad as this since having grown up in Kenya.

Mark's father was one of the first game wardens in British East Africa before the *Mau Mau* uprising and *Kenya* independence from England. His father helped set up the National Parks for the colonial government. Before that, he has been a white hunter for many years. Most of the game wardens had been white hunters. They knew the animals' habits and could see the value of keeping the wildlife alive for the tourists who would come to *Kenya* to view them in their natural habitat. The people in Kenya knew this was the future industry for East Africa.

Now the very existence of the elephants was at stake. Mark felt something had to be done soon or they would be gone. Most of the personnel in the game department felt the same way, but they had families and needed their jobs. They looked the other way when they discovered the illegal ivory poaching was covertly being sponsored in the halls of the government. Mark knew of one man in government who could and would expose the scandal to the public, Minister P.D. *Mnazi.* He has been telling the newspapers and anyone who would listen about corruption in government. The minister had the ear of the people, but he also had enemies who were out to silence him. Mark had made arrangements to meet Minister Mnazi at an abandoned ranger hut outside of *Voi,* which was *Tsavo* Park headquarters. The minister drove down from Nairobi in his white Mercedes Benz.

P.D. *Mnazi,* was a dapper man, who always wore English-style suits with a flower in his lapel. He carried an ebony walking stick that had a large cabochon blue sapphire on the handle. The minister had used his position to acquire land, wealth and notoriety. It was said that he was the owner of a gambling casino outside of Nairobi that he liked to frequent. As well as being a lady's man, P.D. *Mnazi* was one of the power elite, but he had stepped out on his own. He wanted to become president of Kenya.

Mark had never met P.D. until the Minister pulled up in his car and asked Mark to get in. They drove off in the air-conditioned Benz.

"Awf'ly good to meet you, minister. I've turned up some information on illegal poaching in the park," said Mark.

"What do you have?"

"There's a bloody organized gang that operates here. The leader is a Somali, and his men are from the *Liangulu* tribe who are poaching elephants. He makes the arrangements to pick up the ivory and transports it on the Galana River, picking up more ivory from other poachers along the way before he gets to the coast. My informers tell me he sells it to an Arab dealer in *Mombasa* who has ties to the *Kenya* First Family. I'll be informed when the next shipment is sent and I plan on following it to its source."

"Will you be able to bring me proof of who is involved? I need pictures," said P.D.

"You will have them, sir," said Mark.

31

"Tell me. Why are you doing this? You could lose your job if they find out you supplied me with information. I can't protect you if you're caught."

"I bloody well know that. But, if the ivory trade is not stopped, there'll be no more elephants and no more Kenya as we know it today. We Kenyans are responsible for saving the elephants so others can enjoy them. It's a terrible crime against nature if we let this continue."

"You're a good man. I'm glad to know there's someone like you out there, even if we might not have the same motives. I want to change the government. You want to save the elephants; working together we can accomplish both ends. I agree with you. It can't go on like it is. I will use your information the best way I know."

Mark put out his hand for the Minister to shake. P.D. took it and Mark said, "You'll be hearing from me."

P.D. dropped Mark off at his Land Rover and went on his way.

Mark got word that the poachers were on the move. He and his African assistant, Daro, drove over to a camp on the Galana River and waited for them to show up. The poachers kept the ivory undercover, usually buried somewhere close to the river so it could be easily recovered when the time came to pick it up.

Mark and Daro camped out on a ridge near a camp site that had been used by poison makers. Mark recognized the vessels used to make the toxin. Some dead birds lay on the ground around the abandoned fire pit. He knew that any birds that flew over where the poison was being cooked would be killed because of the strength and potency of the lethal fumes. He and Daro looked out onto a long stretch of the Galana where they could observe any poachers' activity on the river for miles.

Mark had been on their trail for months observing their killing of elephants and rhinos. He could have made arrests long ago, but he wanted to know their source and waited for them to move it to the coast. He and Daro waited by the river for two days.

In the early morning of the third day, the poachers arrived with two dugout canoes powered by small outboard engines. They pulled up onto the shore below. Their fellow-poacher tribesmen came out from under the thick low ground cover at the river's edge and loaded the ivory tusks onto the canoes.

Mark photographed the scene with his long lens camera. He was able to get recognizable photos of the poachers. The Somali paid them and headed down river.

Mark and Daro followed from a distance above the river in the Land Rover traveling east toward the coast. The Somali and his gang made another stop and picked up more ivory, which completely filled the dugouts.

When they got to the outskirts of Malindi, a coastal town, the poachers were met by a bulky lorry driven by two Arabs. Mark was able to observe the unloading of the ivory from the dugouts into the lorry and he got the photos he needed for evidence.

He told Daro to stay with the poachers until he could get word to Donald Markham, the head game warden, who later would make arrangements to have them arrested. He knew the poachers would stay on the coast for a few days spending their booty getting drunk on palm wine and prostitutes before they would head back up river into the bush.

Mark sometimes used an Arab disguise he kept in his vehicle for undercover work. He dressed in the Arab robes and turban and followed the lorry toward Mombasa. When they got into the city, he pursued the lorry to a warehouse in the old Arab quarter on the harbor. Mark watched as the driver stopped the vehicle on the back side of the building. They got out and looked around to see if anyone was observing them. A half breed, Arab and Chinese, came out from inside the warehouse and opened up the double doors and directed the backing of the truck inside.

There was a coffee house across the street from the warehouse. Mark sat there on and off for two days as he watched who came and went into the building. He saw a western-dressed middle-aged African woman, whom he recognized as one of President Kenyatta's relatives, come to the warehouse and leave with the Arab-Chinese businessman he suspected as being the exporter for the illegal tusks. Mark had carefully hidden a camera in the Arab robe. He could lift from around his neck a scarf that concealed the camera, and was able to take photos without anyone seeing him.

Mark stayed in a flophouse close to the warehouse. He bedded down in a stuffy room with four cots. Gauzy nets hung over the beds to protect the patrons from mosquitoes and bugs. Malaria, a common disease in the coastal towns, could be gotten from the malaria mosquitoes which made no sound. You never knew if they were about. His roommates would change every night. Mostly Africans.

On the second night, the room had filled up with Africans and it became hot and sultry. No air moved. The sound of snoring and farts filled the room. Candles, which stood in a holder by the cot, were the only light. Mark had recognized a Samburu tribesman by his robes, beads, and his elaborate hairdo stiffened with camel dung and urine mixed with red ocher dirt. When it dried, it stood high on his head in an unusual design resembling a French chignon.

Mark had spent many a night sleeping out under the stars in the bush in the company of Africans, but he had never slept in a small room filled with strangers. He became uneasy. He tossed and turned often under his mosquito net, kept awake by the loud sounds of the Africans. Just as he thought he was going to drop off to sleep he heard a strange noise. It sounded to him like a rat gnawing on rope. He sat up in his cot and listened. The sound came from the next cot. He reached over and lit the candle and pulled back the net from his bed. He held the candle light in the direction of the Samburu tribesman and saw two giant harbor rats chewing on the tribesman's hairdo. He tried to scare them away by putting the candle in front of them, but they wouldn't leave. They kept chewing.

The Samburu awoke and sprang to his feet. The rats ran while he grabbed his spear from alongside his cot. A war-like scream came out of his mouth, which woke the others.

Mark answered him in swahili, which the Samburu didn't understand; instead, he put his spear to Mark's neck. Mark panicked, telling him about the rats and letting him know he had no intention of trying to kill him or whatever he thought Mark had in mind.

The other Africans laughed, making fun of the Samburu, commenting on the rat's poor taste. After that incident, Mark could no longer stay in the room. It had made him apprehensive and claustrophobic. He left the flop house and walked down to the waterfront. He sat down on the old timbered dock and watched the night activity in the harbor.

A light became visible and grew larger as it came in his direction. It was shining from the deck of an Arab *dhow* that sailed toward him. He could hear the sing-song sound of Swahili conversation between the Arab sailors as the dhow got closer. Mark guessed the dhow came to pick up the ivory.

He walked over to the dhow when it tied up and talked in Swahili to the crew.

They told him they were from Aden and had cargo to pick up to take out of the country. He told them he needed work and could they hire him to help them to move the cargo.

The two Arab sailors talked it over among themselves and offered him four hundred shillings, which was nothing. Mark agreed and the sailors knew they had made a good deal. They asked him to come aboard to share some tea. It was being prepared on a makeshift charcoal grill where they did their cooking. They talked about everything from weather to politics.

Mark had been interested in dhows. He knew about their history, how they had traveled the Indian Ocean and the Arabian seas for thousands of years. Their wide beam and single mast with a large triangular sail had made them the most seafaring boat that was ever put in the water. They were once used for the transporting of slaves in the slave-trading days and they still sailed the old routes up the east coast of Africa across to the Arabian Peninsula and around the Gulf States. The dhow owners appeared to be either

Arabs or Africans. Their language was Swahili, and they were known to be the best story-tellers at sea.

While the men were drinking their tea, a Peugeot pulled up to the dock and a slender man in Arab dress got out. He turned on a flashlight and made his way toward the dhow. When he got to the boat, he talked Arabic to the sailors.

Mark recognized him as the half-caste smuggler he had photographed with the Kenyan lady and stayed in the background saying nothing.

The Arab half-caste told them to follow him. Mark and the two sailors walked behind him to the rear of the warehouse building. The half-caste took a key from his pocket, opened the double doors, and turned on a light. Stacked before them stood large mounds of elephant tusks sorted in different piles by their size and weight. Mark figured there were over four hundred, a small fortune in ivory.

The half-caste told them to move the tusks to the dhow. One of the sailors picked up a tusk. It looked to weigh anywhere from fifty to seventy-five pounds. He carried the heavy load onto the dock and onto the dhow and the other sailor followed with more. The half-caste followed the sailors and watched how they loaded the ivory. Mark stayed behind and as soon as he felt no danger of them seeing him, he brought out his concealed camera and took some hurried pictures of the cache. After he was satisfied with the pictures he had taken he picked up a tusk and carried it onto the dhow giving it to one of the men to pack. In about an hour, they had finished the loading and the warehouse stood empty.

The smuggler took out a roll of bills and counted a stack for the *dhow* owner. He walked back to the warehouse and closed and locked the doors and drove off just as dawn started to appear.

Mark was elated. He had done it. He had the evidence he needed. He couldn't do anything more himself. It was too dangerous. He would wait and go to the police headquarters in Mombasa and call his boss at Tsavo to make arrangement for the arrests. It had been a difficult assignment, but the long months and tough days and nights out in the bush stalking poachers had finally paid off. The *Liangulu* were great hunters and hunting elephants their way of life, but to save the elephant, the tribesmen had to be put out of business to help stop the sale of illegal ivory. Mark knew it would be difficult for the tribe to understand. They'd be put in jail for killing elephants, while the white man killing elephants, legally because he had bought a hunting permit.

The dhow owner counted out four hundred shillings and gave Mark the money.

"*Asante, Buana. Kwaheri,*" said Mark.

"*Nime furahi sana kwa kukuona. Kwaheri ya kuonana,*" yelled the sailors as they said goodbye.

Mark left the dock and walked over to the police station on Cliffe Avenue. Dawn came up with its subdued colors of orange, pink and blue- gray over the Indian Ocean as he walked into the *Mombasa* administration building. At counter he showed his ID to the policeman on duty.

"The name's Mark Livingston, I'm the assistant game Warden at Tsavo Park. Is your chief on duty?

"He should be here in an hour, Bwana."

"Can I use your phone to call my superiors in Voi? It's police business."

The policeman took him to a back office and a phone. Mark took off his Arab robes and turban. Under the robes he still wore his khaki shorts and a tee shirt. He knew he smelled bad. He hadn't been near a shower in days. He couldn't wait to get a clean hotel room have a wash and get some sleep. He picked up the phone and made a call to Donald Markham in Tsavo.

"Donald, its Mark Livingston. I'm in Mombasa. I did it. I have the evidence we need to put the entire ivory ring in jail."

Eight

The phone rang in Mark's room at the Castle Hotel in downtown Mombasa. He fumbled with it as he picked it up. "Hello."

"Mark Livingston?"

"Yes."

"Major Darassa, here, with the General Service Unit. Can I come by and have a talk with you?"

"Who told you about me, Major?"

"Your file was turned over to me by the Chief of Police in Mombasa. I'm investigating an ivory case for the Kenyan Government."

"I see. Give me ten minutes. Okay?"

The phone call worried him. Why was the General Service Unit on the case? Arresting poachers was not in their line of work. They're on to me, he thought. The police chief called them in Nairobi. Thank God I didn't give them the film, but the Chief knows I have it and he's told them.

Mark jumped out of bed and into his Arab disguise and checked to see if the film and photos were in his knapsack. He slipped out of the room and took the back fire-escape that came off the hallway at the end of the corridor. When he got to the hotel parking lot at the rear of the hotel he decided to leave the Land

Rover. He couldn't go back to Voi. That would be the first place they would look for him and he didn't want to bring any pressure on Donald Markham to hide him. He wanted to keep Donald out of it. Donald knew about the corruption at the top, but was not about to jeopardize this position with the National Park service for the actions of one of his zealot game wardens. He'd take a bus to Moshi, Tanzania. No one would think of looking for him on a bus. Astrid would hide him and help him get out of East Africa.

Mark walked quickly to the bus station that stood close to the hotel and bought a ticket to Moshi.

The dilapidated bus left Mombasa later that morning full of passengers. Mark sat up front. He had noticed when he got on the rear shocks sat low over the rear wheels. They had loaded bales of *khat* on the top of the bus to be distributed by an attendant on the way. Mark knew that the Africans along the coast chewed *khat*, but he had never tried it. It was an African custom. No white men he knew did. He could always tell who chewed it because it made their teeth brown. It was a stimulant that got you high and gave an narcotic effect. Someone had told him it was similar to the coca leaf in South America.

Across the aisle were a group of Muslim women traveling together. They were covered in black *rindas* with only their eyes and the bridges of their noses showing. Behind them sat some Chagga tribesmen whose home was the foothills under Mt. Kilimanjaro. Two young Germans in shorts and tee shirts sat behind Mark, each carrying canvas backpacks with sleeping bags attached.

Everyone settled in for the hot, long, monotonous trip. Only the *khat* dealer seemed to be active in the group. He kept taking a sprig of the green leaves and putting them in his mouth to chew and pulled the leaves off the stem with his teeth, spitting out the stems on the floor of the bus.

The first stop was a small village of buildings covered with corrugated tin roofs. The bus pulled up in front of a falling down shack used as the bus stop. A lean-to extended from the roof of the building to where a cooler with a Coca Cola emblem stood.

Some of the passengers got off and took a drink from the cool cooler and paid an attendant. The *khat*-man got up on the roof of the bus and threw a bundle of *khat* off to a man waiting. He yelled at the man and the man yelled back. Mark had no idea what was said. The *Khat*-man took payment from the man and the bus was on its way.

They arrived at Voi, Tsavo Park Headquarters. Mark decided to stay on the bus. He might be recognized, he thought, if he got off. As he looked out of the bus window he saw Matthew, an African Park Ranger, getting on with his wife and two children. Mark covered his face with the corner of his turban as they walked by him. He knew they lived in Mwatate, the next stop. After the new passengers had got on and the *Khat*-man had made his delivery to his connection the bus went on.

One of the German youths behind Mark touched his shoulder and asked him in English if he knew anyone that climbed Kilimanjaro.

Mark answered them in sign language that he didn't speak English.

The *Khat*-man offered Mark some *khat* to chew, but he declined. The *Khat*-man was getting higher and higher.

The bus pulled into Mwatate, a small village not far from Voi, and discharged the ranger and his family. By now the Khat-man was flying around up onto the bus then back into it. He had made another delivery. He sat in front of Mark counting the shillings he had collected. He looked out at the African he had just delivered the *khat* and yelled at him. He got up from his seat and jumped off the bus cursing the man in *Swahili*. Mark could make out that the *Khat-ma*n thought the man had cheated him. He screamed and cursed at him. The African became indignant and yelled back at him, demanding he count the money again. The *Khat*-man counted it again with the African looking on. When the African saw that he had given him the proper money, he told him he was crazy pointing to the *Khat*-man's head. He didn't respond, but got back on the bus acting offended. The African went off mumbling to himself as the bus pulled out.

By four o' clock they were traveling in Tsavo West. Kilimanjaro could be seen in the distance. The mountain would be one of the sites he would miss the most when he left the country, he thought. He'd always remember those spectacular sunsets reflecting off the snow- covered crest. Mark knew there had to be few vistas in the world that could match it. The two German hikers got excited as they saw Kilimanjaro on the right.

The terrain shone with hazy brown savannas and valleys. The foothills on the horizon were purple and green with foliage. An occasional lone elephant could be seen eating off some scrub bushes.

Mark remembered a book he had read on travel in East Africa at the turn of the century. It told the story of Teddy Roosevelt, the American President, and his experiences as he traveled over the same area. He had come with a large hunting party overland from Mombasa, traveling over the very same country that Mark had passed though today. It had been extremely dangerous in those days. Loins and elephants filled the land with their presence. The safari caravan had to stop to let thousands of wild animals pass. Once in a while you'd see an occasional elephant. When Mark thought about how different it had become he felt sad. Once there where so many and now so few. The thought fueled his own attitude that what he was doing was right in working to help save the elephant and the rhino from extinction.

They pulled into Taveta on the border of Kenya and Tanzania. Continual border conflicts and been raging between the two countries. Without warning, Tanzania would close its gates and let no one from Kenya enter. You were never sure what was to happen from one day to the next. If Mark could get across the border to Tanzania, he figured he would be safe from Major Darassa's secret police.

Mark stepped off the bus when it arrived at the border. The bus went on to Moshi. He knew another road the big lorries used as they traveled between Arusha and Dar es Salaam. He'd hitch a ride on a lorry across the border from there. The customs never bothered to search lorries unless they were looking for someone. Mark hoped his name had not yet appeared at the border station.

A lorry, loaded with new rubber tires, stopped to pick him up. He talked swahili to the driver and offered him five hundred shillings if he could ride in the back with the tires. The African driver agreed. Mark knew he suspected something, but the money made it possible.

Nine

Major Darassa sat in his office in downtown Nairobi. He had just hung up the phone when his secretary came in. She looked concerned as she adjusted the papers on his desk.

"Major, Minister Mfalme is in the other office. He wishes to speak to you, Sir."

"Show him in."

The minister walked in, dressed in a dark English-tailored suit that showed off his large frame. His hair had a small tint of grey at his temples. He wore a scowl on his wide handsome face. Major Darassa jumped up to greet him.

"I heard from Mombasa about the arrests and the implications of our president's family involvement in the illegal ivory trade. What have you done to locate the game warden who has circulated these lies?"

"We are looking for him, minister. We think he's in Tanzania. I have undercover personnel in the country and they've been alerted. I am expecting a report at anytime, minister."

"Mzee is concerned about the publicity. He doesn't want the information in the hands of his enemies. It's a delicate time for him, he forgets."

"Yes minister. I have personally taken charge of the case. It will be handled discreetly, I assure you."

"I'll count on your discretion. Here's my private number at my home. Call me there if need be. "The minister left the room. Major *Darassa* buzzed for his secretary.

"Get Otieno and Najaro to come to my office."

Ten

A strid pulled up in front of the acacia tree where Mark was waiting in a small lorry. Molo sat in the back behind the cab with the supplies. Mark jumped in the front seat and they were off.

As they made their ascent of Kilimanjaro, the terrain changed from semi-dry to a tropical rain forest. Banana and mango trees grew in patches along the road side. African women could be seen in the fields picking and carrying large stacks of bananas on their heads. Others walked along the narrow road carrying their crops as the lorry passed them by. Ahead in the foothills of the mountain, great expansive tea plantations could be seen. The road narrowed so only one vehicle at a time could pass.

"Dad is leaving tomorrow for Dar es Salaam to pick up his client for a hunting safari. I told him about the trouble you're in. He said you could join him in Selous on safari and pick up some extra money, if you're interested. You'll have to shoot elephants. They plan on culling a herd."

"What? I can't do that. It's against my principles. Why is Helmut doing this? I hope you let him know how you feel."

"I have. He says it's a job, but he also said it could be his last hunting safari. He is coming around to my way of thinking at last.

I've never said much, but he's knows how I feel. He's like your father. They're the old school. It's always been a way of life."

"My father will never understand why I am putting myself in jeopardy over some bloody illegal ivory traders."

"Mark. I understand you and I admire your courage. We have to take a stand. Someone has to or the killing will never stop. It'll be the game's end for all."

They ascended to three thousand feet and the end of the road. From there they traveled by foot. Astrid parked the lorry in a small clearing. They were still in the tea-growing part of the mountain. Rows and rows of tea bushes covered the hillside in a symmetrical pattern. The Chagga farmers in their bright colorful dress gathered the leaves from the teeming bushes.

Astrid helped Mark with his pack as he fastened the straps around his shoulders and they started up the mountainside. *Molo* brought up the rear carrying a light pack of supplies.

They moved easily through the tropical forest. A few Sykes monkeys could be seen in the trees along the trail, but no other wild animals were witnessed. The sweet exotic smell of frangipani drifted through the cool mountain air. The roar of a mountain river could be heard ahead. Heavy rains in the forest and the melting snows of Kilimanjaro had kept the water level high and dangerous.

When they got to the river's edge, they heard a cry from below and looked down. Two hikers stood cramped against the side of a ledge, their bodies hugging the wet rocky wall. Mark recognized them as the two young Germans who had been on the bus with him.

"How did you blokes get down there?" he yelled.

"We lost our footing on the bank. Be careful. It's hollowed out under your feet. Don't get near the edge. It will give way," one of the German youths yelled back.

Mark and Astrid looked down into the steep ravine where the water dropped a thousand feet.

"Molo, go back to the lorry. There's some rope and a block and tackle in the back. Get it and bring it here," said Astrid.

"Yes, Mama." Molo dropped his backpack and went off down the trail.

"Are you men hurt?" Mark yelled over the roar of the water.

"Jacob's leg is broken and he's bleeding."

"Can you make a tourniquet to stop the bleeding?"

"If I move I'll slip, because of the moss on the rocks."

"Hold on, old boy. We'll have you up soon," Mark yelled back. Molo returned with the block and tackle and gave the rope to Mark. Mark made a lasso at the end of the long rope. He and Astrid tied the rope around a large hardwood tree near the river's edge. They attached the tackle and threaded the pulley. Mark moved over to the mist-covered ravine with Astrid behind him. He wrapped one end of the rope around his waist, and Astrid and Molo braced him so he wouldn't go over the edge when he threw the rope. The two Germans were still secure on the ledge, but the water from the river splashed on them making it difficult for Mark to get the rope over for them to grab. Mark had much experience with a lasso for he had used one often in the capture of animals at Tsavo, but every time he threw the rope, the water would interfere and carry it away from the men.

"I need to cross the bridge. The water interferes with the rope and it won't work from here. We can lower the line down to them from over there. Molo untie the rope," he said.

Mark led the way up the river to a crude suspension bridge that extended over the river. The bridge swung precariously back and forth as they walked across. Astrid felt a slight vertigo as she cautiously walked over the raging water toward the other side.

The bank was steep from this point and the Germans were directly below, but Mark couldn't see them from his angle.

"Molo, go back over the bridge and guide me as to where I'm to drop the rope."

"Yes, Bwana."

Astrid and Mark tied the block and tackle to a large pointed rock and made it secure. Molo had gotten back on the other side of the river where he had a view of the scene. He motioned with his hand for Mark to move the line to the right. Mark kept moving along the ledge until Molo gave him a signal to stop and pointed below. Mark let down the line over the edge. Molo could see the noose descending to the Germans. One of them took the rope and put it over the shoulders of his injured partner. Molo signaled Mark and Astrid to bring him up. They pulled. The man lifted off the ledge to the edge of the ravine above. When they saw his head come above the canyon lip they secured the line and got hold of his shoulders and pulled him up on to the embankment.

He seemed barely conscious. His leg bone protruded through his pants leg and his blood flooded the ground. Mark quickly tore off part of his pants leg and made a tourniquet. He applied it around the man's thigh and the blood flow stopped. He sat the man up against a tree and took the noose from around his shoulders and lowered it to the other man below. Mark could feel the line go taut and he and Astrid pulled the second man to safety. They gathered around the injured German.

"There's a hospital in Arusha. We'll take him there. Look how pale he is. He needs blood and look he has a spiral bone fracture. Let's get him down to the lorry," said Astrid.

"I'm going too. There no sense in me going to the hut tonight if I will be leaving with your father tomorrow," said Mark.

"You changed your mind? You're joining dad?"

"I'd like to see him again before I leave. Maybe I can convince him he's wrong."

Astrid looked at Mark and smiled. "Mark, I like you more than ever." She looked at Molo, "Cut down a couple of long tree limbs and we'll make a stretcher."

Astrid and Mark took their backpacks and put them together and Molo brought them two long branches that they assembled into a make-shift cot. They gently put the injured German on the stretcher and they carried him down the mountain to the lorry.

Mark stayed in the lorry as Molo, Astrid and Manfred carried Jacob into the small bougainvillea-covered hospital in Arusha. Before they left, Manfred asked Mark. "Are you leaving us?"

"No. I'll wait here."

"You saved our lives and I have something for you. As soon as I get Jacob taken care of I want to talk to you," said Manfred.

"I'll be here, said Mark. Mark didn't want anyone to see him. The more he stayed out of sight the better, he thought. What a twist of fate. He would be going with Helmut to Selous. He liked the idea of being on the last hunting safari with Helmut, whom he admired, and it gave him some more time to be with Astrid. He liked the idea of being able to spend another night in her bed.

A hour later the front door of the hospital opened. Astrid, Molo and the Manfred walked out and came to join Mark.

"How's your friend?"

"He can't be moved for a while, but he going to be okay. They're operating on him now, putting a pin in his leg," said Manfred.

"Doctor Singh is a wonderful doctor. We're so lucky to have him here. He's been offered a staff position at the hospital in Nairobi, but he likes living in Arusha," said Astrid.

"Mark, can I have a word in private?" asked Manfred.

"Why sure, mate, get in the cab." Manfred climbed in the front seat with Mark.

"I want you to have this." Manfred took from his pocket a large stone and gave it to Mark.

He examined the rock and said. "Is it what I think it is?"

"If you mean an uncut ruby, yes. We found the stone while we were prospecting in Kenya. We're geologists and we're on our way back to Nairobi to stake a claim, but we thought we would try to climb Kilimanjaro. It has been a life-long dream of mine."

"This ruby is worth a bloody fortune. I can't accept it, but thank you." Mark handed the ruby back to Manfred.

"We want you to have it. Please. You saved our lives. We won't miss the stone, we have others. In fact, the mine will make us rich beyond anything we could have imagined. I talked it over with Jacob. He wants you to have it. What good would it do us if we were dead? You saved our lives. You're entitled to this stone. It's yours and your lady friend's reward. Have it cut. I see a part of it hanging around your girlfriend's neck."

"That's a nice thought," said Mark as he tossed the stone in his hand. "I guess I can't refuse."

Eleven

Darkness had fallen by the time they arrived at the lodge. There were cries from the animals as they passed by in the lorry. Something was bothering the animals, thought Astrid. Up ahead the headlights of the lorry shone on a baby elephant in the care of George, an animal attendant, who was trying to make it drink from a bottle of milk.

"It looks like I have a new orphan," said Astrid as she stopped the lorry and jumped out of the cab. Mark and Molo followed.

"Where did the little packy come from, George?"

"We found her in the bush, Mama. Her mama, she dead. Poachers." said George, as he tried to put the bottle in the small elephant's mouth, but the little one wouldn't take the warm milk.

"She weak no wanta eat, Mama," said George.

The baby elephant was about three feet tall. Astrid knew it would be hard for it to survive. She had experience with this size baby elephant before. It seemed too young and needed the potency of mother's milk. Astrid took the bottle from George and drew some milk from it and put it down the soft little trunk for the elephant to smell, but the little elephant didn't move. "It won't live. It needs its mother's milk. I'll give it Molo's formula. It has worked before on these babies." She looked at Mark. "I feel helpless and sad, Mark, when I can't save one of these little ones. Those bloody poachers have got to be stopped."

Mark knelt next to her and put his arm around her shoulders. Astrid said to George. "Stay with her tonight. Keep trying to feed her." She and Mark started back to the lorry.

"Bwana, some men here today ask for you." said George.

"What did you tell them?" he asked.

"I no see Bwana," said George.

"Were they Tanzanian?"

"No. One big one, he have tribal scar on face. He no from here," said George. Mark and Astrid left for the hotel.

"General Service Unit is onto me." I shouldn't stay here tonight."

"Where will you go? They won't be back in the dark. Not out here. It's too remote. Besides you're in Tanzania. They'd have to kidnap you. They can't arrest you in this country. They have no authority." Astrid stopped the lorry next to the main lodge.

"Stay in the cab," she said. "I'm going to check and see if one of the tents is vacant. You can stay there tonight. If they do come back they'll never look for you there. Not with all the hotel guests here"

Astrid went into the lodge while Mark remained in the lorry. She was back in a few minutes. They drove in front of the long row of tents, looking at the numbers. "There it is. Number sixteen," said Astrid. She stopped and Mark picked up his knapsack as Astrid lifted up the front cover of the tent to enter. She struck a match and lit the oil lamp by the cot.

Mark took the pictures out of his knapsack and gave them to her.

"These are for P.D. Mnazi in Nairobi. Tell him that the General Service Unit are after me. Tell him where I am." He drew Astrid to him. "Will you stay with me?" he asked, looking into her wide blue eyes.

"I can't Mark. I'm leaving for Nairobi early in the morning. I still have much to do tonight to be prepared for tomorrow. I'd be bad company. There's too much on my mind." She moved away from him.

"Thanks for today. I love you," he said. Astrid smiled at him.

"You're sweet Mark and I love you too." She lifted up the corner of the tent flap and left.

Mark could hear the sound of the lorry as it drove away. She actually said she loved me. I can't believe it, but she did. What a day this has been, he thought. He blew out the oil lamp by his bed and collapsed on the cot with his clothes on. All he could see in his thoughts was Astrid's beautiful face as he drifted off into a deep sleep.

Astrid drove back to the orphanage. She stopped the lorry in front of where George attended the baby elephant. She picked up a kerosene lamp, lit it and joined George, who still tried to get the baby to drink from the bottle. She sat down next to the small animal who was having a problem breathing. It lay listless making no attempt to move. Thick mucus flowed from its mouth and trunk. She touch its rough hide and the tip of its truck to feel its body temperature. The baby seemed cold to her.

"The baby's sick. How old do you think it is?"

"Maybe two days, Mama. She stand around dead mama when we find. I think no eat from mama. She see poachers cut tusks from Mama. I know she feel sad, to see mama be killed so bad."

"Yes, George, I agree. I miss my Suzy so. She was my pet. She also wouldn't eat when I found her. I had a terrible time getting her to do so. I remember now. George, go to the kitchen and have *Molo* give you some corn syrup and bring it back."

George got up and left. Astrid kept stroking the baby's trunk.

"You poor hungry little girl. Mama wants you to eat. You must be very hungry. Mama has something wonderful for you to taste. I bet you're going to like what Mama gives you." she said stroking the elephant hide around its ears. The elephant didn't move and its breathing remained the same. Astrid started to sneeze. Her eyes watered. She can felt them puffing and swelling. Damn those allergies, she said to herself. She took a large red cloth from her pocket and blew her nose. She looked up and saw Ingrid in her cage close by. Ingrid jumped up and down and screamed, wanting Astrid to come to her. Astrid got up from the elephant and went to Ingrid's cage. She opened the door and Ingrid came to her and gave her a sloppy kiss as she hugged her.

"You poor girl. I haven't forgotten you, Ingrid. Mama has been busy trying to stay out of trouble. Oh, what is going to happen to you, Ingrid, if I go to jail? What is going to happen to all my babies? I'm going to miss all of you," she said as she looked around at the animals staring at her. I think they know, noting how sad they looked, she thought.

George came back with the corn syrup. She handed him Ingrid and she took the corn syrup and sat down next to the baby elephant's head. She opened the bottle and poured the thick liquid on her middle finger and inserted it into the elephant's half-opened mouth as if it were its mother tit. She observed the baby elephant, looking for any movement it might give. Nothing. She pulled out her finger and poured more syrup on it and inserted it again. Nothing happened for a moment or two and then she felt it. Its mouth moved. A slight movement, but it moved. Then she felt its tongue slowing moving, back and forth. It swallowed. She looked up at George. "George, It swallowed." Astrid petted its head. George smiled at her. "George, give me the bottle. Is it warm?" George nodded. She put the bottle in the little elephant's mouth and the baby started to suck.

"She is nursing, George. She is going to make it," she yelled."

Twelve

Everyone got off in the early morning for their destinations. Astrid and Molo *departed for* Nairobi. Astrid in the Land-Rover and Molo followed in the supply lorry with their camping gear. Mark and Helmut flew to Dar es Salaam. Helmut had sent his safari crew ahead two days before to have the camp set up for their arrival to Selous.

Astrid and Molo arrived in Nairobi. He took the lorry to a supply station near the railroad station to purchase the supplies they needed.

Astrid parked in the Parliament Building in downtown Nairobi. She entered the building and looked at the directory in the lobby. She took the elevator to the fourth floor and walked down the hall to suite 430. The sign on the door read: "P. D. Mnazi".

She went inside and addressed the girl at the reception desk.

"May I see the minister. My name is Astrid Dryden. I'm from Moshi in Tanzania. Tell him I have confidential documents from Mark Livingston."

"I'll see if the minister is in. Your name again, Miss," asked the receptionist as she got up from her desk.

"Astrid Dryden."

"Thank you." The receptionist went through a door marked private. A few moments later the door opened a crack and Astrid could see a dark shadow through the opening. The door closed and a minute later opened again. The receptionist came out and said, "You may go in."

Astrid walked into the office. The walls were covered with English eighteenth century hunting prints. P.D. Mnazi stood up as she entered. He wore a dark tailored suit with a bright red tie and a boutonniere in his label. He gave her the impression of being a stylish dandy.

"Sit down, Miss–, Miss—,"

"Dryden. I was asked to give you this, minister." Astrid handed him the envelope.

He opened it and went through the photos slowly, without comment.

"Where is the party that took these?"

"He's hiding out in Tanzania. The GSU is looking for him. He told me you were the only one in the government he could trust and you would know what to do with these." Astrid got up. "I must go. I have clients arriving from London. Here's my number in Moshi if you need to talk to Mark. I will know where he is." She handed him her number. P.D. looked at Astrid with interest and took out of his pocket a stack of gambling chips and handed them to her.

"Here. If you have some time while you're in Nairobi, go and spend these at the casino. Tell them at the door that you're a friend of mine. I'm sure you'll have good luck."

Astrid was a little taken back by his gesture. Is he coming on to me, she thought, but dismissed it as foolish. I hope Mark knows what he is doing, she thought.

"Thank you, minister. I've never gambled, but I might give it a try." She smiled at P.D. and left the office.

Astrid drove down Government Road and stopped and parked the Land Rover by the Hilton Hotel. She crossed the street and entered a three-story building. The door was open to an office on the first floor. A sign on the door said. HEADQUARTERS SAVE THE WILD-LIFE ORGANIZATION. Derek Palmer, Director.

Posters of wildlife hung on the walls. A large graph of a fund-raising campaign was in the window. The office was sparsely furnished with furniture that looked like it could have been donated.

Derek, a young man in his early thirties, with a thin dark beard and a slight bend in his long frame sat at his desk. He wore a tee shirt with SAVE THE WILD-LIFE FUND printed on the front. On his desk were stacks of papers strewn around. You could tell he wasn't the neatest person by his appearance. When he saw Astrid at the door he jumped up to greet her. "Astrid, what brings you to Nairobi? Can we have dinner, tonight?"

"I can't Derek. I'm about to pick up a client at the airport and we're on our way north. Derek, I have a favor to ask."

"Of course. Shoot."

"Promise you never heard this from me?"

"You have my word," said Derek.

"Thank you." Astrid was relieved, she trusted Derek. They had worked together in the past and had the same sympathy for elephants and rhinos. Derek had a little crush on her, but it had never come to anything. "This has been a big decision, I've been wresting with it for days. I'm going against my father's wishes and I feel bad."

"Well, what is it?" asked Derek, concerned.

"Helmut is about to slaughter a hundred and fifty elephants for the Tanzanian government. I can't let that happen." "Good girl." answered Derek. "Where's this massacre to take place?"

"In the Selous." answered Astrid.

"Where in the Selous? It's a million acres."

"Behobeho Camp on the Rufiji river. I know you'll do what you can to save them."

Astrid drove back to the supply warehouse and parked next to her supply lorry. Molo appeared from the cab.

"Have a safe trip, Molo. We'll be in tomorrow afternoon in time for supper. Here's the name at the ranger station. He'll tell you where to set up the camp." Astrid handed him the name.

"Yes, Mama. *Kwaheri.*" Molo waved as she drove off to the Nairobi airport.

Thirteen

The VC10 from London glided down onto the runway. Jim Fielding and Lady Anne Conway smiled at each other as the giant jet came to a stop. Graham Lindley sat across from them in the first-class section.

"I felt we were over the Amazon. I didn't see a sign of life down there for hours. I'm chicken when it comes to large jets. I always feel helpless. Give me a small single engine job I can get down anywhere," said Jim.

"I feel excited when I arrive in Nairobi," said Anne. "It's the only place I have been where you can smell adventure as you depart from the plane. I think it has a lot to do with the wild animals. There's no civilization left in the world today that has this atmosphere."

"I couldn't have said it better." said Jim.

They left their seats and exited the aircraft. The sweet clear Kenyan air filled their lungs with a new fresh feeling of being alive. Jim thought about living in Kenya later in life where he knew he could live to be a hundred. The thought brought a smile to his pallid face.

The flight from London had rumpled them up a bit. A long shower would be refreshing right now, thought Jim. He checked his traveling companions to see how they were holding up as he stood in the line for immigration. Lady Anne's beige linen dress looked wrinkled, but her lovely face was alive with the excitement of arrival. The whiskey Graham had drunk on the flight was visible. It made his skin blotchy and his eyes droop.

It took some time to get the film, cameras and baggage through customs. As they came out, Astrid stood waiting for them. She recognized Jim from her father's description. What a handsome American, she thought. She liked his wide shoulders and lean body. Dad was right about his being attractive, she thought. She wondered about the beautiful woman. She had an aristocratic look that belonged only to upper-class Englishwomen. She joined Jim and introduced herself.

"Is your name Jim Fielding?"

"You must be Astrid," said Jim as they shook hands.

"This is Lady Anne Conway and our cameraman Graham Linley."

Lady Anne gave Astrid a big smile as she looked her over. "Jim, you never told me you were to have such a pretty young guide. Where did you get your experience, darling?" asked Anne.

"Her father is a famous white hunter in East Africa and if I know Helmut he's raised her to know everything about the bush and much more. How is your father?" asked Jim.

"He's disappointed he couldn't be with you and sends his regards. He's busy. An American is arriving tomorrow and he's taking him to Selous and after that he has a film company from Hollywood arriving in Moshi. They're making a film using an old German fort. It seems you picture people all come at the same time."

"It's your sun, no rain this time of year and the public interest in African stories," answered Jim.

"Dad's not complaining, he likes the money and being with movie people can be lots of fun. The Land Rover is outside waiting to load. We'll be driving to Mount Kenya Safari Club today. It's one hundred and thirty miles north and the accommodations are wonderful." Astrid looked to see if everyone had their luggage and equipment. "Are we ready?" They picked up what they could carry. Graham had a porter bring up the rear with the equipment as they exited the airport terminal to the awaiting transportation.

Fourteen

Helmut and Mark got to the airport terminal in *Dar es Salaam* at the same time the airplane with Clay and Tim Nobertson arrived. The air terminal was new and modern with large glass windows that looked out on to the tarmac where airplanes arrived and departed. The building was meant to impress the tourists when they arrived. It had the latest amenities. The floors were a shiny beige marble with green lines running through. All the airport personnel were dressed in starched khaki uniforms that gave the look of efficiency and well being. Helmut and Clay hurried to immigration and customs to await their client.

Otieno and Najaro the two Kikuyus tribesman who worked for Major Darassa in General Service Unit, the Kenyan secret police, were at the Air Terminal observing passengers arriving and departing. The large stocky henchmen dressed in loose white shirts and khaki shorts stood out from the rest of the crowd. Otieno had tribal scars of the Kikuyu tribe tattooed on his forehead and cheeks. Mark and Helmut passed them by as they went to meet Clay. Otieno showed Najaro the photo he had of Mark. They both smiled and followed them to immigration. They stood near by observing their actions.

Sounds of an argument could be heard at the immigration desk. A swarthy looking man stood yelling at the officer.

"What do you mean I need a typhoid shot! Look! It's on the shot record, here. See!" Clay pointed to his immunization record the immigration officer held.

"*Bwana,* it's not up to date. You need a booster before I pass you." The immigration officer motioned to a porter mopping the floor to come over. The porter carried his mop and moved slowly across the room toward Clay and the Immigration officer.

"Give this man a typhoid shot," said the Officer. The porter nodded his head.

"No porter is going to give me a shot. Isn't there a doctor?"

"This man dispenses all inoculations. We do not have a doctor." Clay fumed.

Helmut peered in through the door and asked, "Are you Mr. Nobertson?"

"Helmut?" Helmut nodded his head.

"For Christ's sake do something. Get me a doctor!" Clay yelled out at Helmut.

"I can find one, but it will take some time."

"How long?"

"An hour to get back out here."

"Do you believe this? They want me to have that nigger porter give me a shot," he said to Tim who stood near him.

"Wait till customs sees the guns and ammunition we have. They're going to think we came to start a war," said Tim.

"I never thought about it. But that nigger could give me hepatitis or some fucking disease I have never heard of. God damm it. I'm always so organized. When something stupid like this happens to me my blood pressure goes up. Look at me, I am sweating like a stuck pig." He gave the porter his immunization record.

The porter motioned Clay to follow him over to a closet door and opened it. He put down his mop and motioned for Clay to roll up his sleeve. He took a syringe from the closet and punctured Clay's arm with the needle.

Clay went back to Tim who was waiting for the baggage to arrive on the conveyer belt. "If you send me home in a box, you'll know that stupid nigger is responsible."

The conveyor belt started to move and the passengers' luggage came into the terminal. Tim took their cases off the belt as they passed. They got busy removing their belongings. Six rifles in carrying cases, a submachine gun packed in its case, boxes of cartridges, assorted hunting paraphernalia, cases of liquor and numerous traveling bags. Two porters helped load the equipment and guns onto carts and wheeled them over to customs.

A tall thin customs officer dressed in sharp creased khaki safari uniform looked over the baggage. He took a hard look at the liquor and made a note of the ammunition on a slip of paper.

"Come with me," said the customs officer.

Clay and Tim looked at each other as they followed him into a small office and he closed the door.

"Would you sit, please? We are a poor country. We need American dollars. I need dollars. Do you have five hundred American dollars with you?" Clay nodded. "Good, you can give it to me. If not, I'll confiscate the liquor and cartridges. I think you have some criminal plans for that ammunition, Bwana."

"They never did this to me in Kenya."

"Kenya is a rich country. We are not that fortunate, Bwana."

"Ah shit, give the man five hundred, Tim. I'm starting to feel sick," said Clay as he got up from the chair.

Tim reached into his pocket and brought out his wallet and gave a five hundred dollar bill to the officer who quickly shoved it into his shirt pocket. They walked back to the counter and the officer stamped their baggage and hunting supplies "passed". The porters loaded up the carts again and moved them out through the door as Clay and Tim met Helmut and Mark.

"Sorry about the inconvenience, Mr. Norbertson."

"What bad news do you have for me?" asked Clay.

"You'll have no trouble from me, Mr. Norbertson none, whatsoever. I have a plane waiting to take us to *Selous*. It's an hour flight. This is Mark Livingston, my assistant." Mark shook Clay's limp hand. Mark had a feeling about Clay he didn't like and when he saw the guns and ammunition, he knew this man had to be trouble.

The two Kikuyus followed the group out of the terminal and watched them load a two-engine 310 Cessna airplane. When the small plane rose into the air, they walked to the charter office and went in. Otieno asked in *swahili* of the attendant. "The Cessna airplane, what is the destination?"

"Behobeho Camp in Selous," said the attendant.

"Is there a hotel or camp?"

"A small camp on the Rufifi river. We service it from here. I have a aircraft going tomorrow with supplies. Do you want on?"

Fifteen

Anne could hear Jim in the bathroom taking a long shower as she stepped out on the balcony of their suite at the Mount Kenya Safari Club. From where Anne stood she admired the beauty of Mount Kenya with its sharp snow-covered triangular peak reflecting moon-light in the distance. The cool night mountain air mixed with the smell of olive logs burning in fireplaces of the rooms brought back memories of her youth at her uncle's farm in Nanyuki, not far from where she was standing. She wanted to see her uncle, but her personal life was a mess and he would want to know everything.

I can't answer him, she thought, I don't have the answers. He wouldn't understand me traveling with a man that isn't my husband. As much as she would have liked to see him, she wouldn't subject herself to him about her lifestyle. How different her uncle was from her father who, when he lived, was arrogant and aloof. If she only could have communicated with her father more.

It was the same with her mother. Her mother never went against her father's wishes. She always stood behind him, even when she knew he was wrong. Anne knew that's where her rebellion came from. She wanted to defy her parents and she did. Being a young flower child in London in the sixties seemed the only way she felt she could get back at them. It seemed now so ridiculous when she looked back. The way she dressed, all the dope she consumed, but what fun, she thought.

Her marriage to Alex had been a roller-coaster ride. She loved him, but could she bear him? Alex was so bright and talented. She remembered what he had told her before they got married. "I'm a free soul, love, and I want to remain that way." He wasn't interested in having children and they would have to live on what he made as an artist. He had made the rules, and they were difficult to live by, but she wanted him and she would take him under any circumstances.

The money hadn't come in the way they both thought. She had a small allowance from her estate, but it wasn't enough for them to live on. Finally she got Alex to say yes about her going to work. Their marriage became more and more open. She had her little affairs and he had his. So far no seriousness came of it and they kept discreet with one another to protect each other's feelings. It seemed different with Jim. He remained open and fun and made everything look and sound easy. With Alex it seemed to her one-upmanship that he enjoyed and he became a severe critic of all aspects of life, which made him difficult to live with.

She enjoyed The Mount Kenya Club. It reminded her of a posh resort in the California desert of Palm Springs, where she had visited when she traveled in the States. It had the same kind of bungalows and golf course but its location was the best. In the middle of the highland plateau in central Kenya, one of the best climates in the world. She knew she could sit for hours and watch the white peacocks and the crown cranes prance and show off on the lush green lawns. When someone told her William Holden, the American movie star, had a wild animal complex next door for orphaned and injured animals, she thought, if she had time, she would walk over and have a look.

She felt hungry. All she had eaten today was a roll and a cup of dark Kenyan coffee when they had stopped at a cafe on their way. It had to be a unique landmark because the equator ran through the restaurant.

Anne walked back into the room. Jim hadn't yet come out of shower. She rapped on the door. "Jim, I'm going down to the dining room. I'm so hungry I could eat a Dik Dik. I need a snack before dinner. Join me when you're through." Jim opened the door, and the steam rolled out. He came through the cloud of mist and grabbed her.

"Jim. What are you doing? Look, you're getting my dress wet, you twit."

Jim wrapped his wet lean body around her and gave her a seductive kiss as he pushed his body into hers.

"You're crazy! I'm not going to make love to you now. I'll have to redo my make-up. Get back in there." She pushed him back into the shower and closed the door. "You're dreadful! I'll have to change my dress before I go," she complained through the door.

She walked to the closet and picked out a green shirtdress and looked at it. She took off her damp dress and hung it over a chair and put on the other one. She took a zebra skin belt and cinched it tightly around her small waist. She touched up her makeup. She could hear Jim singing in the bathroom as she left the room. Englishmen talk about sex, but Americans do it, she thought as she smiled to herself.

Sixteen

Anne entered the dinning room and picked a table with a full view of Mount Kenya. She noticed a group of men sitting together in the corner of the bar. Some were dressed in safari clothes. Others were in open shirts and slacks. They didn't look like tourists. In fact they looked odd to Anne. They gave her an interested look. Amazingly, she recognized one of them and at the same time he recognized her. Oh, my God! It's Anthony Roseli. What is he doing here? she thought. Anthony got up from his table and came toward her smiling. Anthony was in his late thirties, tall and thin, Italian-looking with large white teeth and dark slicked-back hair.

"Anthony, what a surprise! What are you doing here?" she asked as she put her hand out to him. He took it and gave it a kiss. "I could ask the same."

"I'm working on a film."

"I didn't know you were an actress. I thought you were a decorator."

"You know I am, but I got this chance to come here to work on a film and get paid, so here I am, darling."

"I'm on business." He looked toward the table he had gotten up from. "Can I sit down?"

"Only for a minute."

"Are you with your husband?"

"No. But I'm with a man. He's an American film director."

"Ah, I understand."

"Anthony. Please do me a favor. Don't let him know you know me. He could be jealous. I don't want to put myself in jeopardy. You can be a bad boy, Anthony, and you know I know it, darling."

Anthony smiled and looked up as Astrid came into the room and approached the table. Astrid was in a pretty light blue dress. Her long blonde hair was piled on top of her head. She wore earrings and a small gold necklace, and had on lipstick and a little rouge on her wide cheeks. Her young blonde looks got the attention of the entire room. Seeing her, Anthony made no attempt to leave the table until he could be introduced. Anne remained uncomfortable and was not about to make an introduction. Anthony realized this and introduced himself.

"You must be in the picture also. My name is Anthony Roseli. What is yours?" He extended his hand.

"I'm Astrid. I work for the film. I'm not in it."

"That is too bad. With your good looks you could easily be the star." Astrid blushed. "I thought I knew this lady from London, but she tells me I'm mistaken," said Anthony showing off his white teeth.

Anne pretended to keep her cool but she felt panicked. How could she get so unlucky as to run into Anthony in the middle of Africa? Anthony put on a good act but he was far from being a gentleman. She had met him over a year ago at the Clermont. He had that dark menacing handsomeness she found exciting, and he came on to her immediately when they met. She found herself attracted to him. When she asked Rene, the maitre d', about him, he told her his business was gambling. He was involved with a syndicate that ran casinos in the Caribbean and around Europe. He had asked Rene to work for him.

When Anthony found out that Anne worked as a decorator, he hired her to do his flat in Eaton Square. She liked the way he spent money. He didn't object to the expensive pieces of furniture she had selected for him. In time, listening to him and overhearing some of his conversation he had with his associates, she realized he was a gangster. For some strange reason she found that exciting. She started sleeping with him. She knew that nothing would ever come of it.

"By the way you speak, you must be from Kenya," Anthony said to Astrid.

"No, I live in Tanzania, near Kilimanjaro."

"Are you making the film here at the Club?"

"No. We're at Marsabit north of here. We'll be there tomorrow," said Astrid.

Jim came into the bar and spotted his group. He looked fresh and relaxed in his clean pressed khaki outfit.

Anthony got up when he arrived. "You must be the film director these ladies have been talking about. Can I have a minute with you? My associates and I have been talking about putting up backing for films. Would you be interested?"

"On that subject I'm all ears. Have you ever done it before? Please sit down. I'm Jim Fielding." Jim gave him his hand.

Anthony took it. "My name is Anthony Roseli. No," he continued, "but I'd like to talk if you have some time. I'm sitting with Ray Ryan, he owns this place and is a friend of William Holden has a script about a lion he would like to film here at Mount Kenya. My associates are thinking about putting up the money. Can I take you to dinner? I'd like to ask some questions about financing movies."

Jim looked at Anne and Astrid for their approval. Anne made a "no" motion with her head out of Anthony's sight.

"I'm sorry but we have many things to discuss about tomorrow. Thank you anyway. Could we talk at breakfast?"

"Why not? I'll call you in the morning," said Anthony. He took Astrid's hand and looked into her clear blue eyes and winked. He acknowledged Anne and left the table to rejoin his group. "Something about that guy I don't trust," said Jim.

"Why do you say that?" asked Anne.

75

"Intuition. Or maybe it's his handshake. I've never trusted a man with a weak handshake. Look at that group he's with. They look like Mafia to me. Let's go to dinner," said Jim, as he rose from the table followed by Anne and Astrid. They walked into the dining room.

The dining room filled with the hotel guests. Graham sent his regrets; he still suffered from jet lag and too much to drink on the airplane.

Anthony and his group came into the dining room and sat opposite, enabling Anthony to look directly at Astrid. Astrid became conscious of his flirtatious looks.

"I never met anybody like Mr. Roseli before. He's handsome."

"His type is quite common around London, darling," said Anne.

"I plan on going to London after I get a problem taken care of. I've never been anywhere and I want to go to school. I have an application in at Cambridge."

"My father was a trustee there. I'll try to see if I can be of some help to you."

"Oh, Lady Anne, would you?"

"Why not, darling? I can tell you're a bright girl. I'd be happy to help you."

Jim listened to them as two bottles of French champagne were delivered to the table by the waiter.

"There must be some mistake. We didn't order champagne," said Jim.

"That gentleman sitting over there sent it, *Bwana*," said the waiter as he made a motion with his head toward Anthony. Anthony picked up his glass and with a smile made a toast to them. The gesture annoyed Jim, but he made no comment. Astrid, he saw, seemed pleased and he watched her smile back. The waiter poured their glasses full. Astrid gulped hers down. Jim could tell Anthony impressed her, but said nothing.

"Astrid, tell me more about the big elephant we're filming," he said.

"He's old. They say his tusks weigh two hundred pounds, which makes him the largest elephant in Kenya. President Kenyatta identifies with him and has made him famous and protected from hunters. Two younger bull elephant live with and guard him. There's respect and hierarchy in their ranks."

"Yes, I have seen it. It's much to be admired. The human race could learn a lot from elephants. It's unfortunate we humans are not that kind to our own," said Jim.

"Let's eat, I'm starved," said Anne as she picked up the menu. "Roast Impala. It has a sweeter taste than beef. And look! Telapia is on the menu. I haven't tasted that delicious fish in years," she said.

"The champagne is making my nose tickle," said Astrid as she laughed. "I'm having such a good time, and you foreigners are interesting. I hope Dad lets me go with his clients more often. I like this kind of work." Astrid drank another glass of champagne. Anne handed her the menu. "I'm not hungry. I'm too excited to eat." She looked back at Anthony's table. "I think Anthony's cute."

"I wouldn't call him cute, darling. He looks more like a wolf to me. I would eat if I were you. That drink will make you wish you did when you get up in the morning. A champagne hangover can be brutal," said Anne.

"I'd listen to Anne, Astrid. I think she knows what she is talking about."

Astrid smiled at Jim. Jim could tell she was getting drunk. He almost wished that Anne wasn't with him. He found himself attracted to this young girl and he could tell Anne suspected he might be. He knew he'd have to be careful. Jim picked up the menu.

"Have you ever wondered why they feed you so much food in Kenya? Look at all the food on the menu. I like eating light, but there's always a seven-course dinner they expect you to eat.

I'm personally into hamburgers. Don't order one, I've made that mistake."

"It's we English did this. It was part of our colonial culture we brought to Kenya and it has stuck to this day," said Anne. The Italian song "*Nel blu ti di pintonto di blu*" was being played on the piano coming from the bar.

Astrid started to hum the tune. "*Vararie,* oh, oh, oh, oh. That's my favorite song. I never get to go anywhere like this. I'm having so much fun. I never realized until now what I've been missing. That music makes me want to dance. Would you excuse me? I'm going to the bar."

Astrid got up from the table. She weaved a little, taking her full glass of champagne with her and walked into the bar. Jim and Anne exchanged looks.

Anthony got up from his table and followed her.

"We better keep an eye on her. She could get into trouble with that guy," said Jim.

"She's a big girl, Jim. She can take care of herself."

"I'm not so sure. She's had no experience with men. Especially that kind of guy. He's a gangster.

Seventeen

In the early morning Anne and Jim were awakened by a thud from the room next to them. Jim sat up in bed and listened. Then he jumped out of bed and took a glass from the nightstand and put it to the wall and listened with his ear against it. He could hear Astrid's muffled voice coming from within.

"Please don't. You're hurting me. I don't want to. Please, please."

Jim rushed to put on his pants and ran out the door of his room to the room next door and rammed it with his shoulder. The door flew open as Jim rushed in.

Anthony had Astrid pinned down on the bed, her dress raised up under his legs, her arms pinned back with his knees. His pants were open and his erect penis stuck in Astrid's face. He tried to force it into her mouth as she lay under him.

Jim ran to him and pulled him off Astrid, and threw him across the room. He followed, kicking him in the stomach. Anthony groaned with pain. Jim grabbed his hair and pounded his head on the floor. Anne came into the room and rushed to Astrid. Astrid tried to sit up, blood running from her mouth from where Anthony had hit her. She started to sob, but then stopped with nausea taking over, vomiting over the side of the bed.

Anne stood in shock watching what happened before her, not knowing what to do or who to help. Anthony lay semi-conscious on the floor. Jim left him there and went into the bathroom. He ran some cold water on a towel and came out and wiped off Astrid's bruised face.

She sat on the bed sobbing. Anne came over to comfort her sitting down on the ruffled bed next to her.

Jim went back to Anthony, who still lay on the floor, and picked him up by his shoulders, dragging him out of the room down the hallway to an empty laundry hamper. He picked him up and threw him in. He rolled the hamper out through the double doors, out onto the terrace to a sloping lawn above a mountain creek. He gave the hamper a shove and watched it roll down the hill into the stream.

He said to himself. "I hope the lions get the son-of-a-bitch." He went back into the hotel to Astrid's room. His body shook as adrenaline pumped into his blood stream, making his voice weak. He looked at Astrid who seemed to be coming to her senses.

"Anne, can you stay with her? We'll try to get out of here at sunrise. I don't like any of that crowd that jerk hangs with. Did you tell him where we're going last night?" he asked.

"I think I did. I'm all right, Anne," said Astrid. "Please, you don't have to stay with me. I'm sorry to be so much trouble. I'll never drink champagne again." She looked at Jim. "Don't tell my father." Jim nodded. "Now, try to get some sleep. I'll wake you in a couple of hours," said Jim as he and Anne left and went back to their room. They got back into bed, but Jim couldn't sleep and when he did, he dreamed of Astrid.

Eighteen

Helmut's camp site stood on the Rufifi, a wide sandy river filled with islands and pools, formed by rain run-off from the blue-violet mountains in the distance. Green canvas tents stood lined up along the river's edge under the shade of palms, acacia and mimosa trees. The tents had outer flaps and an extended roof, so one could sit with the mosquito net down and view the surrounding countryside and wild animals with relative comfort.

Mark, Helmut, Clay and Tim sat around the camp fire after dinner having drinks in their canvas chairs. In a meadow, a short distance from where they gathered, they could see herds of zebra, impala, giraffe and bushbuck acting almost tame grazing in the meadow, and from the river, eyes of crocodiles dotted the fast-moving water. Hippos slept and ate along the shore. A lion's roar came from out of the forest close to the camp. Everyone seemed to be in their own space listening, looking, and observing the unfamiliar surroundings. Clay broke the silence.

"This place is teaming with game. Helmut, you brought us to the right place. With my new ammunition I'll be able to shoot-em-up real good."

Mark became uncomfortable and moved in his chair.

"Tell me, Mr. Nobertson, do you enjoy killing?" he asked matter-of- factly.

"If you're referring to shooting game. I do. I'm a hunter and I publish stories on hunting in my magazine, "Guns and Targets". Mark gave Clay a hard look and got up from his chair.

"Would you excuse me. I've brought along a good book to read." Mark left the fireside and walked into the dark.

"Do I detect an attitude?" asked Clay annoyed.

"Mark has definite ideas how he wants the planet to remain," replied Helmut.

"That young twerp is an unsuitable companion on a hunting safari. Send him back. I won't tolerate environmental fruitcakes looking over my shoulder every time I fire my rifle."

"I'll make sure he doesn't annoy you. I'll keep him busy with the crew." Helmut rose from his camp chair. "I'm turning in. We'll be leaving first thing after breakfast. Good night." Helmut walked off.

Mark came out of the latrine behind Clay's tent and saw a porcupine perched next to a tree stump, and said, "Don't you run off, you bugger. I'll be back." Mark went to the camp kitchen where Mytoto, the camp cook, his hands in a bowl washing up the dishes. He wore a wrap-around print skirt and wearing a bright red turban. Mark saw Mytoto was about to say something, but Mark put his finger to his lips giving him a sign to be quiet. He motioned *him* to join him. Mark whispered so Clay and Tim were out of ear-shot still at the camp table. "Come, follow me," he said to Mytoto.

Mark stayed out of sight as he and Mytoto made their way back to the latrine. The porcupine hadn't moved. Mark opened the flap of the latrine tent. He motioned Mytoto to herd the porcupine into the tent. He flapped his wrap-around skirt like he was herding a gaggle of geese. The porcupine moved forward toward the latrine tent. Mark left the entrance and helped Mytoto drive the porcupine inside the tent and closed the flap. They both seemed to enjoy their little prank and moved off into the night.

Mark and Helmut shared a tent furnished with two cots, a metal safari table and two camp chairs. A canvas wash basin stood outside. A shower tent was set up behind that was used by the whites. The Africans used the river. Clay had his tent similarly furnished. Tim had a tent by himself. The Africans slept outside under the stars behind the main tent, which was used as dining area and the kitchen.

Mark and Helmut lay in their cots listening to the night sounds of the African bush, happy to be back on safari, the lifestyle they both were born to and loved. A lion's roar could be heard on their side of the river not far away, and the laughing cry of a hyena came from the nearby forest. Hippo sounded in the pools down river. The night skies of the southern hemisphere shone with millions of bright stars reflecting in the blue black heavens along with the glittering Southern Cross. The sweet smell of the cool forest along the river bank penetrated the night air.

"Mark, you awake?" asked Helmut.

"Yes sir. I'm thinking this is real Africa. Not t'all like the National Parks. None of those bloody mini-vans with those bloody heads sticking out trying to get a photo of some wild animal that is almost tame from seeing tourists every day. Thank you again for letting me come with you. I'm finished in Kenya. The bloody *Wogs* won't let me back. I burned my bridges, I did. Maybe I should go to England. Astrid said she wants to go to school at Cambridge. What do you think?"

"My father wanted me to go to school in Germany after the war, but I didn't want to leave Tanganyika. If I had, I'd never have married Astrid's mother, Murlee. We were nineteen. You would have liked my wife. She looked like Astrid and had her independence. Sometimes I look at Astrid and I think I'm looking at Murlee. She died when Astrid turned ten. I thought I would never get over the grief, because of our closeness."

"How did she die?"

"A tsetse fly epidemic, carrying the sleeping sickness. Over one hundred died in our area. Everyone stayed cooped up. The clients dried up. No one wanted to go on safari with the epidemic around. But it left as fast as it came and no doctor or scientist could explain why."

"Astrid told me about her mother," said Mark. "She said she remembered her. This is personal, but I wondered why you didn't get married again?"

"I had opportunities, but I had Astrid to raise. She came first. I found it difficult; I was gone so much out on safari. Molo became her surrogate mother, and he and I taught her about the bush. As you know she can keep up to any *Masi* when to comes to hunting or tracking. I did meet a nice lady. We almost got married, she is an American from Chicago and a widow. She came on safari after her husband died. We related to each other, which was sort of odd being that she came from another world than mine. Astrid liked her, too. But I could see she could never live my life out here. I could never live in a big city. What would I do there? I only know how to stalk wild animals. That kind of man has been gone from the American scene a hundred years. If Astrid does go to England I might think about getting married again. I'm only forty two. If I made an effort I'm sure I could get myself a nice woman."

"Jolly good. What do you think of a bloke like me being your son-in-law? I'm in love with Astrid and hope we'll be able to get married, but right now everything is awl'fy up in the air." "You'd make me very happy. Your dad and I would like that." "Jolly good. Now, if I can get Astrid to say she will."

"Keep working on her. She'll come around."

"I have this." Mark reached for his knapsack and took out the stone and showed it to Helmut.

"What is it?"

"It's an uncut ruby, old boy. It must be worth a fortune. I'm hoping it will be our grub stake in a new life."

"Where did you get it?"

"It's a rather long story. Astrid and I....."

Nineteen

Suddenly, they heard loud screams out of the night. Mark and Helmut jumped from their cots and into their walking shorts and ran out of the tent.

"For Christ's sake someone come, help me." yelled Clay's loud voice coming from the toilet tent. They ran to the tent.

Clay came out of the toilet his shorts down around his ankles. Porcupine quills hung from his backside. "Can you believe, I sat on a fucking porcupine, in the shit house. Christ, someone help get these fucking quills out of my ass. The pain's killing me."

Helmut and Mark got to him first. Clay stood bent over. Porcupine quills hung from his bottom as he stumbled over his dropped shorts. He pulled at the quills letting out a yell as he yanked them loose. Helmut took over and pulled the remaining quills from Clay's butt. Clay screamed profanities with each yank.

Helmut yelled to Mytoto, "Mytoto, bring the iodine and some bandages."

"Yes, Bwana." Mytoto ran off toward the kitchen.

Helmut and Mark helped Clay back to his tent where they laid him down on his stomach to inspect the damage. Mytoto came back to the tent with iodine and bandages and handed them to Helmut. He looked to Mark. Mark gave him a half smile and made a sign with his head letting him know to say nothing of their conspiracy. Helmut poured the dark liquid into the wounds.

Clay screamed with pain. "Christ man! What you doing to me?"

"I've got to kill the germs," said Helmut.

"Get me that little black bag over there." Clay pointed to a back bag on the other cot. Mark picked up the bag and gave it to him. Clay took out some pills and put them into his mouth. Pour me a glass of water. No! Forget the water! Pour me a glass of whiskey.

Mark took the bottle of scotch by the bed and poured a little into a metal cup.

"Fill it up. Can't you see the pain I'm in?" Mark handed him the whiskey and Clay gulped it down.

"Try to get some sleep. The game warden will be here in the morning for the hunt. You'll need all your strength," said Helmut.

"I'll be all right, but my ass won't. Get out of here! I'm goin` get drunk. I'll see ya in the morning, boys."

They left and as they walked back to their tent, they heard the loud roar of a lion close by. They looked at each other uneasily. The Africans reacted, too, and did not want to get back into their sleeping bags.

"Mytoto, put some more wood on the fire and keep it going. Have someone stand guard," said Helmut.

"Yes, Bwana."

Mark and Helmut went back into their tent, but slept with one eye open.

Mytoto had breakfast on the long portable table when Mark and Helmut came into the mess tent the next morning. Sausages, eggs, hot rolls and coffee filled the morning air. The sun had just come up and the camp was getting ready for the day's activities. The African gun bearers were busy cleaning the powerful elephant guns and filling ammo jackets with cartridges.

"*Jambo, Bwana.* See *Simba* spoor outside kitchen? He here in camp. I hear him. Lazy Runi said he hear nothing, but I showed him he here, Bwana. Runi sleep. He says he killed two *Simba*, but I know he lie. He frightened of *Simba* and me too," said Mytoto.

"I'll have a talk with him. Have two shifts tonight with one of the other boys who can stay awake." said Helmut.

"Mark, find how Clay is this morning. See if he needs any help."

"Do I have to? I don't like that ugly American."

"Forget your personal feelings. We have a job to do," answered Helmut's stern voice.

Mark left the table for Clay's tent. He looked in. Clay was gone. He heard sounds of rifles being cocked and walked to a clearing in the dense forest a short distance from the camp. Mark saw a herd of impala, Thompson's gazelle and zebra grazing in the dew covered meadow. From a pile of logs that had brought down by elephant he heard firing of guns and looked over and saw Clay with a fast automatic rifle blasting into the herd.

The animals fell like flies. The others ran in every direction. A few ran toward Mark almost knocking him down as they passed. Mark was horrified at what he saw. He raced over to Clay who kept firing away with his automatic. When he ran out of ammunition he turned to his African gun-bearer and handed the gun for him to load again. The bearer handed back a fresh rifle as Mark jumped Clay and tore the gun from him. Clay struggled with Mark, grabbing for his rifle.

Mark yelled, "Stop your madness, you bloody sick human being."

The sound of gunfire brought Helmut into the clearing. Mark saw him and yelled, "Helmut, this man is crazy. Make him stop the killing." Mark was so upset he could hardly talk. He slumped to the ground weak from the encounter.

Helmut ran to Clay and took his rifle. "It's illegal to shoot game in this manner. If the rangers were here they'd arrest you. As your guide I forbid you to continue." Clay calmed down and looked at

87

Tim, who looked upset. "I got a little too carried away, I guess." He turned to Tim and said, "Come, son. Let's have breakfast. I'm hungry." Mark and Helmut watched as Clay followed by Tim walked through the field of dead animals. Mark looked at Helmut. "Do you see what I've been preaching. Am I so wrong?"

Twenty

In downtown Nairobi a meeting had been called in the mammoth Assembly Hall at the Parliament Building. Minister P.D. Mnazi was standing in front of the packed crowd of MPs.

"These are serious times when our leader's family continue to exploit our national treasures. Our rain forests are being burned down for charcoal to sell to the Gulf States. This horror has got to stop or there will be no forest left for our children and their children." A roar came from the assembly. A few of the old MPs exchanged serious looks, whispering to one another as P.D. Mnazi continued with his speech. "Our people died in the forests with a handful of soil in their hands, believing they had fallen in a noble struggle to regain our land. Now that we have it back, our leaders are exploiting it."

This was accompanied by a strong chorus of boos from some of the MP's. One said, "He's gone too far this time. This is treason."

P.D. continued, "We the government have put good laws in place to stop the illegal poaching and selling of ivory, but how can you stop this illegality when people in high government are taking profit from it, and destroying the very foundation of Kenyan wild life? I have here," he lifted this hand into the air, "photos of a recent raid of poachers led by one of our ruthless neighbors to the north, the Somalis, who have bedded down with our country's leaders. One of our own game department personnel took these photos of the illegal buyers in *Mombasa*. Look, gentlemen! See who this illegal buyer is. Someone we all know in Kenya. Someone we respect in our high government. See for yourself!" He handed the photos to the man seated next to him and the photos were passed around the room. They caused a major furor.

"I have nothing more to say. You're looking at the evidence."

The photos were now in the hands of Major Darassa and Minister Mfalme.

Minister Mafalme spoke into Major Darassa's ear. "It's time to put operation "Hyena" in place. I don't want to hear the details. Call me when you have the results," he said

Major Darassa nodded. MP Mnazi walked out of the Assembly and Major Darassa followed a few feet behind.

Twenty One

The sound of helicopters could be heard in the distance as they approached, flying low over the camp. There was no room to land along the shoreline so they settled on a clearing about a one hundred yards from the camp.

Five miles up river at Behobeho camp, the Kikuyys henchmen rented a shallow-hulled aluminum boat with an outboard motor and loaded it with supplies. Otieno handed Najaro two high-powered Holland & Holland 306 caliber rifles. They shoved off from shore on their cautious journey down river.

Ten minutes into the trip the river opened into a large pool filled with a colony of hippos. A loud bellow came from under the boat as it lifted into the air and tilted to its side, almost throwing them into the murky water. The Kikuyus panicked and reached for their rifles. Again the small boat was rammed from the side. They looked into the water. A small calf was caught up in the motor. The mother became confused and hysterical. She came at the boat again. This time Otieno raised his rifle and fired, shooting her between her wide bulging eyes. Blood spurted from her mouth as three other hippos came at the small boat. Both of the tribesmen started firing into the hippo herd. The brownish water turned into a thick red brown as the bleeding hippos rolled over on their backs and sides.

The blood moved through the water rapidly, reaching the banks of the river's edge, exciting a group of crocodiles that had been sunning on the shore. When they got the scent of blood they lunged into the water and swam out to the dying hippos, starting an eating frenzy amongst themselves as they tore at the black bodies with their lacerating teeth and jaws.

The rest of the hippo herd headed for the river bank, and emerged running off, into the forest, *pounding* down the green flora with their weight.

The river ran red. The Kikyus got the boat clear of the feeding orgy. They shakily proceeded again downriver towards Helmut's safari camp.

Ian Parker, the Tanzanian game warden, and two African helicopter pilots walked into camp as everyone finished breakfast. Helmut got up to greet them.

"Good morning, Ian. How was your trip from *Arusha?*"

"Jolly good. Good to see you, Helmut. This is Mathew and John, our pilots."

Helmut and Mark shook their hands. "Mytoto, bring some coffee," said Helmut. They sat down at the metal table facing Mark, Clay and Helmut.

"We spotted the elephant herds twenty minutes by air from here. They're traveling in two large groups. Must be over three hundred of the buggers. We'll round them up with the choppers. There's a box canyon we can drive them into not too far from where they're now. We'll fly you blokes in where you can take a position and knock them off when they come through the canyon entrance."

Clay and Tim looked at each other and smiled.

"I'm Clay Nobertson, publisher of *"Guns and Targets"*. This is my editor and son, Tim. He needs to get some photos from the air of the round-up before the kill. Can you accommodate him?"

"No problem, mate. Are you blokes ready?" asked Ian.

"Mark, you come with me and Ian. Clay and Tim will go with Runi," said Helmut.

Runi told the other gun bearers where they were going. They packed up the guns and ammo and followed Parker and John out of the camp to the choppers, Helmut bringing up the rear.

Twenty Two

Mark, Helmut, Ian and the pilot squeezed into the small helicopter and took off from the clearing and headed out for Mikumi National Park with Helmut's gun-bearer Runi. Clay, Tim and two Tanzania rangers followed in the other helicopter. They followed the Rufifi river as it wandered north. From the air Helmut spotted the red flow of blood in the river below. He motioned to the pilot to circle down to get a better look.

Otieno and Najaro were traveling downriver without the help of their outboard engine, not wanting the sound to bring any attention. They heard the helicopters approaching overhead and brought their small boat into shore under a group of wide-spreading acacia trees and waited as they watched the two copters fly by.

From the helicopter, there was no sign of anything other than the crocs indulging in a feast.

"Someone has killed those hippos. Those crocs would never attack them alive. What do you make of it, Ian?" asked Helmut.

"I agree, but we don't have time to investigate." Ian motioned the pilot to go on.

They flew on for twenty minutes, passing over ravines, thick forests, river valleys and plateaus into a wide valley where a small river flowed making a green belt along its course. As they came closer to the ground, they saw a wide path of devastation: huge trees had been overthrown and were spread asunder: cedars, cypress, mimosas, acacias, all torn to shreds, and tall fields of grass trampled flat. It looked as if a tornado had cut a wide path through the valley floor. The devastation was a sure sign that elephants were up ahead.

Mark saw the elephants first in the distance and pointed them out. A long formation of earth-brown and gray rounded shapes moved in a wide path. They looked larger and larger the closer they got. Their numbers covered a mile of track. The copter came down low over the backs of the moving herd and caused them to panic. The leader, an old female, stopped and flapped her big ears back and forth and pointed her trunk up in the air at the helicopter defiantly.

"I don't want to shoot them from the air. I'll take you blokes up ahead to the mouth of that canyon and drop you there," said Ian. The copter flew on ahead of the herd. The other copter made some circles for Tim's photo purposes and flew on to catch up. They merged into a small-mouthed canyon and landed. Everyone got out and checked the area for cover. Ian sent the two copters back to the camp to pick up the gun bearers and ammunition.

The noon heat, more than a hundred degrees, scorched them. They stood at the rocky canyon entrance with no shade from the African sun, which beat down on them, penetrating their clothing. Stinging black flies buzzed around their bodies, biting any part of their skin that wasn't covered. The sun had cracked and baked the rocky terrain of dry red ocher dirt with its force blinding them. Mark squinted to bring his eyes into focus. A small breeze came up now and then making the condition more bearable.

Helmut and Mark followed Ian as he walked around surveying the area. A large mass of rock stood in the middle of the mouth of the canyon. They scrambled onto the rock pile and looked back into the valley.

"This is a perfect position to set up the guns," said Ian. "Helmut, Mark, and Clay, stay on this side of the pile and I'll take the rest with me on the other side. The elephant will come down through the valley floor and when they get to this point, they'll fan off to each side. We can trap the buggers in the canyon. We should be safe up on the sides of these rocks."

Mark started to feel sick. Could it be the heat, he thought, or the fact that he was going to kill these majestic creatures? He had killed elephants before, but only to put them out of their misery when he came upon them in the bush dying from starvation or lack of water. But now he knew he had to kill for a reason he didn't believe in. He stood on the rock pile about to kill off a herd of healthy elephants, because some government researcher told some officials that the elephant killed all the native flora and fauna in the National Parks and they had become deserts because of it. Mark couldn't believe it. It didn't make sense to him. As far as he was concerned, the elephants stood for everything that meant East Africa. He was about to help slaughter its national resource.

"I feel awf'ly sick, Helmut. I think I got in over my head. I can't kill. My conscience won't let me," said Mark.

"Mark, you have to see this in different light. There're too many elephants in this area. If we don't kill them, they will starve to death. You saw what happened in Kenya during the drought. How did you feel when you had to kill those elephant because they were too weak from starvation to get up on their feet? It's the same here. We're saving them from future misery," said Helmut.

They heard two shots fired. They turned at the sound and hurried over to where Clay stood. He had his .45 caliber handgun in his hand. The chamber still smoked. At his feet laid a four-foot puff adder, its head blown off.

"I almost stepped on the son-of-a-bitch," said Clay as he pushed the snake off the ridge with his foot.

"Keep your eye out for those buggers. They live among these rocks. Have you got your position staked out?" asked Ian.

"I'll stay right here. When my gun-bearer gets here with the Rigby .416 and my .375 Magnum, I'll be in the best position to splatter them. Now don't you guys forget ...the biggest tusker in the herd is mine. No one else can shoot him. You got that?" said Clay. Clay repulsed Mark. What an ugly American, he thought. He knew that he could never become a white hunter like his father or Helmut. He knew he could never put up with people of this sort.

Mark took a long drink from his canteen and handed it to Helmut, who finished it off. He sat on a rock and waited for the copters to return. His thoughts went to Astrid.

Twenty Three

Astrid's hangover woke her early. She knelt in the bathroom, her head over the toilet experiencing the dry heaves. Her sides ached. Everything came back to her about last night, that made her feel worse and embarrassed. She thought she couldn't face Jim and Anne. What a naive fool they must think her. And when she thought about Anthony, she got sicker. Anne had warned her about him, but she didn't listen. She had never drunk champagne before and she was sure she would never touch it again. It affected her judgment. She had to get herself together, she thought. The trip to Marasbit would take at least a day and she had a lot to do to get the camp in shape for the film crew. She heard a knock on the room door. She made her way over to open it, feeling dizzy and unsure on her feet as she walked. She opened the door. Jim stood in front of her with a pot of coffee.

"I thought that you might need this. How you doing today?" he asked, looking her over.

"I'm awf'ly embarrassed and thank you for saving me from that terrible man." She started to cry and went into Jim's arms for comfort. She remained for a moment sobbing on his chest. She could feel Jim's breath becoming shorter as he held her. The smell of his strong warm body aroused her. She could feel his erection against her. She looked up at his face and saw in his eyes that he wanted her. She pushed herself away. What was happening, she thought. Why was she acting this way? Stop, Stop. Get yourself together. You're making a fool of yourself. Her head was pounding. The dizziness had made her sick again. She raced toward the bathroom, getting there just in time as she slammed the door and hit the bowl. Tears came to her eyes as she heaved and heaved. Weakness made her fall to the bathroom floor, her head still over the toilet bowl. I'll never drink again, she thought. She heard Jim at the door. "Are you all right?" his voice asked.

She answered weakly, "Yes, give me a few minutes."

Twenty Four

Ian directed the operation and got everyone in position to the kill elephants. Mark, Helmut and their gun bearers stood on the right side of the rock pile. Clay, Tim and their assistants stood positioned on the left. On the hillside across from them stood one of the Tanzania Park rangers armed with a semi-automatic rifle. On the other side was the other Ranger with a long barrel elephant gun.

Mark watched in the distance as the two helicopters kept the elephant in formation, moving them forward to what would be their graveyard. The red dust blew thick as a rain cloud, as it moved forward toward them with the movement of the herd. The trumpeting from the large bulls could be heard as they tried to keep the herd together. They moved back and forth within the herd to keep the younger elephants moving, encouraging them to keep pace with the rest. The helicopters repeatedly dived at the herd, pushing them on.

When the massive formation got to the mouth of the canyon, the old matriarch, in the lead, got scent of the men in front of her and balked. Her ears moved back and forth and her trunk flew up as she sniffed at the air, backing up. The other elephants stopped behind her, and sniffed at the air and pawed at the ground, not wanting to go on farther. The copter pilot overhead, seeing the

101

herd would go no farther, came down and almost touched the backs of the pack, which frightened them into moving ahead.

Mark looked up at the sky and saw that the vultures were gathering overhead. They came from nowhere anticipating the slaughter. He pointed them out to the rest of the group. How did they know? He wondered. He had seen this before. Another of nature's mysteries. Mark saw a huge bull elephant moving up to the front of the herd. His tusks, Mark figured, would weigh about one hundred pounds. He had never seen that big an elephant before. He stood three feet above the rest of the herd. Mark looked over at Clay, whose attention focused on the bull and watched him raise his powerful rifle and take aim.

"Don't shoot! You bloody fool! You'll panic and scatter the herd," yelled Mark.

"Let the herd get inside the canyon before you shoot. I'll tell you when," yelled Ian.

The herd started to move forward again. They were nervous and cautious as they moved past the hunters, snorting with their raised trunks. The small calves remained close to the underside of their mothers, which made it difficult for the cows to move forward. The hunters had their guns sighted on the animals as they moved by. The big bull saw the Tanzanian ranger up on the side of the canyon and took off up the side of the hill trying to attack him, but it was too steep for him to maneuver. He backed down, moving on as he looked back at the ranger.

Mark felt the excitement of the kill in his stomach. He tried to keep his emotions under control, but he wished he wasn't there. The whirling blades of the helicopter were so close they deafened him. The red dust cloud swirled up around him, blinding him and the rest of the hunters. He could barely see the massive herd in front of him as it moved through the induced tornado cloud into the canyon. Mark opened his dust-covered eyes, which burned as he did. He could see that the copters had done their job well. The elephants were inside the canyon, backed up against its steep walls. They had turned their massive bodies around and were facing the hunters. Screams, roars, and trumpeting cries came from the herd as it anticipated danger.

Ian raised his hand for all to see and gave the command. "Get ready, you blokes! I'll take the leader, the old female, out first, "said Ian.

Twenty Five

Everyone took aim at an elephant in front of him. "Aim, fire!" he yelled.

The roar of so many elephant guns going off at the same time was deafening. The old female dropped to the ground. The other elephant came toward her, confused, not knowing what to do next. As Helmut and the other hunters started to shoot the elephants the animals dropped to their knees in front of them. After the first line of elephants down, the hunters shot the second line and then the third. The gun-bearers took the rifles back from the hunters and loaded them again and again, the empty shells flying in all directions. As fast as they could get the cartridges into the chambers, the hunters fired them again.

Clay dripped with sweat. He had sighted the big bull and shot at him but missed the critical mark to bring him down. The elephant had disappeared into the pack.

"What's the matter, Dad? You missed him," said Tim with a smile.

"Shut up! There was a light in my eye," said Clay.

Mark's emotions had gotten away from him. He put his gun down at his side and from deep within him he felt a terrible sadness. He started to sob. He couldn't do it. He hated himself for being here, as part of the slaughter.

Helmut looked over at him and saw his condition. He said nothing but went back to killing the elephants.

Mark looked up and saw the stream of fresh thick red blood that had dammed up; it broke loose and ran down the hill toward him. He could smell its salty odor as it flowed by him making him sick to his stomach. He turned his head away to vomit. Mark knew that he could never kill another wild animal.

Over the hill to the rear of the canyon, Mark saw another helicopter appear on the horizon. He could make out the name painted on the sides in black letters, SAVE THE WILDLIFE WORLD ORGANIZATION. Derek Palmer, Astrid's friend, had come to save the herd. He flew the copter and another man sat beside him in the small Bell aircraft as it moved over the herd toward the hunters. The helicopter swooped down on the rear of the herd, dropping smoke bombs in its midst, terrifying the elephant pack, making them move out of the gorge toward the hunters.

Just as Clay had the big bull sighted to shoot again, the bull rushed forward through the remaining herd and downed elephant corpses, charging the hunters on the rock pile. Clay fired at the bull as he climbed; unfazed by the bullets, it continued to charge. The loose rock under its feet caused the shale to give away and slide downward.

The falling rock started a avalanche of moving pebbles, making the footing give away under Helmut's feet. Mark, seeing this, left his position on the rock pile to grab Helmut. Mark reached out to hold on to him, but Helmut's feet went out from under him, his rifle flew into the air and he fell down in front of the big bull.

Ian had the bull in his gun sight. As the elephant was about to pick Helmut up with his trunk and stomp him under his feet, Ian pulled the trigger of his high-powered rifle sending the bullet into the elephant's brain. The bull's knees buckled and its massive body fell on the rock in front of Helmet.

Mark slid down the loose slope to Helmut. Ian followed. They brought a shaken Helmut to his feet.

The remaining herd raced from the gorge through the dust and smoke making it impossible for anyone to see them pass. Only the deafening clamor and cries were heard as the sound of the pack disappeared into a red dust cloud.

Everyone was shaken by what had happened.

"Who alerted those environmental assholes? They're taking all the fun from the sport. Just as I was about to get the biggest trophy of my life. I can't believe anyone could find us here." Clay looked at Mark."

"Did you tip those guys off?"

"No, but I wish I had. I'd feel better," said Mark.

"Cut the bickering. Help finish off what we started," said Ian. He left his position on the rock pile and motioned for the others to follow. He ran to the heap of carcasses of the fallen elephant herd. He and the others walked through mountains of dead and dying. Ian and the Rangers fired into the brains of the wounded, to finish them off.

Down from the clear sky came the multitudinous vultures. They landed on dead elephants. With their featherless heads they ripped into the freshly opened wounds, devouring the flesh, as they fought amongst themselves for position.

A long silence took over the hunters. Only Clay seemed to be high with emotion. Mark noticed that no one else made any jokes and seemed to keep their feelings to themselves.

Ian spoke first. "We'll let the carcasses rot in the sun for a few days. It will make it easier to pull the ivory."

"That big bull was mine. I shot him too. I want his ivory now! I'm taking it back with me in the helicopter. You got my money I put up for my license, so I want my ivory," said Clay.

Ian looked at Clay, and then at Mark and Helmut. Mark knew Ian had the same feelings he did.

Ian yelled to the two rangers who were surveying the dead herd. "You blokes, get those tusks off that big bull. We'll take the bloody pair with us back to camp," yelled Ian.

Clay looked pleased and joined the two rangers as they took a chain saw to remove the giant tusks from the skull of the bull elephant.

Twenty Six

The Kikuyus pursuers had arrived on the outskirts of the camp at midday. They hid the light boat upstream under some palm trees and covered it with fronds. They made their way down toward the camp, keeping undercover. They watched Mytoto, the cook, cleaning vegetables outside the mess tent for the evening meal. A big fire crackled in the fire-pit, heating large tin canisters of water for the evening showers. Mytoto's assistant lay under the shade of an acacia tree waving the flies from his face as he rested.

The Kikuyus henchmen sat undercover in the forest. Otieno reached into his rucksack, and brought out some jerky and handed a piece to Najaro. They both chewed on the dried impala meat as they waited for the hunters to return.

The helicopters dropped down on the clearing. Mark, Helmut and Runi, the gun-bearer, got out and proceeded to the camp. Mytoto met them and handed them each a highball. They sat down on camp chairs and relaxed with their drinks. They felt tired, sweaty, and dirty. Helmut's khaki shirt and pants were caked with dried blood.

He took off his shirt and yelled at Mytoto.

"Bring some hot water. I want to take a shower and get into some fresh clothes."

Mark sat in his canvas chair saying nothing but feeling depressed.

"What's the matter? Are you still upset about today?" asked Helmut.

"You're bloody damn right I am. I thought what we did was a bloody crime against nature. Those elephants would have moved on to somewhere else to find food. They're intelligent, they have survival instincts. There's a million acres of wilderness south of here. We didn't have to kill them. It's a bloody awful thing we did."

"You're right, Mark. I have always operated using instinct, but we have scientists telling us what is right and what is wrong with our ecosystem, and they have the ear of the government officials who make the decisions. Today convinced me that I will never shoot another wild animal again, unless it's for food. I guess I can get used to photo tourists on my safaris," said Helmut.

Mytoto ran to Helmut. "Bwana, hot water ready."

"Jolly good." Helmut went to his the tent and came back with a towel wrapped around his waist and went to the shower tent. Mark finished his drink and went into the tent to rest.

Twenty Seven

Watching them with a pair of field glasses from the nearby forest was Otieno. He handed the binoculars to Najaro as he watched Mark enter his tent. He brought the glasses down. He smiled as they waited for nightfall.

Ian Parker brought the rest of the group back from the hunt.

Helmut joined him. "Ian, I owe you my life today. It was a lesson to me. I'm retiring from hunting."

"You'll be missed, Helmut. I'd do the same if I could. I have another five years before I can retire. It's not at all like the old days. The fun is gone. There's no sport left. Just mass killing. I love those packy too much to put them away the way we did today. I know you won't tell anybody, but I was happy to see those crusaders show up. I'd wish them luck if I could." Ian put out his hand. "I'll see ya around, Helmut. Take care."

Ian and the rangers got back in the helicopter and took off, Helmut waving to them.

The sun started to go down and night would soon engulf the camp. The forest started to come alive with sounds of the animals pursuing their evening meal.

Clay and Tim had cleaned up and showered and had come out of their tents to sit around the fire to wait dinner. Mark and Helmut joined them. Clay seemed drunk. "The photos I got today should be a sensation. I shot twenty rolls. I'll soup up the negatives to see how they look," said Tim.

"I can't believe I didn't kill that bull. I must have shot him three times, but the game warden brought him down. That really pissed me off. He could of let me do it."

"Oh, you'd let the bugger kill Helmut, huh?" asked Mark.

"You know kid, you're a trouble maker. I can't figure why you're here. If my kid were chicken like you, I'd of left him home."

"If I had a father like you, I'd of stayed home." Mark looked to Tim, who half smiled at his remark.

"That bull was mine. As far as the world knows I shot him. I know every big game hunter would give his left nut to trade places with me right now. Wait till our readers see the size of that elephant's tusks. They're gonna shit. This elephant has got to be the biggest one in Africa, and I got him."

"He's not the biggest. The biggest is Ahmed," said Mark.

"Where is this Ahmed?" asked Clay becoming suddenly interested in Mark's statement.

"He's up in Marsabit. They say his tusks are over one hundred pounds each."

"Why am I not there hunting him?" asked Clay as he looked at Helmut for an answer.

Mark answered for him. "You can't hunt Ahmed. He's sacred. President Kenyatta has him protected. He's a national treasure. , "When Ahmed *dies… I die" said* Kenyatta. "H*e's* in his eighties," said Mark.

"Where is Marsabit?" asked Clay.

"It's up in the Northern Territory," Helmut said. "My daughter is there now. She's a guide on a film crew. They're photographing Ahmed for a movie."

Clay looked over at Tim and they exchanged looks. "I was telling Tim before we got out here tonight," said Clay, "We should go on back to the States. I got my elephant. He has his photos and a story. I still got a lion and a water buffalo on my license, but I've shot them before. It wouldn't be any new kick for me. I'll pay you guys off. You gave me a great adventure and I'm happy with the results. So what do you say? Let's call it a hunt."

"Fine with me. I can join my daughter and an old friend of mine in Marsabit. Mytoto, another whiskey," said Helmut.

Mark couldn't have been happier about what he heard. He would go to Marsabit with Helmut and see Astrid. He would get away from this awful American. But how? He thought, I'm a wanted man in Kenya. If I fly in a small plane I could get there without going through customs. It would be his only way. He would get Helmut to charter a plane. Mark came back from his thoughts and noticed that Helmut drank more tonight than he had ever seem him drink before. He must be celebrating, he thought. No more hunting.

Mytoto came and said, "Bwana, dinner she served." Everyone got up from their chairs and brought them with them as they moved into the dining tent. Clay poured everyone's glass full of whiskey. Mytoto brought a kettle to the table and poured turtle soup into their bowls. He had caught the turtle in the river that afternoon, but didn't tell them the river was full of blood. Mark noticed everyone's spirits were up. Clay made jokes as Mytoto served the fried telapia.

Twenty Eight

The smell of cooked food drifted across the camp site into the forest where the Kikuyus *sat in the d*ark, watching. The aroma of roasted meat penetrated their nose. Their stomachs growled with hunger. The mosquitoes came up as the sun went down, making their wait uncomfortable. The tattooed Otieno, pulled a *panga* sword from his rucksack. Its large shining blade flashed in the light of the camp fire in the distance as he moved a pumice stone up and down the long blade, making it razor sharp.

When everyone finished their dinner they moved back to the fire for more drinking. Again, a lion's roar was heard close by. Everyone exchanged glances and became uncomfortable.

Helmut went to the kitchen to find Mytoto. "Have Runi watch the fire tonight. Tell him to stay awake this time and keep the fire going."

"Yes, Bwana."

Helmut went to the portable radio. He sat down and put on the earphones. "Helmut Dryden at safari camp on the Rufifi river in Selous calling. Come in, Dar es Salaam."

"Dar es Salaam, *Rufifi*. "Over."

"Rufifi camp. Have a plane pick us up in the morning. We're terminating our safari. Over and out".

Helmut walked back to the camp fire to join the others. By the way he walked, Mark could see the drinks had taken their effect.

"The plane will be here at ten 'o clock in the morning. I'm going to turn in. I'll see you at breakfast. Good night," said Helmut as he went into his tent.

Mark said to Tim. "You got an empty cot in your tent?" Tim nodded his head.

"Jolly good. If you don't mind, old Helmut snores too much and I need some sleep. I didn't get much last night. May I bed down in your tent, old boy?"

"Be my guest," said Tim.

"That's sporting of you," said Mark.

"Hey, kid. Tim and I are going to Nairobi tomorrow. Where should we stay?"

"The city dump. I hear it's jolly good."

Clay looked to Tim. "Wise-ass, this kid. You know something. I could get to appreciate you more, son, after this trip. I'm turning in. Come help me with my wound. It needs a fresh dressing and don't bring iodine." Clay cautiously got up from his camp chair and moved slowing toward his tent carrying a bottle of whiskey in his hand.

Mark sat in front of the fire looking out into the darkness as Tim got up and went into Clay's tent. Mark could hear them talking but couldn't make out what they were saying. He started to think about Astrid. She's going to be surprised to see us tomorrow, he thought. It had been a terrible day for him. He would never forget it. He knew he'd have nightmares tonight because of his experience.

Twenty Nine

The camp fire started to die down. Mark picked up a couple of logs that were lying near by and threw them on the fire. He stood before it as the fresh logs caught. The flames lit up the area, casting a large shadow of his body across the camp clearing.

Mark was observed by the Kikuyus from their position in the undergrowth. They watched him as he left the fireside and walked over into his tent. They got up from where they were and moved slowly and quietly around the campsite keeping out of sight.

At Mark's tent he picked up a few personal things. Helmut was dead asleep, snoring like an old dog. He came out and then went into Tim's tent down from his. He heard Tim and Clay still in conversation in Clay's tent. Mark got into the spare cot and went to sleep as soon as his head hit the pillow. When Tim came in later, Mark remained in a deep sleep.

The camp had quieted down. The Africans were in their sleeping bags. Runi, the Masai, came over to the fire and put some more logs on and sat down in front of it. He wrapped his bright red Masai robe around his body and made himself comfortable for the night watch.

The wild African sounds of the night filtered through the camp. Most everyone slept, except for the Kikuyus had moved to the trees behind Mark and Helmut's tent.

They watched Runi from the jungle's edge. His head would fall from time to time as he tried to keep awake. Otieno got down in a crouch and moved slowly into the camp. He carried his panga in his teeth as he crawled by the sleeping Africans like a black panther in the night. He reached the mess tent, and went to look for something to eat. He opened a tin container filled with part of a roast that had not been eaten for dinner. He took the tin with him as he sneaked back out of the camp to join Najaro in the forest.

After they had eaten the impala roast, they both moved up to the forest side of Helmut's tent. They could hear snoring from within. Otieno lifted his sword and made a long slit in the side of the tent and pulled back the canvas making it large enough to enter. In the darkness of the tent he could make out the shape of a body asleep on the cot. He raised both arms and hands that held the handle of the *panga* and brought it down with the force of a guillotine. Helmut's severed head fell on to the cot and his torso jerked with spasms as his dismembered head fell to the ground. Quietly, Otieno made his way out the tent the way he entered.

Runi still remained in his same position by the fire. He had heard no noise to alarm him.

A lion nearby in the forest got the scent of fresh blood and came toward the camp sniffing at the air as he moved. The fresh smell brought him up behind Helmut's tent. He went in through the hole made by Otieno. The lion picked up Helmut's torso in its mouth and dragged it out of the tent into the forest. The sound of the lion's movements alerted Runi. He left the fireside and went to explore Helmut's tent.

"*Simba! Simba!*" he yelled.

Mark jumped from his cot when he heard Runi call out. He got into his shorts and grabbed his .306 and chased out followed by Clay and Tim. They entered Helmut's tent. Mark stood horrified by what he saw. The tent was full of blood. Helmut's severed head was on the ground, his torso missing.

Runi ran in pursuit of the lion. Mark and the rest followed him into the forest. Runi called from ahead. The darkness and the thick brush made it difficult to move fast. They had to pick their way through as their eyes got adjusted to the dense forest. Mark could see Runi's shadow ahead as they moved on.

The lion stopped and dropped Helmut's torso to challenge the pursuers. It stood over Helmut's torso as Mark and the others approached. Runi had his bright flashlight positioned on him. The lion stood frozen and blinded at the spotlight that reflected in its savage yellow eyes, roaring a defiant sound in their ears. Mark moved up next to Runi and raised his high- powered rifle and sighted the lion between the eyes and pulled the trigger. The snarling beast dropped to the ground, his body falling on top of Helmut's torso.

Mark and Helmut's safari crew were beside themselves with grief as they buried Helmut in the early morning on a small hill back from the river's bank. Mark knew Helmut's death was meant to be his. How could he tell Astrid,? he thought. He had a terrible guilty feeling. If he had been in the tent he might have saved Helmut, but they were after him. He tried to put the thought out of his mind. He should be with Astrid. He had to tell her he loved her and their fate together had been sealed with Helmut's death. He knew Helmut would want that. She would need him. I have to get to Marsabit, he thought, but how?

The small plane landed in the grass clearing. Mark, Clay and Tim loaded their possessions. They tied the large ivory tusks to the landing gear. Clay had insisted that the ivory go with him. Runi and Mytoto, who had worked so many years as part of Helmut's safari team were like part of his family, showed tears when they said goodbye to Mark. Mark could see how much they had loved him. He himself displayed tears as he got on the airplane.

Runi and Mytoto would break camp and bring Helmut's supplies back to Moshi. Clay had given Mark the money he owed Helmut plus a bonus, which gave Mark the money he needed to get to Marsabit and Astrid.

Mark instructed the pilot to circle the camp and to dip the airplane wings in a final salute to Helmut, who lay buried on the Rufifi. Mark thought it had to be a fitting place for Helmut to be beside the great hunter, Ionides, and the explorer, Selous, the two men responsible for making the Selous the greatest wild life sanctuary in the world.

The small aircraft turned east and headed into the sun.

Thirty

Anne had finished packing when Jim came back to their room.

"Did you check on Astrid this morning? Frankly, darling. I suggest we get on straightaway. I don't like those friends of Anthony's. They could cause us trouble. Graham called. He's waiting for us in the Land Rover."

"As you predicted, Astrid has a hangover, she'll be okay," said Jim. He walked over to pick up his bag. "I'm ready. My bag is packed." Anne closed the lid on her *Louis Vuitton* case and gave it to him. "We'll go down the side entrance. We can avoid anyone in the lobby that might be interested in our destination," said Jim."

When they left their room, Jim knocked at Astrid's door. She came out carrying her one bag. She looked sheepish and demure. She kept her head down and wouldn't look up at Anne or Jim.

She murmured, "Good morning." Then after a pause. "I'll go and pay the hotel bill and meet you out front"

"No," said Jim, "I'll have Graham pay the bill. No one saw him last night so we can quietly get on our way."

The red dust flew from under the wheels of the Land Rover as the four sped on their journey northward. They left the green fertile highlands of Kenya behind and moved on into the vast

121

desert wastelands of the northern frontier. For miles they seemed to be alone in the desert. Only a few wild animals were seen on the parched soil. They stopped to have lunch at the Samburu Game Lodge. They sat on the veranda of the hotel that overlooked the Ewaso Nyiro River. For luncheon entertainment, they and the guests of the lodge watched a leopard eat a goat that had been killed previously and tied to the tree for bait across the river. A group of green monkeys came into the dining room and hopped onto the long buffet table and stole food. A couple of waiters tried to scare them off, but they had gotten tame with time and wouldn't leave.

Astrid remained quiet through lunch, her face still flushed from last night's drinking experience. Jim saw her problem and said.

"You'd feel better if you had a beer. It helps with hangovers."

"The thought makes me sick," said Astrid curtly.

"Just trying to be helpful. How far is it from here to *Marsabit?*" asked Jim.

"About a hundred miles. It's all desert until we get there. It will be a relief from all this sand. The forests are thick and alive with animals. Some of the biggest ivory in Africa lives around the area. They call the place old elephant graveyard."

"Isn't it wonderful, darlings, how the elephant take care of their own? It would be nice to see more of that in the human race, but we seem to have gotten to be so selfish in our lives that we ignore our old people."

"Not in America we haven't. We have Social Security," said Jim.

"Oh, I don't mean it that way. England has socialized medicine and pensions, but that's not the same. I'm talking about one-on-one. Being kind to one another," said Anne.

"Elephant have a hierarchy in their ranks, the old take care of the young. We could all learn from them," said Astrid as she looked at her watch. "Let's get on with the journey or it will be dark when we arrive at Marsabit."

The Land Rover stopped to let a camel caravan pass. Two hundred or more camels tied nose to tail in a long procession filed by in front of them. The male camel herders led the caravan. Bringing up the rear were the women, dressed in colorful robes, swathes of brightly colored clothes covering their heads and faces from the sun and the blowing sand. Elaborate jewelry peeked from beneath their garments. "Jim, we've got to follow that caravan and get them to stop," said Anne.

"Why? You have a good view of them from here."

"I know that, darling, but I'm interested in their jewelry! I love what they're wearing. It's gorgeous. I can see a giant jewelry display in Harrods's. It could make me some of money. Oh, please follow them. Here! Let me wave some money at them," she replied, opening her bag and waving a five-hundred-shilling note out of the window.

"They're the Rendelle tribe, they're camel herders. Their route takes them into Ethiopia," said Astrid.

"They're stunning-looking, darling. I love their costumes, and their jewelry is divine! I've got to take some pieces back to London with me. It will be a sensation. I have never seen such original and beautiful designs."

"They make it themselves from iron and a kind of crude copper and steel that they forge in little makeshift furnaces. It's quite fascinating to watch how they do it, and the semi-precious stones are mined in hills somewhere out here in the desert," said Astrid.

"Oh, Jim, please try to stop them. I've got to have that jewelry."

"Graham, let's try to get some footage of the caravan. I might be able to use it somewhere in the feature. Use the Ariflex. It's packed behind your seat."

"Jolly Good. I'll be set up in a jiff."

They must have looked ridiculous to the Rendelle as they chased after them through the desert. Jim raced ahead of them in the Land Rover, making a dust cloud that covered the caravan with a fine gray powder. He stopped in front of the leader. Anne jumped out of the Rover and ran up to the women who were startled by her presence. Anne stared at their jewelry as she motioned to the women to let her see it. "Astrid, darling. Help me. Tell her I want to buy the jewelry they're wearing," said Anne.

"I'm sure they've never seen a white women before. Be careful, they might think you're trying to harm them," said Astrid.

"Don't be silly, darling. They can see I mean no harm. These women look so refined and their taste in jewelry is divine. Tell them I will pay them handsomely," said Anne, moving in closer to examine their wares.

Graham had his Ariflex rolling as he ran between the camels and the herders. The camels smelled and made grotesque sounds and passed wind. Astrid walked over to the herder who looked most like their leader and in Swahili asked if the women would sell their jewelry. The herder told her he knew very little of Swahili and then called out: Hashim. A young man came forward and spoke to her in Swahilli.

"I speak, Memsaab," he said.

Astrid answered him in Swahili and said. "This lady wants to buy your women's jewelry. Could you arrange it?"

Hashim ran to the rear of the caravan and started talking rapidly to the women. A group of them came forward and showed their adornments and ornamentations to Astrid while Anne examined them admiringly. Anne pointed to what she wanted out of the offering. The jewelry looked as if it were part amber, part filigree silver, with semi-precious stones surrounded by arabesque designs. The Rendelle women laughed among themselves and their eyes grew wide when Anne handed them money. They thanked Anne and began counting it. "They think they made a great deal with you", said Astrid.

"I know that I have, but don't tell them," said Anne as she put a large string of amber up to her neck. "Isn't it divine, darling? I can hardly wait to get to London to show it to my friends." She waved goodbye to the camel herders who started up the caravan and moved on their way.

"Well, Graham, are you happy with the footage?"

"Right O. All we need is a desert epic." They climbed back into the Land Rover and continued on.

As they returned from the open desert to the road they saw a gray Range Rover speed by as it threw up a cloud of red dust in its path. Jim didn't see the driver; he was more interested in the vehicle itself. He had never seen the new Range Rover before. If he *had* seen the driver he would have kept it to himself. Anthony Roseli sat behind the wheel.

Thirty One

A white four-door Mercedes sedan pulled up in front of the Hilton Hotel coffee shop in downtown Nairobi. An attendant dressed in a white uniform took the car as Minister Mnazi got out. He was dressed in a pin-striped English suit with a red carnation in his lapel and wore black and white wing-tipped shoes.

"Good day, Minister. Major Darassa is inside looking for you," said the attendant, concerned. "Minister, my wife woke this morning and told me about a dream she had. She is frightened about your safety. In her dream a hyena carried your body away. Be careful, Minister," begged the attendant.

Mnazi looked at him with a nervous smile. "Don't worry, old man. Nothing is going to happen to me."

He walked into the crowded coffee shop. Most of the regular crowd had gathered. Undercover police, tour operators, dope traffickers, tourists and government officials. The Minister recognized most of them. He spotted Major Darassa and went to his table. The Major got up to greet him. The Major had on his aviator dark glasses, which made him look more menacing. His fresh starched khaki uniform custom-fitted his large frame. A beret that he never seemed to remove accented his wide face and head.

"Good morning, Major. Can I join you?" Minister and the Major sat down. "You've been inquiring about me."

"Yes, Minister. That speech you made yesterday in Parliament has caused controversy in the party. Some of the MPs are concerned about your accusations. Mzee wants to see you. You have hurt him with your insinuations about his family. He wants to make amends and begs to see you. He's at his farm in Kiambu. I can drive you there."

"I have not seen our President for over six months, and the last time we talked wasn't a pleasant experience."

"Minister, you go back too far with him. No one knows him as well. You were at his side in those early years of our cause to free our country from the British. For old times' sake please see him. He misses your counsel." Mnazi thought for a minute and said. "How long will it take?"

"We should be there for lunch. I'll have you back by four o' clock at the latest."

"Very well, after you."

They got up from the table and walked outside to Major Darassa's waiting car. As they opened their doors to get in, two uniformed men got into the back of car with Mnazi and Major Darassa.

The old attendant watched as the Minister and Major Darassa's men sped off. A shadow passed over his head. He looked up into the cloudless sky and saw a vulture circling.

Thirty Two

Later that day they arrived in the small village of Marsabit. The gray Range Rover sat empty in front of a small concrete building that said, "HEADQUARTERS MARSABIT RESERVE."

Jim said, "There's that Range Rover. I've never seen one of those up close. I'd like to stop and look it over."

"It will be here tomorrow, Jim. It's late and everyone is tired. Let's get on to the camp," said Astrid.

Jim looked around and saw that everyone agreed. They drove on.

Anthony Roseli stood inside at the front desk in the ranger headquarters office. A Baron tribesman, dressed in ranger uniform, approached him.

"There's a film company camped somewhere around the area. Do you know its location?"

The ranger pointed. "Up that road, Bwana, one mile and a half. On south side, Bwana. Many tents. You see."

"Thanks, governor." Anthony walked back to his Range Rover. He looked in and then looked down the street. Two Somalis stood in front of the village store drinking beer. Anthony motioned to them, and they dropped their beers and came running. They then climbed into the back of the Range-Rover and Anthony drove off.

Jim drove past a tall handsome African carrying a spear. Anne asked Astrid, "What tribe is that attractive man from?"

"He's a *Boran*. Marsabit is their home. At one time, they were the most feared tribe in Northern Kenya. Even the Somalis kept their distance. They're nomads like the Rendelle, the camel herders we just met. The Boron, like their cousins the Masai in the south, live for their cattle," said Astrid as they drove by a large group of Boron around an open pit water well.

They had formed a double line for bailing water. A line of men and women, their black glistening bodies toiling in the setting sun, brought the water up from the source, passing it to one an other in large tin cans. When the water got to the surface, they poured it into a long wooden trough as their thin, underfed cattle drank from it.

"I bet they've been taking the water from there the same way for a thousand years," said Jim.

"They look to be a friendly and happy people the way they look and smile at us," said Anne.

As they got into the foothills, up ahead, a big bull elephant could be seen eating off a tamarind tree.

"Look," said Anne. "Ahmed."

"No, he is one of the bulls that live around here. I told you elephant are big at Marsabit. Ahmed's a giant and his tusks are mammoth. When you see him you'll know," said Astrid.

"I'm so excited, but let's get to that camp. I need a bathroom," said Anne.

"I can stop now if you want. You can go over behind that tree," said Jim.

"Oh, Jim, you're terrible. I can imagine some wild creature waiting for me behind that tree and you'll have to save me. No Jim, I'm not going to let you get that on me, darling."

Jim laughed and drove on faster up the mountainside.

Thirty Three

Molo stood in front of the turn-off on the road waiting for Astrid to arrive. The green safari tents stood ready, and a giant camp fire blazed in the pit when they drove in and stopped.

Everyone went to the tents that Astrid had assigned for a rest and to freshen up before dinner. Molo had their towels laid out on their camp cots and the water steamed hot in the shower tent.

An hour later, everyone left their tents dressed in fresh clothing and sat around the campfire having drinks, except Astrid, who nursed an iced tea. The aromatic smell from the cedar and olive log fire penetrated the evening air. The sun had gone down and the African night crept in around them. They had put on sweaters and jackets because the night air on the mountain remained clear but cool.

"Our sound man and my assistant cameraman should be here tomorrow," said Graham.

"Good, we can go around and have a look before they get in. Let's hope our luck is good in finding Ahmed. When looking for something deliberately, it always seems you can't find it, especially when you have a movie camera. That's been my experience," said Jim. "Don't you find that to happen, Graham?"

"Most times, old boy."

"This is one of the last places in Kenya where you can find black panthers," said Astrid. "They're almost impossible to see in the wild. Maybe we'll have some luck while we're here."

"I'd love to see a black panther, but I hope I don't see one in my tent," said Anne.

"I wouldn't worry. They're very shy," said Jim. "And besides you've got me to protect you."

"That's what I like to hear. A man who will protect me. What a luxury in life," said Anne.

"You sound as if that doesn't happen to you. If I were you I'd change the company I kept," said Jim.

Anne gazed out into the night and said, "I just might do that." And that person could be you, Jim, thought Anne.

The loud trumpeting sound of a male wild elephant could be heard in the distance.

"That's Ahmed," said Astrid. He's letting us know he's aware we're here."

Thirty Four

Anthony Roseli, with his two *Somali* henchmen, stood in the forest looking down on the safari camp. Anthony watched Jim through binoculars as Jim got up from his chair in front of the fire and moved over to the dining table and sat down. Anthony dropped the binoculars that hung on a strap around his neck and motioned to one of the Somalis to hand him his .350 Magnum rifle with a telescope lens attached. The light from the lamps on the table and the firelight illuminated the group enough for Anthony to get a clear sight on Jim's forehead. He smiled to himself as he started to pull the trigger.

At that moment Jim stood up and raised his glass. Anthony followed him with the rifle. Then Anne stood up in front of Jim and remained there. Anthony dropped his rifle in disgust. "Move out, you English bitch," he said to himself.

From behind he heard the sound of a charge of a large cat and the scream from his *Somali*. He turned and saw a black panther had one of his men down on the ground. Anthony tried to take aim with his rifle to kill the panther but in the darkness he couldn't see and wasn't sure what he was aiming at.

The panther had his jaw gripped on the Somali, rolling him over and over on the ground, the African screaming and yelling in pain. The other *Somali* ran off through the bush.

Anthony backed off and took aim again and pulled the trigger. The man and the panther remained still. Anthony crept up to investigate and saw the power of the bullet had put a hole through the panther and had passed on into the Somali, killing them both. Afraid, he looked around to see if any other wild animal were in sight and then took off racing through the bush and forest back toward his Range Rover on the road. He blindly fled, bumping into trees and scrubs, tearing his clothes and bruising his body along the way. As he ran, he stepped on a trap and felt himself being yanked into the air. A crude rope surrounded him with its grip; his body swung back and forth in the sling. He yelled for help, but no one could hear, only the wild animals of the forest.

Thirty Five

The Cessna two engine sat down at midday at the airport in Dar es Salaam. Mark stayed at the charter service to hire a plane to Marsabit. He said goodbyes to Clay and Tim, happy to be rid of them. They told him they would leave that afternoon on an East African flight to Nairobi. Clay said he wanted to visit with someone he knew from his previous trips to Kenya.

Mark chartered a Cessna 180 for the next morning for *Marsabit*. The owner of the charter service inquired as to Helmut. Mark told him that Helmut had gone by ground transportation back to *Moshi* with his crew. Mark wanted to keep Helmut's death quiet for now. He knew if it got out, the assassins would realize that they killed the wrong man and would be looking for him again. In his best Swahili he inquired if anyone had chartered a plane to the Selous besides his party.

"Yes, Bwana, two Kenyans booked passage on the supply plane the next day." The manager looked into a book on the counter and leafed through some pages.

"Do you have their names?" Mark asked. The manager looked reluctant. Mark reached in his pocket and took a one-thousand-shilling note and gave it to him.

"Here, Bwana." He pointed to two names. Mark copied them down.

"Where are they now?"

"No have returned through here, *Bwana*. They still be in Selous," said the manager.

Mark thought, I have no proof these men killed Helmut, so I can't have them arrested, but I'll make sure Mnazi knows about what happened. He can have them arrested in Kenya.

"Can you give me a description?"

"Yes, Bwana, big men. Over six feet. Maybe thirty. One had face tattooed with the scars of a Kikuku."

Mark spent the night at a hotel in downtown Dar es Salaam. He saw Helmut's decapitated head in his dreams. He woke up dripping in sweat. He tried to go back to sleep but he couldn't. As he laid turning in his damp bed, his thoughts went to Astrid. What will she do now? She has a hotel she'll have to operate by herself, and the orphanage she has to oversee. How could she go to England to school with those responsibilities, he asked himself. He had to help her work out those decisions. When dawn finally arrived, he felt more tired than when he had gone to bed. He took a long shower, dressed and went down to the lobby and checked out. It was too early to go to the airport, so he walked around downtown Dar es Salaam observing the classical architecture of the old buildings, which were decaying from age and deferred maintenance. The Arab influence of the filigree balconies on the old houses gave a mystery to them. The occupants could see out, but he couldn't see in. What an interesting city Dar es Salaam must have been in its day, he thought. Not like the ugly buildings and jumbled planning of downtown Nairobi, which grew much too fast.

Mark walked past a glass and concrete government building that had been put up in the last few years by the socialist regime of Julius Nyerere. It had changed the face of the past. The city and the country now gave the feeling of hard times and poverty. The new socialist government was not working; he could tell. How different it seemed here from Nairobi, he thought, with that city's hustle of capitalist activities and working conditions. Mark looked at his watch and saw he'd better get to the airport.

Thirty Six

At seven in the morning Mark tried to find a taxi, but no cabs seemed to be in the streets. As he crossed the avenue to return to the hotel he noticed a jewelry store. He looked up at the sign over the door which read: L.E. PATEL & SONS, QUALITY JEWELS. He looked in the window and saw a middle-aged East Indian in a white short-sleeve shirt putting merchandise on display in the shop window. The store had not yet opened so Mark made a signal to the man to open up for him. The man ignored him at first, but Mark reached into his rucksack and pulled out the uncut ruby and held it up to the window for the man to see. The Indian immediately left the window and pulled open the protective metal door to greet him.

"Oh, good morning, sir. What have you there?" he asked.

"It's an uncut ruby. Would you like to buy it?"

"That all depends, sir. Please, come in." Mark followed him into the shop and over to a counter where the man stood in front of a bright light.

"Can I see the stone?" Mark handed him the rock. The stone didn't look like much. Its surface bore the look of sand and minerals. If you didn't know what it was, you would have passed it by as rock with some color to it. The East Indian examined it carefully. Little bits of perspiration came out on his forehead as he did.

"Tell me, sir. Where did it come from?"

"A mine in Kenya."

"Do you own the mine?"

"No."

"Can you tell me who they are?"

"I'd rather not."

"How much do you want for it?"

"How much will you give me?"

"I would like to check its color," he said as he took the stone with him and turned to go out of the room.

"I'll go with you," said Mark as he followed him toward the back. The Indian looked annoyed but answered, "very well, sir."

The Indian turned on a polishing wheel and put the stone against the wheel to smooth its surface. He picked up a jeweler's glass to examine it.

"I'll give you a hundred thousand shillings," he said. Mark took the stone back from him and examined it also.

He said, "That's ten thousand U.S." The jeweler nodded.

"Thank you, but that's not enough," and he started to make an exit.

"One minute, sir, how much do you want for the ruby?"

"One hundred thousand. U.S."

"Oh, sir. I am a poor man. We are a poor country. No one has that kind of money."

"The jewel is worth twice that, and you know it. Mineralogy has been a hobby of mine. Even I recognize the color of this stone as superior quality and when it's broken up it will bring a big price."

"Let me do this, sir. Let me take a picture and measure its size. I have an associate in Bombay. I will see if he would be interested in buying it."

"I'll agree to that." The jeweler used a measuring device while Mark watched him. He took out a camera and took pictures of the ruby from different angles.

"How big is it? How many carats?" he asked.

"One hundred and thirty-seven. A big stone," said Mr. Patel.

"It's a Maharajah's jewel," said Mark and smiled. "Do you still have any of those rich blokes left in India?"

"Oh, my, yes. By all means, sir. There're many, but they do not have the money they once had."

"I'm out on safari, but will call when I return. Give me your phone number," said Mark. Mr.Patel wrote down his number and Mark left the shop. Mr. *Patel* looked after him.

Mark went back to his hotel and had the concierge arrange to get him a ride to the airport.

Thirty Seven

The cab pulled up to the charter office and Mark saw the Cessna was ready for take-off. He gave his small bag to the pilot, an African, and climbed in.

They took off and flew along the coastline. In the distance, Mark could see the harbor of Tanga ahead with dozens of ships in port. There was more activity in Tanga than the main port of Dar es Salaam. He pointed below and asked the pilot. "What's going on down there? It looks like an armada."

"It's the Chinese. They're building a railroad in the interior of the country. They use the port as their supply station."

Mark had heard that Tanzania did business with the Chinese. The plane left the coast and flew on into the interior passing over the Kenya and Tanzania border. Mark could see Mount Kilimanjaro in the distance. They flew at eleven thousand five hundred feet. The closer they got to the great mountain, the larger it became. All of sudden the smell of smoke filled Mark's nostrils. The airplane's cockpit filled up with smoke. They started to choke and panic. They couldn't see in front of them. Mark knew that a fire on an airplane could be the end of them. The pilot eyes teared as he tried to check all the instruments.

"What's going on?" asked Mark as he tried to see out the window. Mount Kilimanjaro loomed up before them.

"No place to land... we have no parachutes," said Mark as he looked to the pilot for reassurance. The smoke cleared in the cabin as fast as it appeared.

"I can't figure it. Our oil pressure is okay, the manifold pressure is normal and we've lost no RPMs." Again the cabin filled with smoke. Mark opened a little side widow to let it out, but the smoke kept coming in from the cabin floor.

"I'm going to take it down. I've got to get away from Kilimanjaro," said the pilot, keeping cool. "Look and see if you see a clearing to land."

Mark and Dan scoured the terrain for some kind of open space. None could be seen, only ravines and canyons below. They moved away from the mountain at five thousand feet. Mark saw that they had passed over Lake Amboseli Game Reserve. The smoke had again disappeared, with no changes indicated on the instrument gauges.

"I'm going to bring it down to a lower altitude and follow the road into Nairobi. If we have to go down we can make an emergency landing on the highway," said the pilot.

Mark remained quiet. He watched ahead and kept his eye on the gauges for any change, hoping they would not have to go down or that the airplane wouldn't explode in the air. When he saw the Nong Hills straight ahead he knew Wilson Field outside Nairobi was not far away. The plane skimmed the plateaus and hills. Mark felt he could reach out and touch the tops of the trees with his hand. He couldn't believe he could be calm considering the danger. Up ahead he could see the Wilson airstrip. He looked over at the pilot, who smiled with relief.

The pilot brought the small plane down on the runway without a mishap and taxied over to a hanger. With a nervous sigh, Mark unbuckled his seat-belt. He looked up to the heavens and said to himself. Thanks, old boy, you got us here.

It took about a half a day for the airplane mechanics to figure out the problem.

"It's the oil line," said the mechanic. "The vibration of the heater exhaust pipe against the top of the oil line caused a tiny hole in the line that dripped oil into the heater causing a combustion," he said. "A small problem", he continued, "but a major one if you didn't know what it meant. I don't have the part in stock, but we found it in Entebbe. The part will be here in the morning."

Mark looked reassured, but didn't feel happy about staying in Nairobi for the evening. He laid low and stayed out of sight during their time on the ground. He called Minister Mnazi. His secretary told him she hadn't heard from the Minister in over twenty-four hours, but would let him know that Mark called.

While he talked on the phone, Mark saw a Land Rover drive up to the Charter Service and Clay and Tim Nobertson got out followed by Nigel Bartlett, a white hunter. Mark knew him to be of dubious reputation. He had been charged with inhumane treatment of one of his safari boys. So the story went, the boy had been badly beaten by him, but Nigel had gotten off. The newspapers wrote about the scandal every day and it caused a lot of controversy between the black and white Kenyans. Mark thought, "birds of a feather" when he saw the three load their guns and equipment into a Beech twin engine Baron and take off.

Mark went into the office and asked. "What was the destination of the Beech Baron that just took off?" "Marsabit," said the attendant".

Thirty Eight

After a big breakfast Jim, Astrid, and Anne left camp in the Land Rover and Graham followed in the lorry to look for *Ahmed*. They drove up the mountain through a shroud of low morning fog onto a narrow dirt road that wandered through the dense forest. They disturbed the morning grazing of small herds of impala and *Grevy* zebra that ran off when their caravan appeared. The fog lifted as they got to the top of the mountain. Jim drove the lumbering Land Rover onto a game trail that led down into the crater of the old volcano. As they got closer to the lake, they saw a group of elephants bathing along the shore. Jim stopped as they sat looking at the lake and the elephants below.

"I love them...it's their size...their gentleness...their innocence...but I get sad when I think of their future. If the poaching continues there will be no more elephants," said Astrid as she looked down on the herd.

"What a magical location this is for your movie, Jim," said Anne.

"Thank Astrid, it was her idea." Astrid blushed and said. "*Ahmed* brought us. I had nothing to do with it."

Astrid thought, why is he giving me all this praise?

"I remember seeing this place in one of the first documentary films ever made in the twenties on Africa. The camera was one of those old crank jobs. The film-makers were Martin and Osa

145

Johnson, who made their home on this lake for years. They called it Lake Paradise. He built his own lab. Osa did the cooking and hunting for their table. She was a great shot and as brave as a *Masai* warrior. Can you imagine how tough that must've been back then? They flew a double-wing aircraft with an open cockpit. It's all coming back. I can still see those white long scarves they wore, blowing in the wind as they landed on that lake. Those Johnsons had guts and became big adventure-movie heroes. Their fans would stand in line for blocks to see one of their films," said Jim.

"This lake is a perfect place for our camp, it's so picturesque. Can we move here instead of where we are?" asked Anne.

"It's too dangerous. The lake is a watering hole. We'd never get any sleep. We'd have visitors all night at our tents," said Astrid.

"I don't think I'd be happy with that arrangement, darling," said Anne.

Jim turned to Graham in the lorry. "Graham, bring the camera and set up for some shots of the lake. Anne, you drive the Land Rover in from the right and stop. I'll match it up in the studio later with shots of my leading lady," said Jim.

"Who is your leading lady? Do I know her?" asked Anne.

"I haven't cast her yet, but you can bet she'll have to look like you."

"Jim, darling, you're sweet. Let me help you. I'd just die to have Jane Fonda play me, no I mean, I play her, oh I don't know what I mean, darling."

"I'd say you learn fast. I haven't shot one foot of film and you're already sounding like a Hollywood actress," said Jim smiling.

"Don't tease me, Jim. I'm excited, that's all. I know I'm the stand-in."

"Look! the elephants are moving into the forest. They must have gotten our scent, "said Graham.

Jim drove the Land Rover down to the lake shore. Graham got back in the lorry and followed. As they got down to the water's edge they stopped. Graham took the 35MM Ariflex camera from the rear of the vehicle and loaded it with film and set it up on a tripod.

"Where do you want the camera?" asked Graham.

"Anne comes in from screen right to screen left. Set the camera up on that little knoll over there." Jim pointed to a small hill. "Anne, drive the Land Rover over there." He pointed to a group of trees at the far end of the lake. "Drive back along the lake shore passing the camera position and stop," he said.

Anne got into the Land Rover looking very serious and drove off.

The sound of an airplane could be heard. Jim and Astrid looked up and saw a small aircraft circling in the distance.

"It's our crew. Graham, go and pick them up. We're going to continue scouting," said Jim.

"Right-O, old boy. Will be good to see my lads," said Graham.

"Wait for me at the camp, Graham. I know where the airstrip is located," said Astrid. Jim looked and saw Anne waiting at the other end of the lake. Jim yelled. "ACTION." The Land Rover came toward them as the camera rolled.

Thirty Nine

After they had completed the camera work, they left the lake and kept scouting the area for *Ahmed*. They drove onto an off-road trail that wound back and forth along the mountainside. They remained silent as they rode through the moss-hung forest, keeping their eyes alert. Astrid noticed two white-headed vultures circling overhead. Their large wing span made shadows on the ground in front of them as they flew above. She knew they had spotted something that had their attention. Astrid kept her eyes peeled looking for what it could be. Up ahead, near an opening in the forest, she spotted something that looked like a small black animal. "Stop, Jim, I'll investigate."

"What is it, darling? Can I come too?" asked Anne.

"Come if you like," she said as she got out of the Rover. Anne followed her, taking her camera. They approached the black furry form cautiously until Astrid could see what it was.

"I knew it. It's a black panther cub. Be careful. Its mother should be close." She looked for fallen trees and saw the den. She moved slowly forward to have a look. She picked up a stone and threw it into the opening. No sound came from within. Then she looked further into the forest and saw a group of white-headed vultures on the ground feasting on some corpses and went to investigate. When she got closer she could see the corpse of an African and

149

a black panther. The giant birds flew off as she approached. She looked back at Anne who had followed her. "Don't come any closer. Get Jim," she said with alarm. "What is it, darling?" asked Anne, nervous.

"It's the mother of the panther cub and an African. He must have tried to poach her and she killed him."

Anne ran off and Astrid moved closer to the bodies. She saw a bullet hole in the African and further investigation showed the panther had one also. She looked around and saw a rifle lying near a bush. On the ground leading into the forest were fresh footprints of a man. She took off to follow them. About a thousand yards into the woods she found a poacher's sling hanging from a large tamarind tree, a man trapped inside.

She heard Jim's voice calling out, "Astrid, where are you?"

She called back, "I'm over here. Come quick!"

Jim and Anne arrived and recognized Anthony in the sling.

"Look what the cat dragged in. Come on, ladies," said Jim as he turned the girls around to leave.

"Let's go."

"Wait, don't leave me here," screamed Anthony.

Jim looked back. "Why not? What do you think, Astrid?"

Astrid looked at Anne. "Jim cut him down. It's inhuman. He'll die in that sling," said Anne.

"I haven't heard from Astrid, you're the judge in this trial," said Jim looking at Astrid.

"Jim, he's an awful human, cut him down." Astrid replied.

"You got saved, buddy. I bet that's more than you would have done for her." Jim climbed into the tree and cut the rope. The sling fell to the ground with a thud. Anthony groaned. Jim came down from the tree and untied the rope and pulled it back.

Anthony lay for a minute and then as he started to get up he rushed Jim and knocked him down, hitting Jim in the face with his fist. "That's for Mt. Kenya," he said.

Jim rolled over and as they both got to their feet. Anthony hit Jim again and knocked him back. Anthony hit Jim and hit him in the jaw and then to the stomach.

"That's from Astrid, you chicken shit gangster."

Anthony fell back onto the rope sling and tried to get up again, but he couldn't. He lay holding his jaw as fresh blood came from his mouth.

"Get up. You've got a lot of explaining to do. What happened here?"

"I had to shoot the panther or he would have killed me."

"What about the African? Did you have to kill him too?"

"That was an accident. I didn't mean to kill him. He got in the way."

"You've killed a black panther and an African. Those are both criminal offences in Kenya. I bet you're about to kill Ahmed. I'm taking you the ranger's station and make sure they put irons on you. Don't try to run off. I'm a good shot." said Jim.

"Listen to the mighty big shot American, You're nothing. chap."

"I'm someone you wished you'd never met. Come on, get up. We'll see how you like staying in Kenyan jails." Anthony got up on his feet and Jim pushed him ahead with Anthony's rifle as they walked out of the forest to the Land Rover.

Anthony looked around. "Where's my Range Rover?"

"You have the Range Rover I saw in the village yesterday?" Anthony said, "That bloody Somali took it, the fucking coward." Jim pushed him in the back seat.

"Wait! The panther cub." Astrid ran to where she left the cub. She picked up the little panther to examine it. It was alive. She looked up into the sky and saw the vultures were still circling. "Sorry, boys. This one's mine." She took off a sweater she had tied around her waist and wrapped the cub and brought it to the Rover.

"I'm in back with Anthony. Anne, you drive," said Jim.

They got in and drove off. Astrid in the front seat with the cub warmly wrapped on her lap. Her eyes started tearing and she started to sniff. Jim noticed her and said. "Are you all right? Why are you crying?"

"I'm not. I'm allergic to animal hair."

When they got to the camp, Astrid jumped out of the Rover and went to find *Molo*. Jim took off in the Rover with Anthony for the ranger station.

Astrid found *Molo* in the kitchen. "Look! We have a new orphan. Do you have something to feed it?"

"No, Mama. I need milk from a goat."

"Come. I'll drop you off in the village." She gave the cub to *Molo* who took it to the side of the stove leaving it there to keep warm. He picked up a small aluminum milk can and followed her to the lorry. Graham sat in the cab and they left for the village and airstrip.

Forty

The plane had landed when they arrived at the small dirt airstrip in the arid valley, a small distance from the village. The heat of the midday sun reflected off the hot desert in thermal waves as the lorry drove toward two men waiting under the wing of the parked Piper Comanche. Their sound and camera equipment stood on the ground beside them. Graham got out of the Land Rover and went to greet them. Astrid followed.

"Good to see you, lads. How was your trip?" he asked. Astrid came up behind him. "This is our guide, Astrid Dryden." Astrid put out her hand. "This is Noel Harper and Reg Lane." The two men shook Astrid's hand and smiled.

"Don't just stare, lads. Haven't you ever seen a pretty lady before?" asked Graham. Astrid blushed from the attention.

"Come on, chaps. Get a move on. Put your equipment in and get in the back so we can get to the camp for a highball, lads," said Graham. As they loaded, another airplane could be heard approaching the landing strip.

"They got a bit of traffic here today, wouldn't you say"? said Graham. The twin-engine plane touched down, taxied up and parked next to the Comanche.

The door opened and Clay Norbertson stepped out onto the ground followed by Tim and their white hunter, Nigel Bartlett.

Astrid recognized Nigel. He had once come on to her drunk. She had no time for him, but she remained courteous when he brought his safari clients to her hotel. Nigel recognized Astrid.

"Well, look who's here. The blonde German from *Moshi*. Aren't you out of your territory, old girl?" asked Nigel being vitriolic. "What are you doing here?" she asked. "I thought there's no hunting in this area."

"We have a hunting license for elephant in a hunting block outside the Reserve," said Nigel.

Clay and Tim stayed back from the others, not wanting to be introduced while they unloaded their guns and ammo from the plane. Nigel left Astrid and walked back to them and said, "I want you gentlemen to meet a pretty girl I know. You know her father, Helmut Dryden." Clay pulled Nigel back and said. "I'll introduce myself and say nothing to her about my knowing her father."

Nigel looked puzzled as Clay approached Astrid followed by Tim. "Hello, I'm Jack Smith. This is my partner Terry Jones. What are you hunting for?" asked Clay.

"We're not hunting. We're here to film Ahmed, the old bull elephant," said Astrid.

"You don't say. Have you seen him yet?" asked Clay.

"No, but we'll find him, we just got in yesterday. Nice to meet you. I have to get our group back to camp. They tell me they need a whisky, *Kwaheri*." she said. She looked back at Nigel as she got into the lorry and drove off.

"Would you mind telling me what that was all about?" asked Nigel

"Later, kid, later," said Clay as he turned to help Tim with the hunting gear. Nigel's face was a blank as he began taking the gear from the airplane.

Forty One

The speeding white Mercedes sedan churned up a red dust cloud as it left the main highway onto a dirt road through standing fields of yellow maize on both sides. It stopped at a small farmhouse. The two policemen emerged from the back of the car. One of them pulled Mnazi out from the back seat and the other ran around to help him. The minister's hands were handcuffed behind his back. Major *Darassa* got out from the front seat while the driver remained at the wheel. Major *Darassa* opened the door of the stone farmhouse for the two policemen, who pushed *Mnazi* through the doorway. They moved him into a small room in the back of the house and tied him to a plain wooden chair with his hands behind him. The room, bare except for a small table and three chairs, smelled of urine and tobacco. Major *Darassa* sat down at the table and looked at *Mnazi*, who looked back at him menacingly. The two policeman sat on each side.

"Minister, shame on you. Why are you causing our party and leaders a deliberate conspiracy? What can you possibly achieve with your plot to overthrow our government?" *Mnazi* looked defiant and said nothing. "The party decides who will be the new president, and your name is not on the list. You're embarrassing *Kenyatta* with your talk of corruption. He's your old friend. He loves you like a brother. You have hurt him with the lies you spread against his family." *Mnazi* stared at the Major. "I have here," said the major, taking a document from this briefcase, an affidavit you will sign. It states your information on the ivory poaching is false and you're retracting it." *Mnazi* gave the Major a smirk.

"Mark Livingston, the man you had spying from the game department, is dead. He had an unfortunate accident in *Tanzania*," said the Major. *Mnazi* bristled with anger. "You can't get away with this. If you do any harm to me, it will bring you down. I have the common people on my side. They don't want a nation of ten millionaires and ten million beggars. They're tired of the abuse of power by a few *Kikuyus*. You have forgotten about the other tribes in our nation. They want more say in the government and with me they will have it. You remember what happened when Tom *Moboya* was murdered, the people took to the streets and almost brought the government down. If you do anything to me, my people will burn down Parliament. There'll be a revolution," said Mnazi, sweat rolling off his wide face.

"Bring him over to the table. He'll sign this statement," said the major to the policemen.

The two powerful men picked up *Mnazi,* still tied to the chair and carried him over and set him down in front of Major *Darassa* at the table. *Mnazi* looked up at Major *Darassa* and spat in his face.

In the early evening, lights of a car could be seen in the distance coming toward a *Masai Many*atta beyond the *Ngong* Hills thirty miles west of Nairobi. Two teenage *Masai* boys sat outside the *manyatta* attending to their father's cattle. They watched as the car stopped by a nearby stream. They remembered other cars that had come in the night and dropped off human bodies for the hyenas to feast on. This was a graveyard for a few of the government's enemies, because no trace could ever be found of these humans after the hyenas had eaten them. At night this area belonged to the hyenas as they gathered to drink and hunt the game along the stream's edge.

The sound of gunshots startled the boys who ran off frightened by the scene that took place.

Mnazi's body lay face down on the trampled ground. His hands tied behind him, a bullet hole in the back of his head. The two men dragged his body over to the stream's edge. One of them opened a bottle and threw acid onto *Mnazi*'s face. A puff of smoke rose from the minister's burning flesh. In the dark the shrill laughing cry of the hyena could be heard a short distance away. The two men walked back to the Mercedes, got in and drove off into the night.

A few minutes later two powerful hyenas appeared out of the darkness. They approached cautiously and sniffed at *Mnazi*'s corpse, half submerged in the running stream, but they left his body there, undisturbed, and walked back into the dark shadows.

Forty Two

Jim drove Anthony to the Ranger station in the village.

"Get out." Anthony opened the door of the Rover and stepped out. Jim came around the front with Anthony's rifle and shoved him into the entrance of the station. A ranger stood behind a desk and looked up when they entered.

"Do you speak English?" asked Jim.

"Yes, *Bwana.*"

"Put this man under arrest. He killed a black panther and his guide and he plans on shooting *Ahmed.* You'll find the man's body up on the mountain with the dead panther. I suggest you get there quick before the hyenas and vultures. They're eating your evidence."

"*Ahmed!* He kill Ahmed. It will be most unfortunate for him if he tried. Who are you, Bwana?"

"My name is Jim Fielding. I'm a movie director making a film here. This man is Anthony Roseli. He's an international gangster. Be careful with him. He'll try to bribe you. Here, take his rifle. There might be more weapons in his Ranger Rover, it's stolen. Call the head ranger in Nairobi. He should be notified."

"Yes, Bwana." The ranger took the rifle and put it aside. He came from behind the desk, put a pair of iron shackles on Anthony and led him back through a rear door. Anthony said as he left, "Keep an eye out, governor. When it comes, it will be me."

The Ranger led him away.

159

Forty Three

Nigel Bartlett had set up camp in a valley not far from the *Marsabit* village. The terrain appeared semi-dry with giant termite mounds, scrub brush, and thorn trees here and there. Clay started to drink as soon as he arrived at camp and Nigel joined him, keeping up drink for drink. Tim seemed uneasy and drank less, and remained quiet as he listened to the bragging hunting adventures of Clay and Nigel. Clay played with his rhino whip, stroking it and pounding it on the table from time to time to make a point.

His voice got louder and coarser the more he drank. "What do you know of Ahmed?" asked Clay.

"A bloody monster! The old boy's the biggest bull elephant in Kenya. The Wogs that knew him when he lived on the *Tana* River tell me he's been shot by both rifles and poison arrows, but he's still farting and shows no signs of kicking off. Every so often someone sees him up close and takes his picture and it turns up in the Kenyan newspapers. He's like that bloody *Kenyatta*; he's old and indestructible. The old man identifies with him and had him declared a national monument." Clay showed interest.

"Let me ask you something? Would you shoot him if you came across him?"

"No way, old chap. They'd hang me up fast. As far as I'm concerned, that bloody elephant is a god and let him be that way."
"What if you came upon him tomorrow and he charged you. What would you do?"

"I'd think first before I took aim, and to tell the bloody truth I'd risk being trampled on rather than being hanged by those bloody *Wogs*."

Nigel's camp cook approached them as they sat in front of the bright burning camp fire. Nigel gave him his glass and said. "

"*Martini mobile.*" Nigel looked at Clay and Clay gave him his glass. "Me, too, and I want to eat. I'm hungry."

"Leti supi *leo epana kesho*," said Nigel.

"Yes, *Bwana*." The cook left for the fresh drinks and returned.

"*Bwana*, can eat. Come to table," he said.

Clay stumbled over to the dining table in the mess tent. A young *Boran* boy about fifteen, dressed in a *kanus*, helped him with his chair as he sat down. Nigel and Tim joined him. The young boy brought out the soup and served it. Clay looked at it with disgust.

"What is this shit? It looks like a fetus fell in it. Boy, take it away." The boy seemed nervous and upset with Clay's manner as he picked up the soup bowl. Clay pushed it away at the same time and the hot soup spilled onto his lap. Clay jumped up from the table screaming.

"Jeeez, you dumb little nigger son of bitch. You burned me," he yelled and grabbed the arm of the terrified boy as he picked up his rhino whip.

"You need whipping, you little fucker." Clay dragged the frightened boy over by the fire holding onto his arm. The boy started to cry but didn't try to run away. "Lift up that dress you got on," he said. The boy looked at him confused. "You heard me. Lift up your dress." Clay pulled the boy across the small camp table and pulled up his *kansu.* The boy lay stretched over the table, his naked buttocks glittering with sweat that reflected the fire. Clay began beating the boy's buttocks violently with the rhino whip as he held the boy's hand firmly with his other hand to keep the boy down on the table. The boy screamed in pain as welts came up on his soft black skin causing them to open up with each stroke of the cutting whip.

Tim ran to Clay and pulled the lash from his hand. He looked into Clay's fixed blazing eyes making him think he looked into the eyes of the devil. "That's enough! Leave the boy alone."

Clay's eyes had a glint of sexuality as he watched the young boy run off into the darkness, sobbing.

Forty Four

U p on the mountainside at Jim's camp, the new arrivals along with Jim, Graham and Astrid sat around the fire having an after-dinner brandy. A light wind had come up causing the fire to burn bright and flood everyone's face with its light. Anne had excused herself and skipped dinner, saying she didn't feel well. She remained in her tent.

Jim said, "Tomorrow, Graham, you, Reg, and Noel take the big lorry and check the area on the north side of the mountain. Astrid, myself, and Anne will work the south side. *Molo* will pack our lunches and meet up on the crater lake shore for lunch and I hope one of us has some luck and sees *Ahmed.*"

"What if one of us does? What should we do?" asked Graham.

"Don't do anything. Remember where. And find us. It's too dangerous not to have someone to protect us just in case *Ahmed* goes after us. I want to have some gun back up," said Jim as he looked at Astrid.

"Jim, my instructions from the park service are no guns allowed anywhere near *Ahmed.* It says so on the permit," said Astrid. Everyone exchanged looks.

"If those are the bloody rules I'll have to shoot the old boy with a long lens, and the quality won't be there," said Graham.

"I need a full frame shot of *Ahmed's* head to fill the screen, trunk raised in the air, and his ears moving back and forth as he prepares to charge. I'll match it in the studio later with special effects," said Jim.

"We'll get it, old boy, even if we don't have any bloody back up rifles," said Graham.

"Jim, elephants can run thirty miles a hour, so don't let anyone take any chances," said Astrid as she got up from her camp chair. "I'm turning in. Good night." She turned and left for her tent.

"Bloody gorgeous bird, wouldn't you say? Do me a favor old boy. Tell her what a great old bloke I am, "said Reg to Graham.

"Speak for yourself, Reg. If I do any promoting it will be for me," said Graham. "Do you know if she has a boyfriend, Jim?"

"She's a private person. She doesn't say much about herself, but her father told me she has a boyfriend who's a game warden at *Tsvao* Game Park," replied Jim

"Too bad. I like these African birds. It's their independent nature that attracts me," said Reg.

"Any bird you see does that, Reg," said Noel.

Jim got up from his camp chair smiling. "See you in the morning, guys. Watch that brandy. It creeps up on you, and so do the lions. Good night."

Reg and Noel exchanged looks.

Jim walked toward Astrid's tent. Her light still shone and Jim could see her shapely shadow through the heavy canvas.

He stopped, walked up to the tent and scratched the canvas flap with his fingernails. "Hello, its Jim. May I come in?"

Astrid pulled back the tent flap. "What is it?" Astrid stood dressed in a white cotton tee shirt.

"I saw your light and I wondered if you wanted any company?"

"Not really. I was about to put the candle out. Don't you think you should see how Anne is doing?"

"She's all right. She has some stomach cramps, that's all. She says it always happens when it's her time. Are you all right? You looked a little feverish." Jim put the back of his hand to her face. "You seem very warm."

"Yes, I am fine. I think you'd better go." Astrid could see that Jim wasn't about to. "If you have any ideas and think I'm going to fall into your arms, you'd better forget it. You caught me at a weak moment at Mount Kenya. I wasn't myself then, but I am now. I suggest you leave before you ruin a respectable relationship."

The tent flap opened and Anne entered. "Can you stand more company, darlings? I was walking by and heard your voices. I was curious to know what you had to be up to. I hope you don't mind?"

"I stopped to tell Astrid the schedule for tomorrow." said Jim. Anne looked at them saying nothing. Jim had guilt written on his face.

"You shouldn't be out walking around by yourself, you know it's dangerous," said Jim.

"That depends on what kind of animal you might run into, wouldn't you say? Don't wolves live in the northern part of the world? I should have known, they're everywhere."

Forty Five

Molo and his helper were preparing breakfast when he reached down and pulled back the canvas flap that covered the cooking utensils under his kerosene stove. As he picked up a skillet, a large spitting cobra sprang up. Its head flattened as it raised in position to strike. *Molo* backed out and ran from the tent in terror.

"Mama, Mama, come quick. Get gun. Cobra, he in kitchen," he yelled, running for Astrid's tent.

Astrid came out of her tent with a .45 caliber hand gun and ran back with *Molo* to the mess tent. The snake had sunk back down to the ground to retreat when *Molo* had left, but when Astrid ran into the camp kitchen the snake returned to its erect position, the back of his head expanded, his extended upright body weaving back and forth, his cold eyes defying Astrid as she tried to take aim to shoot.

"Stay back. He can spit his venom over four feet." *Molo* stood in back of Astrid as he watched her aim, ringing his hands in distress. Astrid pulled the trigger. The powerful .45 fired twice in succession, blowing the snake's head off with one of the bullets. The noise of gunshots got everyone out of their tents.

Jim arrived first. Astrid stood before him with the gun in her hand. She bent down and picked up the dead cobra by the tail.

Jim stared at her, but said nothing. Astrid walked out of the mess tent over to the fire that still smoldered and threw the dead snake on the embers.

Jim followed. "There's nothing like roasted cobra in the morning to get one's day started," he said. Astrid smiled. "So, you have eaten it before?"

"No, and I'm not about to start."

"It's a delicate meal. It tastes like fowl."

"I'll stick to ham and eggs in the morning. You constantly impress me."

"Because I killed a snake?"

"That's part of it. You're so organized. Your knowledge of the country, the bush, the animals, the people and most of all your beauty. I'm in love."

"Are you trying to seduce me?"

"Well, let's put it this way. If I had known what was waiting for me when I arrived at the Nairobi airport, I wouldn't have made the arrangements I had."

"I don't know if I like that. It sounds fickle of you, trying to make up your mind about all the pretty girls you meet and hire."

"You don't think much of me, do you?"

"I wouldn't go that far. You have some nice qualities. You're sort of handsome. Let's remain friends," Astrid said.

"That's easy to say, but I can't get you out of my thoughts." They heard Anne's voice calling. "Jim. Jim, please come to the tent, darling. I need some advice on my camera."

Astrid looked at Jim and smiled as he walked away.

Forty Six

The excitement of Astrid killing the cobra and the scouting trip to find *Ahmed* had everyone in the camp up with enthusiasm and anticipation of adventure. *Molo* had packed a lunch of cold ham and cheese sandwiches, along with an orange and apple and some Tusker beer on ice. Graham got his group together and they took off in the lorry. Jim drove the Land Rover with Astrid and Anne as passengers.

Again, the morning mist covered the ground as they left camp. The fog lifted as they drove up the mountainside. Up ahead, another Land Rover had stopped on the road. Out from the forest came the biggest elephant that anyone had every seen.

"My God! It must be *Ahmed*! Look at his tusks; they're mammoth. He's a behemoth," said Jim. "Give me my camera. It's in the back somewhere," he said to Anne, who looked ahead at the elephant with wonderment.

Ahmed walked across the road in front of the other Land Rover. He towered over it, making it look like a toy. Jim stopped the Rover. He got out and grabbed his camera and ran toward Ahmed.

Astrid yelled. "Jim you're crazy? Get back here. His *asskaris* are around somewhere. Don't be foolish! Look! He's coming this way." Astrid moved over to the driver's seat. Anne panicked. "Let's get the hell out of here!" She yelled out the window at Jim. "Jim, for God's sake get back here!"

Jim stood a short distance from *Ahmed*, taking his picture. *Ahmed* passed by the other Land Rover and came after Jim. *Ahmed's* tusks looked heavy. He seemed to have a problem raising his head as he ran for Jim. Jim ran back to the vehicle. He looked out of the corner of his eye and saw two smaller elephant come out of the trees up ahead as he jumped into the Rover.

"Let's get out of here!" he said.

"No!" said Astrid. "Remain perfectly quiet. Quiet, quiet," she whispered.

Ahmed stopped. His ears kept moving back and forth. His trunk sniffed at the Land Rover.

Jim's heart came up in his throat as he looked into the gnarled old face of the world's largest elephant. *Ahmed's* two companions joined him. They walked up and then stepped back sniffing the air with their trunks. Their giant ears moved back and forth as they did. One of the beasts let out a loud trumpeting sound and looked as if he might charge, but backed off. Slowly they all turned and walked back into the forest. Before disappearing, they looked back again in the direction of the Land Rover as if to say, "stay away from us or else."

"Christ, what a close call. How in the name of God did you know they wouldn't charge us?" asked Jim.

"I didn't really, but from experience I discovered they must not like the sound of an engine. It must bother them and they won't charge. They seem to change their minds and move off, but if you turn the engine off, I've seen them demolish a Land Rover and the passengers," said Astrid.

"That was one of the most terrifying experiences in my life and a lady doesn't do what I just did to myself. I'll have to change my clothes when we get back to camp, darlings. I'm so embarrassed." Anne's remarks broke the tension.

"Jim, you did something real stupid when you got out of the Land Rover to take that picture. You could have easily been killed. I thought you knew better," said Astrid.

"I do know better, but like you say I was stupid. Now I'll have to figure out how I'll film that old boy when I see him again. You see I've got a problem."

Molo was waiting for them at the camp base. "Mama, airplane he flew over the camp. He signal to pick up. And need milk for panther baby."

"Get in. I'll pick up who whomever is at the airstrip, and we can go by the village and get milk on the way," said Astrid.

Jim and Anne got out of the Rover. "*Molo*, I need some hot water. Could you have someone bring it to my tent?" asked Anne.

"Yes, Mama," he said as he ran to the mess tent to tell one of his helpers to bring the water. Astrid waited in the Rover.

Jim stood by the cab and said. "Were you expecting anyone?"

No, I have no idea who it could be," she said. *Molo* came back to the Rover and got into the passenger side and they took off down the mountain.

Astrid dropped off *Molo* in the village and went on to the airstrip. Mark stood waiting. By the look on his face, Astrid knew he brought bad news. She got out of the Rover as Mark came to her.

She looked at him closely before she said anything. "It's Dad isn't it? Where is he?"

"Your father is dead." Mark put his arms around her as she started to cry.

"How, why?" she cried.

"It was a bloody accident. A lion got him."

"I can't believe that."

Mark looked at Astrid. The pain he saw in her face made him feel weak and guiltier. I can't tell her now, he thought. I can't tell her I'm the one that's supposed to be dead.

Forty Seven

M ark and Astrid returned to the village to pick up *Molo*, who stood on the road waiting for them. *Molo* got in the back. Astrid cried to herself as Mark tried to comfort her.

"*Molo*, Dad's been killed by a lion."

"*Bwana*, Helmut great hunter, know wild animal. No believe *Simba* kill *Bwana*. Many sorry Mama," he said, as he put his calloused hand out to take hers and held it.

"An accident," said Mark. "The bloody lion came into the camp and tried to steal fresh meat from the mess tent. Helmut heard him and ran to chase him away. He followed him into the forest to shoot him, but his gun didn't fire. The lion killed him." Mark thought he would let this story out, but would later tell Astrid the truth.

"What will I do without Dad?. Oh, Mark, he was the tree I leaned on."

"Mama, *Molo* no leave. *Molo* stay with Mama."

"Astrid, I'll never leave you. I'll be there for you," replied Mark.

"Thank you, I love you both. Mark, the trial is in a week. I've done nothing about it. I have no one to represent me. I'm frightened, I don't want to go to jail," she said.

"We'll get a delay. The *Wogs* won't put you in jail. You're a white woman. They don't dare."

"I said that, but Dad disagreed with me. It could very well happen. Oh, Mark, I'm scared."

"Mama, what will happen to the orphanage and the hotel if Mama goes to jail?" asked *Molo*.

"I don't know, *Molo*. I really don't know. I'll have to sell the hotel. Nobody will want the orphanage. It costs too much for upkeep. I can't bear to think of what will happen to my babies. And how will I ever get on without Dad?" Astrid started to cry. *Molo* reached over the front seat to try to comfort her as Mark drove on to the mountain camp.

Jim met them as they pulled into camp. Mark introduced himself, helped Astrid out of the Rover and took her to her tent. Jim could tell that something had happened. He tried to question Astrid, but she seemed unable to talk. He asked *Molo*, who told him what had happened. He wondered why Helmut, an experienced hunter, could have made such a terrible mistake. *Molo* went on to the mess tent to give the baby panther the fresh goat's milk.

Mark came out of Astrid's tent and joined Jim at the mess tent. Graham, Noel and Reg still had not returned from the scouting trip.

"Any sign of Ahmed?" asked Mark.

"Yes, this morning, but I have no film of him yet, except for a few shots with my *Nikkon*."

"Have you seen two American hunters? One's about forty-five, heavy-set. Black hair and eyes; a shifty eyed bloke. The other one young, wears steel-rimmed glasses, slight in stature," said Mark.

"They arrived yesterday in a Beech Baron," replied Jim.

"Did you speak to them?" asked Mark.

"I didn't, but Astrid did. Who are they?"

"Ugly Americans, that's the only term to describe them. Bloody trophy hunters who want *Ahmed's* tusks," said Mark.

"That's impossible. Surely they know *Ahmed* is protected."

"I told them myself, but it doesn't mean a bloody thing to those blokes. They'll kill him and smuggle his ivory out of the country."

"I suggest you get a hold of the rangers and have them arrested," said Mark.

Jim became alarmed. "Jesus, I've got to find him again before they do or I won't have a film to make. Where's everybody? We've got to get back out there," said Jim.

Anne came out of her tent and approached them. She had changed her clothes and now wore a pair of high boots and jodhpurs.

"Hello, I'm Anne. I am so sorry to hear about Astrid's father. Can I do anything?"

"I'm Mark. Yes, would you look in on Astrid? She could use a woman's sympathy."

Graham and his crew pulled in.

"What happened? We waited up at the lake," said Graham.

"We found Ahmed. Get the gear together, we're going back out. This time I know where he's at, but we have to move fast."

"Jolly good. You're the boss. Is Astrid joining us?"

"She's resting in her tent." Graham looked concerned. "I'll tell you about it later. Let's go!"

"This is Mark, he's going with us," said Jim. Jim and Mark got into the Land-Rover and Graham with the others followed in the lorry

Forty Eight

Astrid lay on her cot staring into space when Anne opened the tent flap and entered.

"I hope I'm not disturbing you. I thought you might want some company. Is there anything I can get for you?"

"Thank you, that's thoughtful. Sit down. I've been thinking about the difficulty I'm in. You came at the right time. I want to forget my troubles. Could you tell me something about your life? I've never had the opportunity to talk to anyone like you before. I grew up in the bush, playing by myself or with *Masai* boys. Ask me anything about wildlife, or birds, the tribes who live in East Africa, how they're different from the others. I can tell you, but I don't know much about Europeans. To me you're like a princess from a tale my mother read to me. Have you ever lived in a castle?"

"Yes, matter of fact I did when I was very young. It wasn't exactly a castle, but a very old stone manor. I do remember it was always cold. I never thought of myself as a princess, more like an orphan. I got shipped off to Kenya when I was eleven to stay with my uncle. I remember I liked that most. So we do have some similar background. I hate to talk about myself."

"Please, do it as a favor to me," said Astrid taking Anne's hand.

"If you insist. My family's been around since the time of Elizabeth the First and I'm the last of our line, which is sort of sad

179

because I have no children and if I don't start soon the family name will die with me. I've been stupid about my life. I have a husband, but we don't live together. I got caught up in the swinging life of London in the sixties. Frightfully loads of fun. I enjoyed myself. I was rebelling. My mother divorced my father, which in itself was a scandal. My father gambled his and my inheritance away. He had to sell our lands to pay his gambling debts and estate taxes. It made him heartsick and he drank himself to death. They said he killed himself, but I never wanted to believe it. Depressing isn't it? Do you want to hear more?"

"I'm sorry. My mother died when I was ten. It was a hard period for me. I loved her so. She loved the bush and taught me so much about it. It took a long time to get over her death, but my father and I became closer because of it. I will miss him terribly." Astrid started to cry. "Excuse me, I'm sorry."

Anne moved closer. Astrid put her head on Anne's shoulder. After a few moments Astrid pulled herself together and said, "What about Jim, do you love him?"

"What is this, darling? I came to console you and you have me talking about my family and love life."

"I'm sorry. I hope you don't think I'm prying, but I've never talked intimately like this with a woman before."

"I'll try to answer your question about Jim. I adore him. He's handsome, sexy, intelligent and fun, but he's a wolf. I don't think I could trust him for long. He's the type that could break a woman's heart."

Astrid said nothing.

"What about you, darling? Your friend Mark looks like he adores you."

"Mark and I grew up with the same kind of backgrounds and attended the same schools in Nairobi. He tells me all the time he loves me and I might just love him, but I know nothing about men. I was hoping to learn more from you."

"Let me give you a little advice, darling. Don't take too long to say yes to Mark. He looks to me to be a fine young man. You might not know that now, but a good man is hard to find. Take it from me, darling. I know. Remember Anthony?"

"I hope you're not telling me all men are like Anthony and Jim."

"Almost, darling. Almost."

They looked up as *Molo* appeared at the tent entrance. He had the panther cub in his arms with a bottle. "Look Mama, he eats." *Molo* put the small bottle filled with milk into the cub's mouth who started to suck it eagerly.

"Let me have him, *Molo*" said Astrid as she raised her hands to take him. He handed her the rolled little ball of fur. She continued to feed the cub smiling at *Molo* and Anne as she did so. "We've got a new orphan to raise, she said."

Forty Nine

Nigel drove his Land Rover drove down a trail close to where Jim had seen *Ahmed*. They moved along slowly and watched for any sign of movement in the moss hung forest. Clay sat in the front seat with Nigel. Tim sat in the back with the young *Boron* boy and another *Boron* tribesman who acted as gun bearers. They held Clay's Rigby .416 and his semi-automatic Masher elephant guns.

"Listen to me. We're not supposed to be in the Reserve with rifles. It's illegal. I'll lose my bloody license for this," said Nigel.

"Why do ya think you're getting that extra bonus money out of me? It's not because you tell a good story, pal. You're not supposed to see what I am doing. You got blinders on, sport. Right! said Clay." Sweat soaked his shirt and pants.

"I have a feeling you're looking specifically for *Ahmed* and if you think I'll go along with your killing him, you got the wrong bloke. I'm not going to hang. No sir, old boy, not me." Nigel looked back at Tim. "What's your father up to?" Tim said nothing and shrugged his shoulders.

The young boy put his hand on Nigel's back and said as he pointed. "*Tempo! Tempo, Bwana!*" Up ahead in a clearing stood a giant elephant pulling some branches off a tree. He had not seen the Land Rover because his back was turned to them. The big elephant dwarfed the large tree which he ate from.

"That's Ahmed," said Nigel.

Clay focused himself on the elephant who stood before him. "Stop! Give me my rifle," he said to the Boron boy as he got out of the Land Rover. "Are you coming, Tim?" he whispered.

"Who me?"

"Yes, you."

"I'll take photos from here."

"I always knew you where a pussy," said Clay as he looked at Tim, who looked uncomfortable. "What about you, my famous white hunter? Where are your balls?" he asked.

"I'm staying right here. You're on you own, old boy," Nigel whispered.

"That, I have always been," said Clay.

The sound of the wind was heard, coming from the forest in *Ahmed's* direction, *Ahmed* ripping off the branches of the tree with his huge trunk and the crunching of his jaws.

The young boy and *Boron* gun-bearer got out from the rear of the Rover. The boy handed Clay his semi automatic elephant gun. He kept the other rifle as they followed Clay along a path through the trees. *Ahmed* had not yet got their scent because of the wind's direction. They moved in closer. Clay observed the aging, battle-scarred hide that hung from *Ahmed's* massive body. He turned in Clay's direction, his brown stained mammoth tusks which curved inward toward each other, looking like they had rooted up thousands of trees in his life time. Clay's heart kept racing. The ultimate trophy stood before him, the greatest prize of his hunting career. He could already see those massive tusks framing the entrance door to his office. As he took aim, he stumbled over a branch on the path, which made a cracking sound. Ahmed raised his head and his giant ears moved back and forth. He turned his head and then his body. Clay moved out into the clearing and took aim. *Ahmed* threw his massive head into the air, his snake-like trunk sniffing at Clay. His giant ears moved to signal a charge and a terrifying trumpeting sound came up from his cavernous lungs.

Tim and Nigel looked at the scene with terror. "Why doesn't he shoot? What's wrong with him." Tim yelled. The sound of a Land Rover could be heard behind them. Tim looked around and saw Mark Livingston and a group of men. They had motion picture cameras out filming as they moved into the scene.

Ahmed started to charge. His head down, his heavy tusks just above the ground, he raced towards Clay.

Clay sighted his rifle between Ahmed's watering eyes hoping the bullet would find the elephant's small brain. He pulled the trigger. Nothing happened. Just a click. No shot fired. He pulled the trigger again with *Ahmed* almost in his face.

He dropped the gun and turned around to run and saw the young *Boron* boy standing back by a tree, a full smile on his small shining face.

"The little fucker took out the bullets," Clay screamed.

Ahmed picked Clay up with his tusks and threw him into the air. His body flew up over *Ahmed*'s head and came down hard landing on the ground with the crunching sound of Clay's bones breaking. *Ahmed* seemed not yet content. He pushed one of his huge tusks through Clay's body and lifted him high as if in triumph. Then *Ahmed* shook his mammoth head to jolt the impaled body loose from his tusk.

Out of the trees rushed the two young bulls, *Ahmed's com*panions. One charged at the Land Rover and the other rammed the lorry where Graham and his crew were filming. When the young bull hit the lorry it went up on its side and almost tipped over. Jim had his camera on them filming the action as it happened. The young elephant backed off and turned and walked back towards *Ahmed* and sniffed to see if he was okay. *Ahmed* had not moved from his position standing over Clay's body. The other young bull chased after the young boy and his companion who had run from the scene into the forest. After displaying a lot of hostile movement toward the Land Rover, the elephant turned and moved back into the trees and disappeared.

Mark and Jim looked at each other, speechless and shaken from what they had witnessed. Nigel walked over from his Land Rover to Mark.

"The man tricked me. He never told me he wanted to take *Ahmed* as a bloody trophy. So help me, it's the bloody truth." Mark looked at him but made no reply. He looked at Tim, who seemed to have a smirk.

"Will you bury him here?" he asked.

"Let the hyenas have him." answered Tim.

"What will you tell your family?" asked Jim.

"Clay Norbertson, America foremost big game hunter, was killed at what he loved, giving his readers adventure."

"You don't seem to have any remorse," said Jim.

"I hated the sonofabitch."

Fifty

Jim called a meeting with his crew. They sat for drinks and snacks around the mess table. The sun had set in the west and a cool breeze came up that brought the scent of the tropical forest, mixed with the smell of fried bananas *Molo* had cooked. Cold Tusker beer and Red Label whiskey sat on the table. Everyone sat down, helped themselves to the refreshments and to hear what Jim had to say.

"Graham, do you have the entire footage of *Ahmed's* attack?"

"The camera rolled during the whole event, and Reg, here, had his camera on close-ups. We've got the whole bloody massacre. Poor chap, didn't have a chance with no bullets. It seems to me like a bloody suicide, it was," said Graham.

"I hate to say this but we got lucky on the man's tragedy. As a result I have almost all the footage I need, and it shortened the process." Jim continued. "Tomorrow we will get more shots of Ahmed for backup and then wrap it up."

Mark walked into the mess tent. He looked tired and worried.

"Astrid and I will be leaving in the morning. She has some pressing business to get back to. *Molo* will break camp and get the safari gear back to *Moshi* when you're finished," he said.

"We should be finished in a day," said Jim. "When you talked to Tim, did he say if he was going to take Clay's body back to the States or bury him here?"

"He's taking the bloke, what's left of him, to *Nairobi* tomorrow by air and then on to New York for burial", said Mark.

"I guess that covers everything. I'll see you all at dinner," said Jim. Everyone took their drinks and left to clean up for the evening meal.

Jim walked into his tent. Anne lay on her cot resting.

"I need a shot of you tomorrow in the Land Rover, but it's dangerous, and if you don't want to do it I'll understand."

"What do I have to do?"

"You and I will drive in front of *Ahmed* in the Rover. Graham and his crew will have the cameras on us. You'll have no protection in case he comes for us except my driving skill. What do you think?"

"Well, darling. I came to *Kenya* to be a stand-in, and it's part of the job."

"Not this. This is stunt work, and dangerous. If the insurance company knew I was doing the stunt they would cancel my completion bond."

"Winston Churchill said during the war that English women were a brave lot, so I guess I can't let the tradition down."

Jim smiled. "This isn't war, sweetheart, this is film-making reality." Jim sat down and took Anne in his arms and held her as he looked deeply into her eyes. Anne moved into his touch.

"We're going to spend a couple of days in *Nairobi* by ourselves and have some R&R. Maybe we can go up to Lake *Naivasha* to fish for a couple of days. The bass, there, are over five pounds. Or maybe you'd prefer the beach at *Mombasa*? Would you like that?"

"I'd love it," she said. Jim started kissing her earlobe as they fell back on the cot in an embrace.

That night Astrid got on the short-wave radio and called Wilson Field in Nairobi to have an airplane pick she and Mark up to fly to *Moshi* in the morning.

Everyone sat around the fire for the last night in camp. Everybody's mood seemed restored. The full moon picked up their spirits and filled the night with brightness of day. Jim stood to make a toast. "Astrid and Mark will be leaving us in the morning. Astrid, I can only say, you have been the greatest help to us and showed us another part of Africa we'll never forget. If there's a heaven, Helmut is looking down on us tonight, proud of his daughter."

Tears came to Astrid's eyes as Mark took her hand. I'm so lucky to have Mark, she thought, and Jim was thoughtful to mention Dad. What would she do with him gone, she thought. She didn't care about his safari business, but it brought a good cash flow. I'll keep his Hollywood movie clients, she thought. They're not killers. England for me seems out of the question. I'll miss dad, she thought And if I go to prison, *Molo*, could keep the orphanage and hotel together. *Molo* will know what to do, she thought.

"Thank you," said Astrid.

Jim sat and everyone applauded.

"Three cheers for a jolly good, bloke. Hip, Hip, Hurray. Hip, Hip Hurray, Hip, Hip, Hurray," cheered Graham as everyone chimed in.

Fifty One

The next morning Mark and Astrid got off on their charter to *Moshi*. Jim, Anne and the crew left early looking for *Ahmed*. *Molo* had been in the village that day getting new supplies and one of the *Boron* tribesmen told him that he had seen *Ahmed* in the desert that day with his two *askaris*. When he came back to camp he told Jim of the sighting of *Ahmed*.

The entire party went down the mountain to the desert area around *Marsabit*. The intensity of the heat bothered them. Jim worried that filming in the area wouldn't match, because of the difference in terrain. No trees with moss growing on them; just a thorn tree here and there, some giant termite mounds, cactus and a few desert scrub.

Jim and Anne were in the Land Rover and Graham, Reg and Noel followed in the lorry. Jim drove off the highway to circle the base of the mountain. The sand ran soft in spots, making driving difficult. His vehicle got stuck. The sand came up over the wheels. Even the four-wheel drive gave him a problem. He finally got the Land Rover freed from the dune after he had worked the vehicle back and forth for ten minutes. All the frustration from being stuck got Jim hot and he kept perspiring as the sun got higher and began sending its thermal waves off the desert floor.

Eland and *Topi* grazed on desert plants along the way. They disturbed a family of baboons who scampered in front of the vehicle, led by a huge male who showed his sharp fangs in a warning scream.

"How can you look so serene and cool when it must be a hundred degrees? It must be because you're English," Jim said as he wiped his face and neck with a white cloth.

Anne laughed. "Do I look cool to you? Well I'm bloody hot, but you're right about the English. We don't perspire much. We don't see the sun that often. Look! There's a big elephant up ahead." In the distance stood *Ahmed*.

"Good girl, that's him." Jim stopped the Rover and looked behind him. They had made a dust cloud across the desert that blew to the north. The lorry stopped and Jim got out and approached Graham.

"Our elephant is up ahead. The wind is going to let him know we're here. Use two cameras. Anne and I will drive the Rover in front of him. Just have us covered."

"Right-O, lad. That you'll be," said Graham.

Jim got back in the Rover and drove on. Graham followed. When they got within one hundred yards of Ahmed, his trunk picked up their scent.

"We're lucky. I don't see his pals anywhere," said Jim. Anne looked out on the horizon to check Jim's observation.

"We'll make a couple of passes in front of him if he will let us." Jim put his hand on Anne's knee and patted it. "You're one hell of a lady and a great sport."

Anne gave him a nervous smile and Jim turned the Land Rover around. Everything seemed perfect. Ahmed's giant shadow dwarfed the Land-Rover as they drove in front of him. He stood silent with only his trunk moving in their direction. Jim looked at him out of the corner of his eye and saw he made no attempt to charge.

"So far so good," said Jim as he turned the Rover around to drive by him again. He saw Graham in the camera lorry and gave him the sign to go again. Anne remained silent, but she nervously had her fingernails in her mouth. Jim started another pass moving at about ten miles per hour. When he got directly in front of *Ahmed,* who still hadn't moved, the front wheels of the Land Rover hit a soft spot in the sand and the wheels dug in stopping them in their tracks. Jim shifted into low gear four-wheel drive and stepped on the gas. The Rover dug deeper into the sand, not budging a foot. Jim looked out of the cab and saw Ahmed racing down on them. Jim reacted and turned the engine off. Anne reached for the door to jump out. Jim grabbed her and held her back.

"Quiet! Don't move," he whispered. Anne looked at him terrified. Ahmed stopped his charge. His bulk stood a few feet from the open window on Jim's door side. He placed his giant trunk inside the Land Rover cab sniffing at Jim's body then moved over to Anne's. His smell was wild and musky and the feel of his black hairy trunk up against Anne's skin turned it to goose bumps. She wanted to let out a scream, but Jim put his hand over her mouth. The enormous trunk moved around the cab as it felt, sniffed, expanded, contracted, snorted and dripped thick mucous on them. Finally, *Ahmed* stopped his investigation and pulled his trunk from the cab. Jim looked out the side of the Rover and saw *Ahmed* had turned and walked off. The smell of fear came from their bodies as they looked at each other.

"Was that an introduction?" If it was, I've never had a sloppier kiss, darling. I said my prayers," said Anne, color coming back to her face.

Graham drove up in the lorry and stopped beside them.

Jim looked at him hopefully. "Did you get it?" he asked.

"No," Graham answered, "You're going to have to do it again."

Fifty Two

The orphaned animals screamed when they recognized Astrid as she and Mark walked into the compound. Ingrid flew to the door of her cage, as Astrid opened it to let her out. She gave her a kiss and clung to Astrid's neck as though she said. "Don't leave again."

Two female lion cubs paced in a spacious cage as Astrid came near them. One of them, whom Astrid called Lucy, came to the wire closure and pushed her body against the cage rubbing herself on the wire. Astrid scratched her back.

"Lucy, did you miss me?" The young lioness stood for a moment as Astrid rubbed her coat vigorously and let out a playful roar. The other female came to get her share of the attention. Astrid smiled and said. "I missed you, too."

She and Mark walked on to the next compound. A baby elephant stood being fed from a bottle by George. The little elephant pushed against George's body as he devoured the meal.

"Look, Mark, it's the baby elephant I found before we left. He's grown in a week," said Astrid as she and Mark observed it. "George, he looks healthy and fit."

"He eat all time, *Memsahib*," said George who had difficulty holding the bottle in the little elephant's mouth because of its eagerness.

"Give me the bottle. I want to feed him."

George removed the bottle from the elephant's mouth, and handed it to Astrid. She laughed as the little pachyderm pushed himself against her trying to get at the bottle.

"Isn't it a darling, Mark? We have to name her." Astrid looked to make sure it was a girl. "I love the name Prudy. From now on you're "Prudy". Do you like Prudy, Mark?"

He nodded.

"Here, take Ingrid." She handed the chimp to Mark, but Ingrid didn't want to leave Astrid and screamed.

"Ingrid, you're spoiled. Mark loves you, too. Ingrid is jealous, she wants the bottle." Astrid put the bottle in Prudy's mouth, who pushed against her as if Astrid was its dead mother. Tears came to Astrid's eyes.

"What's wrong?" asked Mark.

"My allergies. I wonder what will happen to my babies when I go to jail."

"Why do you always bloody well say that! Believe me, you're not going to jail."

Astrid didn't reply and continued to feed the small elephant. *Molo* came into the compound followed by Malcolm, the district magistrate.

"I offer my sympathy, Astrid," said Malcolm and lowered his head. "Helmut was a good man and a true friend. I will miss his wisdom and kindness."

"Thank you, magistrate. We considered you close to us."

"I have bad news for you. *Dar es Salaam* removed me from your case and put a Judge in from there. I'm sorry."

"Oh, No! Why?"

"Because of the nature of the crime. It has the attention of the government. They found out I'm a friend of yours and have taken me off the case, but I know a barrister in *Dar*. I told him everything.

He's the best defense lawyer in *Tanzania,* with lots of connections in high places. He'd be willing to handle your trial. My advice is to talk to him." Astrid looked at Mark, who looked worried.

"I told you. Dad warned me they'd put me in jail." She gave the bottle back to George and said, "How do I find this man?"

Fifty Three

The phone rang in a home in *Karin*, a rich suburb of *Nairobi*; an attractive middle-aged African woman picked it up.

"Hello," a man's voice said. "I'm not going to tell you who I am, but listen to me. There's an unidentified body at the police morgue. It's your husband, the minister."

The woman became suspicious. "Why would it be my husband? He's well known."

"He's missing isn't he?"

"How do you know?"

"My business is to know. They won't let you in if you give them your name. I suggest you wear a disguise," said the voice. The phone went dead.

The woman sat down and put her hand to her face and thought, they killed him. I tried to tell him, but he wouldn't listen. Oh Peter, why? She began to sob.

The next morning the minister's wife, wearing a blonde wig and dark glasses, walked into the police station in downtown *Nairobi*. She went to the officer at the desk and said, "I'm Miss *Nugonga*. My boyfriend is missing. He might be in the morgue. Is there a body of an unidentified man here? He would be fifty, about five foot ten. I hope he's not, but I've looked everywhere."

The officer looked at a list in front of him. "A dead man found yesterday that answers to that description, but he has no face. The lady looked horrified. "Do you want to see him?" She nodded. "Go down those stairs." The officer pointed to a stairway. "Push the bell." The lady took the stairway. She hesitated, then put he finger on the bell. A tall young African in a white coat opened the door. "I was sent here. I would like to see the man with no face. It could be my missing man," said the woman nervously.

"Sign the form, Miss." He gave her a form to sign. She signed it and gave it back to him. He looked at it and said. "Follow me, Miss *Nugonga*."

She followed the attendant through a door and he turned on a light. The room showed her breath and smelled of antiseptic. She saw a row of tables. On them lay canvas bags covering the corpses.

The attendant walked in front of one of the tables and looked at the name tags tied to a bag. He picked up a tag and put it down and went on to another table. "Here, Miss," he said and pulled a zipper down to reveal a naked man.

The lady became hesitant as she walked up to the corpse. The man's face appeared burned away and unrecognizable. There was no nose nor eyes. His lips had been burned off, only his teeth showing. She could look no more and turned away.

The attendant opened a manila envelope and poured out its contents. The woman recognized a small gold ring and picked it up. She had given the ring to him when they met. She remembered he used to wear it on his ring finger, but he had gotten heavier and wore the ring on his pinky. She started to cry.

The attendant looked at her and said, "Can you make identification?"

She shook her head and said, "No, that's not him." And left the morgue.

Nairobi appeared to be in chaos when the news got out about finding minister *Mnazi's* body in the morgue. His murderers had made a mistake in pouring acid on his face. It kept the hyenas from eating him.

The Standard ran the headline: "MINISTER P.D. MNAZI MURDERED BY UNKNOWN ASSAILANTS", but everyone knew that *Mnazi* had gone too far with his attacks on the government. It seems to be unfortunate for the officials that the hyenas did not eat *Mnazi's* corpse; otherwise no one would have found his body and *Mnazi* would have disappeared.

In Parliament later, an MP stated: "God being what he is, the hyenas could not feed off the body because Mnazi was a good man."

Fifty Four

Angry Kenyans stood on the sidewalk in front of the New Stanley Hotel in the center of downtown Nairobi as Jim and Anne checked in. The Kenyans carrying signs demanding the government find P.D. *Mnazi's* murderer.

A short time later, Jim and Anne came down from their room and went outside to the Thorn Tree Cafe. Jim recognized Anthony Roseli's picture on the front page of the Standard. He bought the paper and looked at the headline, "GANGSTERS PLOT TO KILL AHMED FOULED". The article went on and said that Anthony had been deported that day and his guns confiscated by the government for a plot to kill one of Kenya's most valued treasures, *Ahmed*. President *Kenyatta* was reached for comment. He stated that...Jim handed the newspaper to Anne who read it as they sat down in the outdoor restaurant in front of the hotel.

The cafe was alive and packed with tourists from all nations. A different language could be heard at every table. A thorn tree stood in the center courtyard from which the name derived. Outdoor umbrellas hung over the metal tables surrounded by white plastic chairs. They served short order food, hamburgers etc. The waiter took their order for two burgers and two pints of Tusker beer. They were dressed in fresh khakis, and Anne wore the native amber jewelry on her wrist and around her neck she had bought from the *Rendelle* women. They surveyed the crowd looking for someone they might know, because the Thorn Tree had the reputation for being the place you could run into someone from your past.

"This cafe is the only place I've found in my travels where the hamburgers taste as good as they do in the States. Must be the good meat they have in Kenya and the way they age it like they do at home. I like Tusker beer also, I don't drink beer, but this brew gives me a glow."

"I'm glad Anthony got his comeuppance," said Anne.

"I wish they'd kept him in prison. He got off easy. I hope that's the last of him. I'm tired of that guy." Jim looked around at the irate crowd milling around in front of the hotel. "*Nairobi* is no place for us to hang out. It's too dangerous. Let's catch the train in the morning for *Mombassa* and spend some time on the beach."

"Lovely, darling. I always wanted to travel on an African train." Their waiter brought the beers. Jim turned to pay him and recognized a man sitting at the back of the terrace.

"There's someone I know over there."

"Who is it?" asked Anne as she looked.

"*Seychelles* Pete. He's a dope dealer and has the best ganja I've every smoked."

"Why, Jim darling, you never told me you're a doper."

"I'm not, but I do it once in awhile."

"Invite him over for a drink," said Anne as she gave Jim a mischievous smile.

Jim got up and went to Pete's table. Anne watched as he did. Pete sat with a couple of young, unkempt white men drinking beer. Pete was a *Creole*, from the *Seychelles* Islands off the coast of *Kenya*. He looked thirty or so, with thinning hair and a beer belly. He wore a soiled white shirt, and looked up and squinted at Jim when he appeared.

"Hello Pete, remember me?"

"*Oui*, the movie man. How's everything, man?"

"Great, man," said Jim, getting into his hip talk. "Come over to my table when you can. I'd like to talk with you and to introduce you to a lady friend." He looked toward Anne and smiled.

"Gotcha, man. Be right over." Jim walked back to his table and Pete followed.

"Anne, meet *Seychelles* Pete."

Pete grunted pleasantly and smiled showing off his uneven brownish tinted-teeth.

"Good to see you, man," said Pete, trying to make his accent sound American.

"We need a little of the special smoke you have. Is it possible?"

"Sure man. Where ya staying?"

"Here at the hotel. Room 412."

"Cool, man. I'll be in your room at six. Would you like to take some back with you?" he asked.

"How would I carry it?" asked Anne, interested.

"Leave it to Pete. He fix you up. I show you when I come to your room, man." Pete got up from the table and walked back to his group.

"How did you meet him?" asked Anne.

"Dian Fossey introduced us. He's her friend."

At six-ten they heard a knock on their room door. Jim went to answer. Anne straightened her skirt and looked in the mirror to check her hair. When Jim opened the door, *Seychelles* Pete stood in the hallway holding a shoe box in one hand and a zebra drum in the other.

"Come in, Pete, we've been waiting."

"Good to see you, man," he said as he closed the door. He opened the shoe box and shoved it in Jim's nose. "Smell, man. It's the best, man. It comes from Lake Victoria. Jim looked into the box and saw dried dark green marijuana. He smiled as he smelled it, looking pleased.

Anne came to have a look and smell. "It smells of mangos," she said.

"Let me roll one, man."

They sat down, Anne on her twin bed and Jim in a chair by the window as they watched Pete roll up a thick reefer. When he finished, he handed it to Jim to light. Jim lit the joint and took a deep drag. He handed it to Anne who inhaled deeply and then handed to Pete, who made a vulgar sucking sound as he took in the smoke. The distinctive smell of marijuana filled the room and before long, everyone's mood elevated.

"Very good, Pete," said Jim as he took another drag.

"The best, man the best," said Pete as he gave them a smile.

"What's the zebra drum for?" asked Anne.

"You transport some ganja in drum back with you."

"What ingeniousness you have," said Anne. Pete picked up the drum and showed Anne how it worked. He removed the zebra skin from the top. Anne could see a cardboard cylinder in the center of the hollow drum.

"I pack for you the ganja around the cylinder and I sew back on hide cover. See." Pete put the cover back over the drum and started to pound on the drum. "Listen, still sound good, man."

Anne smiled. "You're a clever one," she said laughing. "How much is this going to cost me?"

"One hundred. U.S."

"You're not going to carry this stuff back with you, are you?" asked Jim.

"Why not, darling? Pete seems to have a good method to get it through customs and my London friends will enjoy my ingenuity."

"What happens if you're caught?"

"Oh, Jim, you're such a party pooper." Anne looked at Pete.

"When will you have the drum ready for me, Pete?"

"Tomorrow," he said.

Seychelles Pete delivered Anne her Zebra drum in the morning with it's cache of powerful African marijuana. The hide was still moist, recently slaughtered which upset her. She hadn't realized when Pete had showed her the drum that she would be getting a freshly killed zebra's hide to carry back to London on the airplane. Jim remained aloof about her purchase. She knew he didn't approve of what she was doing so she kept her feelings to herself.

Fifty Five

The train left *Nairobi* Station at noon and would arrive in *Mombasa* early the next morning. Jim got a compartment. They went directly to their quarters and got comfortable. You could not compare this train to a European or an American one. The sleeping cars were old, and had been worked to death already in another part of the world. Double doors had been cut between their compartment and another next to them. A loose board held the doors together, so you could make the compartment twice its size by removing the board. Jim pushed on the doors to see if they would open; they seemed secure, but a crack showed between them and daylight shone through. Jim made out the shape of a woman seated there.

Anne made herself comfortable and brought out some ganja. She rolled a few joints for their trip.

Jim went to the bar car and brought back some beer.

Anne had a joint going when he returned. "Here, darling. Have some of this," she said as she handed him the burning joint.

Jim took a drag and sat down next to her and opened a beer. "It's so nice to relax and not have to worry if we're going to see an elephant," he said as he looked at Anne who seemed to be in euphoria looking out the window. God, she's pretty, he thought, smart as hell, too. These English girls know what a man is all about.

She's never once said anything to upset me. I think she knows that I've been interested in Astrid and hasn't mentioned it. If she were an American girl she would have been on me about it and I would have to send her home and we'd both be miserable. That's what I mean. She's cool, cool as they get. Damn, this African weed gets me horny. Oh, Oh, it's hitting me again.

"Have you ever felt like you'd like to be a baboon? asked Jim. Anne looked at him amused. "No, not really. Have you?"

"Sometimes when I get horny I do."

"The way you're looking at me I can tell you are."

"It shows, huh? Why don't we play a little game? Let's get out of our clothes and play baboon."

"Jim, you're kinky. What do I know about baboons?" she laughed. "What do you want me to do?"

"You've watched baboons. You know how they groom each other. We don't have their body hair, but we have our own and we can start there."

"What happens after that?" she asked in a low voice. "What do we do then?" She moved down in her seat.

"We use our noses. You've seen how baboons smell each other to see if they're ready to mate."

Anne reached for her bag.

"What are you doing?"

"I'm looking for my perfume."

"Perfume. Baboons don't wear perfume."

"Oh!"

"Well, are you going to play with me?" Anne looked at him and nodded her head.

"From now on we don't talk to each other. We talk like baboons."

"Jim, you're silly. How do baboons talk? I can't talk like a baboon."

"Sure you can. You do this. You take short breaths in and out and say "ugaa ugaa ugaa ugaa", real fast. That's all you have to do. The rest will come easy when we do it."

The train was moving fast and lunged, throwing them against each other.

"This is a bumpy ride," said Anne. She took another couple puffs off the joint and handed it to Jim who did the same. She looked at Jim who seemed as high as she was and said. "Let's be baboons. "ugaa ugaa ugaa". She stood to remove her clothes. She slipped out of her khaki shorts and removed her loose shirt and then her brassiere and panties. She stood naked except for her safari boots and jewelry. Jim was out of his clothes in a flash. They looked at each other and started to laugh.

"Baboons don't kiss, do they?" she asked.

Jim shook his head and Anne sat down in front of him and looked at his thick wavy brown hair. She picked up a few strands, looked at them closely and scratched his scalp. Jim picked up her long shiny black hair and examined it and then smelled her scalp. They looked into each other's eyes. They started sniffing at each other's bodies. Jim was making "ugaa ugaa ugaa" sounds while getting an erection.

Anne saw he looked hard and took hold of his penis. She turned her body around, her back to him, holding on to his erection, and guided it in. Jim started moving against her rear like he had seen a baboon do. They both made sounds like the animals as they knelt on the compartment seat in rear to front position. At that moment the train made a sudden lunge to the right, throwing them off the long mohair couch across the small compartment and into the double doors with such a force they broke the latch.

The doors burst open. They flew into the next compartment with their bodies still in dog-fashion position in front of a startled African lady.

Anne refused to look at the woman when she realized where she was. They both got up off the floor not saying that they were sorry or apologizing to the lady and left her compartment. Jim looked back as he closed the double doors. The lady stared at him and then put her hands over her eyes.

Jim secured the doors back in place as he looked at Anne. They both screamed with laughter, and were unable to stop. Anne laughed so hard she had to grasp her stomach.

"I've cramps in my stomach, it hurts. Jim, please do something. I can't stop laughing. It hurts so. Please help me." She said as she rolled on the seat holding her stomach. Jim sat down and pulled her over his knees and slapped her bare buttocks and her laughter turned from howls to sobs.

"Stop it," she yelled, "you're hurting me."

It was dark when they made their entrance into the dining car.

They were dressed in fresh clothes. Anne had her hair pulled back and wore dark glasses. Jim followed her as the waiter sat them down at a table in the middle of the car. Anne looked around at the other diners.

The dining car came from another era. It had sterling silver carriage lamps, that glowed warmly between each table. The dark oak paneling gave an inviting atmosphere to the room. The linens were thick and heavily starched. Anne picked up a piece of silver laid out on the table and examined it. It was old and heavy, a seven-piece place setting made in Sheffield, England.

"What a divine experience. I feel like we've gone back to the twenties. Do you see what we are eating off? The china is *Limoges* and the silver is English and look at the crystal. It's *Irish*. Oh, Jim, it's wonderful. I love the atmosphere. Don't you, darling?"

"Why are you wearing dark glasses? It's dark as hell in here."

"I'm so embarrassed, darling. I don't want that woman from the next compartment to recognize me if she is having dinner."

"How could she? You were naked. But I think she's sitting in back of you."

"How can you tell?"

"It's the way she's been looking at us."

"Oh my God, I don't think I can eat."

"Forget it. I have something important that has to do with us. I want to discuss it with you. I never told you much about my past and the life I had when I was married. I did a lot of traveling then, but I won't have to do that much anymore. I want to have a home again and be with someone I love. I think I'm falling in love with you. Do you think there's a place for me in your life?"

Anne took off her dark glasses, looked up from the table, and looked into Jim's eyes.

"Jim, you're sweet. I do love you. You make me feel wonderful, darling. Really, I adore you. You're so handsome, intelligent and organized, but I couldn't stand the idea that you might cheat on me and I have a feeling you're that kind of man. I want a man that believes I'm the only woman in the world and that would be difficult for you. My husband should have been that kind of man, but he wasn't. I loved him so when we met. I would do anything for him. My friends told me not to marry him because he would make me unhappy and they were right. He has."

"You're reading me wrong. I admit I like women, but is that so bad?"

"There's nothing wrong, darling, and women adore you for it, but you don't have to go to bed with them."

"That hurt. Who told you that? Did Graham? He doesn't know me. I only work with him. He knows nothing of my personal life."

"Don't be upset, Jim dear. I told you I love you, but..."

"Not enough to marry me, is that it?"

"We'll see. Remember, we just met."

"I knew I wanted to marry you the first time I saw you that night at my hotel in London."

"Jim, we have time to make the marriage decision. Remember, darling, I'm still married. But I'll tell you this. I want children. How do you feel about children?"

"I want children. I have a daughter, but I want more, especially before I get too old to enjoy them."

"Jim, you're a lovable man." Anne picked up the menu. "What are you going to have for dinner, darling?"

Fifty Six

Astrid hired Charles *Nandanga* as her barrister. He arrived in *Moshi* to get Astrid's defense ready for the courtroom. The newspapers ran stories about what Astrid had done to the poacher, leaving him in his own trap to die. It was the first time a white women stood trial for a such a crime. She had the sympathy of most whites who thought flogging seemed a cruel punishment and should be removed from the penal code, but others thought she should to go to jail, especially Africans, who said it was time whites got their due.

Charles was fifty, bright and articulate. He had been educated in England and spoke with an English accent. He dressed in a formal manner, dark suits, white shirts and sober ties even when the outside temperature was over ninety. He stayed at the Mount *Kilimanjaro* Lodge so he could be near Astrid.

Charles sat with Astrid in her office. Mark stood near listening to what he had to say.

"I'm changing your plea to not guilty because of temporary insanity. This type of case doesn't qualify for a jury in *Tanzania*. We'd be better with one. This judge is a government man. I'll prove to the judge you were not thinking properly when you came upon your pet elephant in the trap. It was like seeing your child murdered in the most heinous way and your mind snapped. The rangers told you of your actions when they arrested you later."

Astrid looked at Mark. "But I said I was guilty," she said.

Mark, with anguish in his voice, said, "Listen to the man. He's trying to save you from prison." He looked at Charles. "Her animals mean more to her than humans, they always have." Mark shook his head. "Which seems ironic because she's allergic to their hair."

Astrid gave Mark a searching look. "Do you want me to lie? I can't."

"Astrid," said Charles, "I respect your feelings and your love of animals, but you've got to help me. I'm to prove to the judge you weren't thinking properly, your mind snapped, to save you."

"What about *Molo*? He was with her," said Mark. "I'll discuss our plea with *Molo* when I'm through with Astrid." Charles looked into Astrid's eyes. "Do you want to go to prison? To be flogged? You could be raped or killed. They've never heard of human rights in *Tanzania*," he said cold heartedly.

Astrid got up from the chair. She paced. She tried to control her feelings but Mark could see she was devastated by what Charles had said. He said to Charles, "You don't have to be so bloody rough."

"I'm trying to get to her. She has to tell the judge she blanked out. I see no other way to save her."

Newspaper reporters from *Kenya* and *Tanzania* and a crowd of onlookers stood outside the small government district building when Astrid, Mark and Charles *Nandanga* arrived. Mark shielded Astrid from the cameras and rushed her into the small courtroom. Locals overcrowded the room. Charles escorted Astrid to the front of the room and they sat behind a long table. Mark took a seat behind them.

The clerk stood and said. "Please rise. The Honorable *Kirubai* presiding." The judge, a stern-looking man in his fifties dressed in a coat and tie, came into the stuffy room as everyone stood. He put a pair of glasses on and looked down at a paper in front of him and then looked up.

"Is the prosecution ready?" he asked.

Mr. Baku stood up. "Yes, your honor."

"Is the defense ready for sentencing?" Charles stood up and said, "Your honor, we've changed our plea to not guilty by reason of temporary insanity."

The crowd in the court whispered among themselves and moved around in their cramped seats.

The judge brought down his gavel. "Order in the courtroom. Mr. *Baku*, is your witness present?" Mr. *Baku* turned to see his witness who he motioned to come forward. The poacher, a thin African who looked middle-aged, rose from a bench and came forward on crutches, his leg wrapped in a large bandage. A yellow greasy cream on his face covered sun blisters. He moved slowly to the front of the room and stepped up to the witness chair next to the judge. He stared at Astrid in front of him.

Astrid looked uncomfortable with his gaze and turned to Mark behind her, who put his hand on her shoulder to reassure her.

Mr. *Baku* approached the witness and directed his remarks to the judge. "Your honor, Mr. *Farasi* does not speak English. I will be his interpreter."

Charles stood and said, "Your honor, I would like an interpreter appointed by the court."

"Very well," the judge replied. "What tribal dialect does Mr. *Farasi* speak?"

"He's a *Chagga*, your honor," said Mr. *Bakua*.

"The court will appoint an interpreter. Recess until one o' clock. Mr. Nandanga and Mr. Baku please come to my office."

Astrid looked concerned and she asked Charles. "What is going on?"

"He'll ask us to quiz some Chagga for an interpreter. I'll meet you and Mark at the *Moshi* Hotel for lunch," he said as he went to meet with the judge.

Mark and Astrid left the courtroom by a side entrance and walked to the *Moshi* Hotel a short distance away, avoiding the onlookers outside.

The hotel, a tall concrete and glass building with outside balconies on each room constructed in the sixties, lacked charm but had conveniences: baths in every room, a good restaurant, and views of *Kilimanjaro*.

A generator truck stood parked in front of the hotel along with another truck loaded with klieg lights and reflectors. Mark and Astrid looked at the equipment closely.

"I say there's a movie company staying at the hotel." Mark remarked.

"Ja, They wanted dad, but he'd been booked."

At the mention of her father, Mark felt guilty. He had to tell Astrid what really happened in the *Selous*. He had to get it off his chest. "Did your dad say what it's about?"

"Yes, World War I, when the Germans occupied *Tanganyika*. Dad got permission to film at *Sani Maui* prison."

They entered the empty dining room and took a table by a large window that gave them a view of *Kilimanjaro*. The waiter came and they ordered two cups of coffee.

"Astrid, your dad… he wasn't killed by a lion. He was murdered."

"Murdered! Who would murder him?" She covered her face with trembling hands.

"Two Kenyans were sent to murder me, but I changed tents that night. It was dark and the killers didn't know it was Helmut." "I'm too confused. I knew Dad couldn't be killed by a lion, he was careful about his firearms, he always had them prepared, and he was always cleaning them. It didn't make sense to me. Oh Mark, how senseless it all is. Poor Dad murdered. He never did anything bad to anyone. He was the kindest man anyone could have ever known. Mark, I'm so sorry. It must be a terrible feeling you have. You can't blame yourself."

"But I do. If I hadn't got involved in this bloody business of saving the elephant, P.D. *Mnazi* would still be alive, your dad would be alive. It's all my fault; I've ruined my life, your life. I'll never be able to come back to *Kenya*, at least while *Kenyatta* is alive."

"Oh Mark, you shouldn't be seen. If they find out you're not dead they'll be after you again. You've got to get out of East Africa." "I can't leave you. When I go, you'll go with me?" Astrid took Mark's hand and held it. Mark looked into her eyes, and tears came to hers. "Astrid, I love you so. I don't know how something so terrible could happen to us. I loved your father. He was more of a father than my own. He encouraged me to pursue you. He'd be happy if you and I got married." Astrid started to cry and Mark moved over next to her and held her in his arms.

"Mark, I need you. Don't leave me. Please don't leave me." Astrid put her head on his shoulder.

"I will never leave you. I promise."

Fifty Seven

By one o'clock the courtroom had filled up. The room baked in the noonday sun. A clerk walked over and turned on the overhead fans. The still air started to circulate. Astrid sat with Charles at the front table with Mark behind her. The judge made his entrance and everyone stood. Mr. *Baku* got up from his seat and said, "Mr. *Murani Farasi,* come to the stand."

The poacher came into the room from the rear and slowly made his way to the front on to the witness stand and sat.

"Would the interpreter, Mr. *Murunga,* please come forward?" A young *Chagga* walked up and stood next to Mr. *Farasi.* The clerk asked the witness to say the oath, which he did though Mr. *Murgunga.*

"Mr. *Murgunga,* I'll ask you questions. Repeat to the court what the witness answers." The interpreter nodded his head.

"What happened to you on March fourth, nineteen-seventy four?"

"I check trap I hide on trail. Out come *Memsahib* and African." He pointed to Astrid.

"What happened then?" asked Mr. Baku through the interpreter.

"The white lady, she have gun. She asked, is trap mine? A small dead elephant in trap. I frightened. I say, "No, trap not mine." She

221

curse in *Swahili*, bad words. She take whip, beat me. I run. African, he chase me down. He tied me," he said.

Astrid looked directly at the witness with no expression on her face.

"What happened then?" asked the prosecutor through the interpreter.

"*Memsahib*, and African dragged to trap. Lady with African put in trap. I scream pain. Lady no care." The courtroom was quiet. Everyone remained still as the questioning continued.

"Did you notice anything about the accused? Was she acting in a strange manner?" An uncomfortable laugh came from the crowd.

"She mad. A crazy look in eyes."

"What was the African servant doing?"

"He stand. He do nothing."

"Then what happened?" asked Mr. *Baku.*

"They leave me. They go off. The pain made me go out a long time. I wake. It dark. I hear hyena. I see hyena shadow. I make noise. I yell at him. I cry at him. Hyena he run away. Pain made me out. God make hyena not eat. I wonder why. I think he know I good man, love my kids. He know who feed kids. The sun it come up hot on me. I need water. I have no water. I go out. I wake up, it is almost dark. I hear something. I think it lion, but happy for me I see number one son. He look for me cause I not home at night. He take me from trap and bring to hospital in *Arusha.*"

"I have no further questions, your honor," said Mr. Baku and sat down.

Charles *Nandangaa* rose from the table. He moved to a easel that was set up in front of the courtroom and put up photos for the judge to see. The photos were of wild animals caught in poachers traps; one was a rhino caught in a wire snare, its horn cut from its head, blood covering the animal; another was a small elephant, similar to Astrid's Susie, its tusk cut from its bloated body, decaying in the African sun. Another was a skinned leopard. Astrid looked away when she saw the photo displayed in front of her.

The judge looked at the photos and said, "Mr. *Nandanga*, are these photographs of the actual crime?"

"No, your honor," answered Charles.

"Remove them, they're irrelevant to this case."

"Your honor, I wanted to show the court the kind of scene Miss Dryden witnessed. It caused her mind to snap, and to do what she did."

"Turn the photos around and get on with the questioning."

Charles looked disappointed and turned the photos over and set them on the floor. He turned to the poacher who sat straight at attention.

"Mr. *Farasi*, how many times have you been arrested for poaching?" Mr. *Baku* jumped up and said, "Your honor, that question is irrelevant. The witness is not on trial."

"Proceed with the questioning," said the judge.

"I'll repeat the question. Mr. *Farasi*, how many times have you been arrested for poaching?" asked Charles. The witness looked puzzled and said, "One time."

"Your record tells me you have been arrested three times. Did you go to prison?"

Mr. *Farasi* nodded.

The court clerk said, "Tell the witness to speak up."

The interpreter said something in *Chagga*.

"Were you flogged?"

"Yes."

"Do you know you can be flogged and go to prison again?" The witness looked puzzled.

"I no kill elephant."

"It was your trap he died in and the ivory was removed. You admitted it was your trap earlier. What you did is against the law, you poached an elephant for his ivory, Mr. *Farasi*. You can go to jail again. I have no more questions for the witness."

Farasi got up and said to the judge. "Master. Family poor. Have ten children. Need ivory to buy food for family. Two sons sick. Have polio. Please, no go jail. Family no money."

A policeman removed the witness from the courtroom.

Mr. Baku stood and called Astrid to the witness stand. Astrid sat in the witness chair. The clerk administered the oath.

"Would you state your full name and where you live? said Mr. *Baku*.

"Astrid Marie Dryden. I live on Highway A23, *Moshi, Tanzania.*"

"What is your occupation?"

"I own a hotel outside of *Moshi* with my father...I'm sorry, my father is dead. I own a hotel and a safari business."

"Would you tell the court what happened when you found your elephant in a poacher's trap?."

Astrid cleared her throat and began to tell her story. "My elephant, Susie, was missing four days. She had gone off before so I wasn't worried. She hears the calls of the wild elephant around my orphanage from time to time. I take in motherless animals to raise until they're able to go back to the wild. They leave on their own when they mature. That usually happens when they come into mating season. Since Susie was too young to mate, I went out looking for her."

"Can I interrupt you, Miss Dryden.

Were you by yourself?" asked Mr. *Baku*.

"Yes."

Mr. *Baku* made a note.

"Go on, miss." said the judge.

"I hiked along a trail and caught a strong odor of a dead animal and I went to investigate. It was a small elephant, decomposed in a poacher's trap. Susie had a toe missing, and the elephant in the trap had no toe. Her small tusks were pulled and her tail cut off. The buzzards and the hyenas had already eaten half of her. I went crazy with grief. Then I heard someone coming along the trail. The poacher, *Farsi.* I knew he poached her." Astrid stopped. "Could I have a glass of water?" The clerk handed her the water.

"What did you do then?" asked Mr. *Baku*.

"I went crazy! My baby dead! You might think it is silly to call an elephant my baby, but that's how I thought of her. I had given her life. I had a gun and I jumped out at *Farasi* and accused him of killing my baby. I got hysterical and I don't remember much after that."

"Miss Dryden, are you going to tell the court that you don't remember beating and putting Mr. *Farasi* in his trap to die? I call that attempted murder."

"That's not true! I didn't! It's a nightmare! I don't remember."

"Where was your servant? He helped you, didn't he?"

"I was by myself."

"Mr. *Farasi* said your servant was with you. Why would he say that?" asked Mr. *Baku.*

"He was mistaken. I was by myself."

"I have no more questions. I would like, your honor for the court to issue a subpoena to Miss Dryden's servant to appear," said the prosecutor.

"Very well. Please give the clerk the witness's name," said the judge. Astrid wrote out *Molo's* name and gave it to the clerk. Charles *Nandanga* stood and walked over to cross-examine Astrid.

"Miss Dryden, are you married?"

"No, sir."

"Do you have any children?"

"Yes, my animals are my children."

"Can you tell the judge about raising a motherless elephant? What kind of care do you give so the elephant will survive?"

"Usually if they are too young they don't survive. They need constant care. The mother's milk is necessary. *Molo*, my servant, makes a special formula from goat's milk and the *Moringa* tree leaves that seems to work for some."

"Is it true that you become very attached to these small orphans?" asked Charles.

"They're my babies. Many a night I've been up with a sick animal."

"Would you say the animals you have, respond to you like their mother?"

"I'm the only mother some have ever known."

225

"So you acted like a mother would act if she saw her child killed in the manner that you saw your Susie in that trap?"

"Yes, a mother's rage took over my emotions and caused me to act the way I did. I had no control over myself." Astrid took a handkerchief from her pocket and dried the tears coming down her cheeks.

"I have no further questions," said Charles.

"We'll recess until tomorrow at ten o clock," said the judge.

Astrid let Mark stay with her that night. She needed him next to her to feel his warmth and strength. The day in the courtroom had made her restless. Charles told her she did a fine job of telling her story. He felt the poacher had a weak position because of his prior arrests. But she worried about *Molo*. Could he lie on the stand? It was difficult for her to go to sleep and when she finally did, she woke up a short time later in a heavy sweat. She pushed off her blankets, went to the refrigerator, took out some milk and poured herself a glass. Mark remained asleep. She kept quiet not wanting to wake him. She sat in the early morning light and her thoughts went back to her mother when she was a little girl.

She remembered her mother's long blonde hair. She liked to brush it for her when she and her father sat down in the evening after the day's chores. Her mother would sing in German in her soft soprano voice "*Guten Abend, gute Nacht, mit Rosen bedacjtcht*". Her mother hated killing of any kind and never wanted to hear any of her father's stories about what he or his clients killed when he was on safari. I wonder what mother's advice would be if she were here now, she thought. I bet she would have done the same thing. She looked out and saw daylight appearing in the east.

Fifty Eight

Major *Darassa* sat reading the Tanzania morning newspaper in his office in Nairobi. He looked at a picture of Mark Livingston shielding a young girl from a photographer. The caption read: TRIAL STARTS TODAY IN MOSHI. "Astrid Dryden, local hotel operator in court for sentencing, with Mark Livingston. Could face public flogging." He pushed the button on his office intercom.

"Find *Otieno* and *Najaro*. Tell them I want them in my office... now."

"Yes, Major. Straightaway."

Fifteen minutes later, the two *Kikuyus henchmen* stood before the major at attention. They wore uniforms of the GSU.

"Look! You hyenas need new eyes. You told me this man was dead. You lied to me! I'll have you staked out for the vultures."

Otieno took the paper and looked at it closely. *Najaro* stood next to him doing the same.

"Major, I don't understand. I killed this man. I am sure of it. His head fell at my feet," said *Otieno* as he looked first at *Najaro* and then at the major.

"You thought you killed him. But he is alive. You stupid hyena."
"He tricked us major. We killed someone else, but who?" They
both looked at each other.

"You killed the wrong man is the point. This time get him. He
is dangerous to us. He could bring down the government. Find
him in *Moshi* and this time make sure he's dead."

"Yes, sir," they repeated together stood at attention, saluted,
turned and left the office.

The phone rang on the Major's desk. "Major, Minster *Mafalme*
is on the line," said his secretary's voice.

"Good morning, Minister. Yes, I have seen the "paper". I have
it in front of me.

Fifty Nine

A larger group of locals had gathered in front of the court building as Astrid and Mark made their entrance. *Molo* had joined them. He looked regal in his red *fez* and his long white *kan*su.

A reporter from one of the newspapers shoved in next to Astrid and asked, "*Memsahib,* what kind of treatment do you think you will get when you go to prison?"

Astrid's face turned to fright. She said nothing to the reporter and moved quickly into the courtroom and took her seat down front.

The judge entered as everyone got to their feet. The clerk read his name and the agenda.

The prosecutor, Mr. *Baku* got up and said, "Will *Molo Kampi* take the stand." *Molo* moved walked to the witness chair and sat down.

The clerk asked him to stand and raise his right hand and to repeat the oath after him. *Molo* sat down and Mr. *Baku* proceeded.

"Would you state your name and where you live."

"My name is *Molo Kampi.* I live at the Mount *Kilimanjaro* Hotel and *Safari* camp. Route A23, *Moshi, Tanzania.*"

"Who is your employer?" *Molo* looked confused.

"Who do you work for?" Mr. *Baku* asked again.

"*Memsahib* Astrid Dryden."

"How long have you been employed, have you worked for her?"

"Many, many years. I boy I come to *Memsahib* father and mother to work."

"Have they been good to you?"

Molo smiled. "Oh yes, mister. They love *Molo* and *Molo* love them." he said with a bright smile.

"On the day of March fourth this year, where were you?"

"*Molo* in kitchen. He had big group Tour Company that day. Make lunch for group."

Mr. *Farasi* said you were with Miss Dryden and held him down for Miss Astrid while she beat him with a whip."

"Bad man, he lie. *Molo* in kitchen at hotel. No with *Memsahib*. *Molo* in kitchen."

"Did Mr. Charles *Nandanga,* your mistress's barrister, talk to you about being a witness and going on the stand?"

Molo became uncomfortable. He moved in his chair and looked at Charles and Astrid sitting before him. "*Molo* in kitchen."

"Did Mister Charles tell you to lie and say that you where not with Miss Astrid that day? Remember if you lie, you can go to jail."

"No lie. *Molo* in kitchen."

"I have no further questions." Mr. *Baku* looked at Charles and said, "He's your witness."

Molo looked uncomfortable. His face was wet with perspiration. He took the glass of water in front of him and drank it down.

Charles got up and walked over to *Molo*. "When your mistress came back that day from finding her elephant in the trap, what did she say to you?"

"Mama say nothing. Mama upset and cry. She went to her cabin and not come out until ranger come get her."

"Was her father, Helmut, there when she came back to the hotel?"

"No, he out. He come later when rangers come." Charles looked at the judge and said. "I have no more questions for the witness."

Molo got up from the witness chair. His *kansu* clung to his body with perspiration.

The judge looked up from his desk and said, "The court will take a twenty minute recess and I will be back with my decision." He left the room.

Mark sat down with Astrid and Charles. *Molo* waited in the back of the room. Everyone remained in the courtroom waiting for the judge to reenter Astrid looked up at the clock on the wall. It said eleven- thirty. She nervously looked at her wristwatch, which was a few minutes slower. The judge's door finally opened and as he entered, everyone stood.

"Be seated," he said. "Will *Molo Kampi* come forward."

Molo looked surprised and came forward and stood before the Judge.

"Would the accused please stand." Astrid rose from her seat and Charles stood next to her.

"After hearing the testimony and details of this case it is obvious that someone is lying. It is the decision of this court that you, Astrid Marie Dryden, be retained at *Sani Maui* prison where you will receive ten lashes and will be confined for thirty days. And you, *Molo Kampi*, you were Ms. Dryden's accomplice. It is the decision of the court that you be given ten lashes and thirty days."

Astrid rushed to *Molo* side. He was in shock and moved his arm over his eyes. "Your honor. *Molo* is innocent. I told him what to do." The judge brought down his gavel. "Ms. Dryden, this is a court of law. You are out of order." A cry went up from the crowd. The Judge brought down his gavel "Order in the court." He looked menacingly at the spectators and continued. "I was going to say hard labor, but being a woman, they will decide what they will do with you. This court is adjourned." The judge rose.

Astrid approached the bench. "Your honor, I want to say something." The judge looked down on her. "You had your chance during trial. There's no more to say."

"But, your honor. Every day we Africans murder thousands of wild animals. We have to save them before it's too late. Enforce stronger laws, your honor. Tell the government to make them stop this senseless poaching."

The rangers came forward and put Astrid and *Molo* in chains. Charles broke away from Astrid and stopped the judge before he went through the courtroom door.

"Your honor. There're no facilities for women at *Sani Maui* prison. You can't send her there." said Charles.

Then they'll have to make some," he said defiantly to Charles. Astrid started to cry. Mark came forward to embrace her, but the rangers pushed him away. The rangers led Astrid and *Molo* from the room. She looked back at Mark who stood helpless.

Mark looked to Charles, who had his head down on the pine table. He said frantically, "Charles, do something. She'll die in prison, for Christ sake. She'll bloody die."

Sixty

The policemen led Astrid and *Molo* in shackles through the crowd to the district police commissioner's Toyota Land Cruiser parked outside the courtroom. They pushed Astrid in the back with an African prisoner and *Molo* into a seat behind her. They locked the door. The guard got into the front seat as he other policeman started the vehicle and they drove off.

The prisoner next to Astrid smelled of whiskey and vomit. He made her stomach churn. The windows remain closed and the heat combined with the odor made the trip unbearable. She asked in *Swahili* for the guard to open a window. He reached around and pulled back the glass. Fresh air quickly revived her.

She was frightened. The sweat ran off of her as she worried about what to expect in prison. "Piss pot", she thought. She tried to block her thoughts. She looked out and saw they had moved down from the highlands into the plains toward *Kabe*. She had seen the German fort many times when she and her father had driven through the area, but not in her worst nightmare would she have believed she would be incarcerated behind its decaying parapet.

The prisoner next to her moved his body against her. She pulled her leg away. He smiled with a sexual leer, showing his worn-down brown teeth, stained from chewing *khat*. She cursed him in *Swahili.* The guard turned around but said nothing. She realized this would be the kind of treatment she would receive at *Sani Maui* and somehow she had to prepare herself.

Up ahead, a steel corrugated building similar to a tobacco drying shed could be seen. A sign, needing paint said, STOP, in *Swahili* and English TSETSE FLY CONTROL POST. Two *Tanzanian* soldiers stood in uniform before the open double doors directing the Toyota to enter. They drove into the dark chamber and stopped. The two guards got out of the front seat and left Astrid, *Molo* and the African prisoner in the van. Astrid asked in alarm, "You're not leaving us in here? DDT is hazardous. Let us out," she yelled to the guards as they walked from the building.

The two soldiers closed the double doors. No light shone, only a crack between the double doors. Astrid could hear a hiss and could see a white cloud swirling in front of the Toyota. She struggled and moved her body to the open window to block the incoming DDT mist. At the same time the African prisoner moved toward her trying to kiss her. The smell of the prisoner's breath in her face and the feel of his rough tongue made her react like a mad dog, she bit him on his lip. The prisoner screamed, "Ahhhi."

Astrid could feel the man's warm blood running down her face. *Molo* jumped over his seat on to the prisoner. He twisted his body at the prisoner and brought down his arms, beating the man with his shackled hands.

The double doors of the shed opened and the outside bright light broke into the building. The two guards ran in and opened he door of the Toyota. Astrid, the African prisoner and *Molo* fell from the vehicle on to the concrete floor.

One of the guards helped Astrid to her feet. Her arms were bruised. Her clothes were covered with the prisoner's blood. She felt she wanted to cry, but controlled herself. She knew this was the start of some very trying times, and she had to have strength to face what could be ahead.

After the uncomfortable drive, the Toyota approached a large granite stone quarry. A guard on the road stopped them to let prisoners who worked in the quarry pass. As Astrid looked from the window she saw prison guards on the edge of a giant opening. A huge crane extended down into the pit. She could see a dozen prisoners hoisting a block of cut granite up to the surface. The hoist swung over the quarry's edge and six men pushed it over to the side and lowered the block to the ground.

Up ahead stood the looming German fortress of *Sani Maui* prison. She looked up at the guards along the top of the stone wall looking down on them as they drove up to the stone arch entrance of the fort. The driver put his hand on the horn and a shabbily dressed-guard in a soiled uniform came from the guard shack to the waiting Toyota. The driver handed him a paper. He squinted and handed it back. He looked in the rear seat and saw Astrid. He stared at her with a half smile.

"Take the girl to the commandant's office," he said, "Leave the other prisoners at admittance."

The double steel and wood-beamed gates opened and the Land Cruiser drove into a cut stone prison yard the size of a football field. In the center stood a stone post that Astrid immediately recognized as a flogging post. It terrified her. She broke into a nervous sweat.

A two-story granite building surrounded the prison yard with open windows covered by iron bars. Astrid could see black faces behind the slot windows peering down on her. Prison guards wore hats similar to the French Foreign Legion, with cloth hanging down from the back to shield their necks. A group of prisoners, in gray loose pants and shirts with no collar, prison uniforms, sat in the prison yard. An armed guard stood near. Another group marched in a small formation with two uniformed guards carrying bull whips. The Toyota stopped at the entrance of the main building. The guard in the front got out and opened the rear door for Astrid.

The African prisoner made a remark that Astrid didn't understand. *Molo* frowned at him. Astrid thought it had to be something obscene. As Astrid looked back into the Toyota she could see how sad *Molo* was. "Be strong. Don't fight them. You'll make it worse," she said as the Toyota drove off.

When the prisoners saw Astrid get out of the back of the vehicle, the ones that were sitting got up and yelled and whistled and made obscene gestures with their hands. The guards took their bull whips and cracked them over the convicts' heads like cattle to calm them down.

The prisoners in formation kept marching but stumbled over each other trying to catch a peek at the girl in chains. Obscene calls and remarks came down from the open slotted windows. Astrid looked up and saw black hands coming through the iron bars pounding metal cups and plates against the walls while the men called out foul words. A guard came from the building and escorted Astrid inside. The smell of a female seemed to drift through the prison and caused uneasiness among the half-starved prisoners.

Inside, the stone walls in the hallway appeared high and felt cool. The guards escorted her down the hall and stopped in front of a door that said, "Office of the Commandant." The guard opened the door and escorted them in.

The room was dark. The only light came from a small iron-barred window near the ceiling. A shabby-looking wooden desk sat in the center of the room with two straight-backed chairs in front of it. Behind the desk sat a half Arab and half African in his late forties. He wore the uniform of the prison system. His hair was kinky black and slicked back from his low forehead with pomade. His light brown facial skin was covered with dark brown freckles.

Astrid stood before him trying to keep her composure. She felt weak from fright, but she didn't want to let this man see her condition. She had made up her mind before she entered she wouldn't show how terrified she felt. She hoped she had the inner strength to bluff her way through.

The guard removed the shackles from her wrists. The pressure from the metal cuffs had made them numb. She shook her hands trying to get some feeling back.

The commandant stared at her and smiled. "Are you comfortable now, *Memsahib*? I'm Major Mohammed, the commandant."

Astrid laughed. "Major, you make me laugh. Do you think I'm going to be comfortable here? I've been sentenced to hell."

The major looked up at the guard and said, "Wait outside." The guard turned and left the room. The commandant looked to Astrid. "I was told only this day you would be here. You're causing me a great inconvenience. I need extra security to protect you from these mad animals locked up behind these walls." He smiled, showing off some gold front teeth. He rose from his chair and walked around her slowly, looking her up and down.

"How old are you?"

"Eighteen."

"You a virgin?" Astrid shook her head.

"How unfortunate. Take off your clothes." Astrid thought. This is it.

"Why?"

"You don't ask me why. You do."

"What are you going to do to me?" she asked as she reluctantly unbuttoned her blouse and removed it.

"Let me see your naked body. After that I will tell you, *Memsahib*."

Astrid removed her skirt and took off her brassiere and finally her panties. She stood in front of him naked. A cold shiver took over her body as he examined her.

He felt her breasts and said, "Your existence depends on me to protect you. If I put you out in the corridor, they would come at you like wild animals. They'd rape and possibly kill you for sport. You're a beautiful white woman, a fantasy, a goddess on a pillar, never to touch, or ogle, but now you're in their midst. You're the fantasy of their desire. They would kill one another for you. You could cause a prison riot. I can't take that chance. I'm going to hide you. You'll be safe in the infirmary. A guard will be positioned in front of the door. Expect a visit. You will reward me for my kindness." The commandant pinched her and bent down and kissed her naked behind. His gesture gave her goose bumps. As he stood up he said. "Get into your clothes. I'm bringing the guard back." Astrid dressed as he watched. She could see the pleasure on his face.

Sixty One

Mark knew if he didn't find a way to get Astrid out of *Sani Maui* prison she would be raped or dead soon. Just thinking about what could happen to her put him in a deep depression, but he knew that money could do almost anything in *Tanzania*: the prison system had to be corrupt, too.

That night when he got back to the hotel he saw the NATION, with his picture and name on the front page. He knew they must have seen it in Nairobi and realized their assassins had killed the wrong man. They would be after him again, he thought. He'd have to move fast. Jim Fielding had called from *Mombasa*. He picked up the phone and made a call to *Dar es Salaam*.

"Mr. *Patel*, this is Mark Livingston. The chap with the ruby."

"Oh, most certainly, Mr. Livingston. I had a conversation with my associate in *Bombay*, Mr. *Singh*. He would be most interested in buying your stone and would come to *Dar es Salaam* to finalize the transaction, Mr. Livingston."

"Is Mr. *Singh* willing to pay my price of one hundred thousand U.S. dollars?"

Oh, yes, most certainly, Mr. Livingston, he is willing."

"I'll come to *Dar* tomorrow."

"Mr. *Singh* is waiting in *Bombay*. He will most certainly come tomorrow also. There is a flight from *Bombay* in the morning."

"Tell him to have five thousand U.S. changed into one-and five-hundred-dollar bills", said Mark as he hung up. Good news, he thought. I'll have the money, but how would he get Astrid out? That he didn't know. He picked the phone again and called Jim in *Mombasa* and found him in his hotel room.

"It's Mark. What are you doing in *Mombasa?*"

"*Nairobi* was a rat race, so we came here to swim and get sun and rest. We read in the NATION about Astrid. What can we do?"

"Jim, it's bloody awful. They've got her in a gruesome place. If I don't get her out, she'll bloody die there."

"We'll think of something. Anne and I will be in *Moshi* tomorrow."

"I'm in Dar tomorrow, but will be back late. I'll fill you in when I see you."

The next morning Jim and Anne checked out of the *Nayali* Beach Hotel and rented a Toyota 4-door. They spent the full day driving to *Moshi*. When they were near *Kilimanjaro,* Jim left the main road and took off over the savannahs.

"Are you taking a short cut, darling?"

"This heat is getting to me. I remember a cold stream that drains off *Kilimanjaro* into pools. We can take a swim and cool off."

"Jim, have I ever told you how much fun it is to travel with you?"

"Why do you say that?"

"You're always inventive. You have the innate ability to come up with the right thing at the right time for the right occasion. I can't think of anything else I would like to do right now," she laughingly said.

The Toyota bounced over the flat grassy plain chasing off herds of wildebeest and zebra and stopped at clear blue pools surrounded by a marsh of papyrus. They jumped from the car taking their clothes off as they ran toward the cold water.

Jim stripped down to his shorts, Anne to her panties and bra. Jim got to the water first and jumped in. The clean mountain water felt like it was full of ice cubes. He came out of the water breathless.

He yelled to Anne, "You won't believe it."

Anne stepped in and submerged her body in the cold running stream. The shock of the cold water after the long hot drive exhilarated her. She stood and felt the hot dry air drying her skin in seconds. She looked over at Kilimanjaro and saw the sun setting in the west and reflecting off the mountain top. The color of the snowcapped peak changed in front of them from blue white to soft pink. It reminded her of a giant birthday cake with pink frosting running down its sides that she had seen once as a young girl.

After a few minutes they got out and sat on some flat rocks that surrounded the pools as a hot breeze dried them off. They watched the bird life among the tall papyrus. Multi-colored song birds sang soft melodic sounds, and the tranquil running water that came down from *Kilimanjaro* made them feel they had discovered paradise.

"Jim, I don't want to leave. It's the most divine place I have ever visited. If you'd build a little cabin here I'd marry you tomorrow." Jim laughed. "This land belongs to the *Masai*. Maybe if I offered them twenty head of cattle we could pull it off– "Look! Over there." Jim pointed to a low-hanging black cloud that moved toward them.

"What is that, darling?"

"They're flies. Millions and millions of them following a herd of *Masai* cattle."

"I don't see any cattle."

"You will soon. The flies have them surrounded. Do you see them now?"

Anne stood up. In the distance she saw a large herd of skinny, long-eared cattle moving in their direction herded by a group of *Masai* boys in their colorful red robes.

"Should we leave? This is their land. We're trespassing."

"They won't bother us. They're bringing their cattle to water."

The young *Masai Murani,* brought the cattle to the water's edge as Jim and Anne watched. The skinny cattle looked hot and thirsty as they rushed to the water to drink. The *Masai* knelt down on the stream edge and drank the water with the cattle. Anne admired their graceful long bodies. The boys smiled at them while staying at a polite distance, as curious about Anne and Jim as they were about the *Masai* boys.

Suddenly, millions of black flies hit, flying over and around them and biting them everywhere.

"Mother Mary, let's get out of here. This paradise as turned to hell," said Anne as she and Jim grabbed their clothes and ran for the Toyota.

Sixty Two

Jim and Anne arrived late in *Moshi*. George had waited up for and put them into a cabin.

The next morning Anne was awakened early by the sounds of the orphaned animals milling around in their compounds. Jim remained asleep. She got out of bed and dressed quietly in her usual khakis and went to the orphanage to investigate.

She watched as the attendants fed the animals, who responded to them like pets. Even the black rhino nuzzled the attendant like a family dog. She found herself fascinated with the animals, amazed they were so tame and docile. Ingrid, the chimpanzee, took to her immediately. The chimp jumped into Anne's arms and gave her a friendly sloppy kiss. Anne felt a maternal feeling rise and she knew she'd better do something soon about having children before it was too late.

Jim had gone when she returned to the cabin, but left a note saying he had gone into town to visit with Tony Morse, a film director who was making a movie in the area. After she freshened up she walked to the dining room to have a meal. She ran into George, and asked him to sit with her.

"George, who's the manager of this complex?"

"*Molo* takes care of hotel, with *Memsahib* Astrid."

"Is Astrid going to sell?" she asked.

"*Memsahib* no say she sell."

"If I were to buy the hotel would you stay?"

"Oh, yes, Memsahib. I work for you. Is Memsahib going to buy?"

"It has entered my mind. Does it make money?"

"Oh, yes. Hotel popular. Occupancy good, *Memsahib. Molo show me in office where* accounting is. You want to see?"

"Please." Anne went off in her thoughts. Would she like living in East Africa again? This could be an opportunity she'd give some thought to.

When Jim returned later that day, he joined Anne in their cabin.

"I had the most interesting day. I've been hired to direct the second unit on a picture Tony Morse is doing here. He's a director I know from Hollywood. He's here directing a picture in the fort where they have Astrid locked up. Tony came down with dysentery. Was he glad to see me! We went over the script and he told me what he wanted. While I was there they took him off to the hospital in *Arusha*. He's sick man, on the frail side. He thinks it was water. The film is using the prison as a location. I got a way in. Now to find a way to get Astrid out."

Mark had gotten back from *Dar es Salaam* late at night. He went directly to Astrid's cabin where he slept. He took out of his knapsack several bundles of U.S. dollars and counted them. He had counted them earlier in *Dar* when Mr. *Singh* and he made their deal, but he wanted to count them again for his own pleasure. One hundred thousand dollars; his and Astrid's new start in life in England. He hid the money in the fireplace chimney and collapsed on the bed too tired to remove his clothes.

The animals woke him in the morning. He realized it had been the first good night's sleep he'd had in a week. He showered and got into some fresh khakis and went to find Jim and Anne.

They were in the dining room having breakfast when he walked in. He pulled up a chair and joined them. He told them about the trial and his trip to *Dar.*

"Eat some breakfast, Mark. This is going to be a long day," said Jim. "Anne, you have your instructions."

"I'll be there," she said.

"What's bloody happening?" asked Mark.

"I'll tell you on the way to the *Moshi* Hotel."

Sixty Three

The two *Kikuyus from the secret service* arrived in *Moshi* in the dark of night and checked into the hotel. They rose early the next day and went to the lobby. They watched the activities of the Hollywood film crew, who had taken over the hotel.

Chagga tribesmen were waiting in line to be fitted for costumes as extras in the film. As the *Chaggas* passed, a man gave them khaki shorts and shirts that had been British Army regulation issue in World War I. Others in the line were handed green cotton German uniforms. Afterwards they went outside and changed into their costumes on the hotel lawn. They seem to be enjoying themselves laughing at how funny they looked. Another of the film crew herded them to a bus that would take them to the film location at the prison.

Mark and Jim arrived at the hotel and walked into the lobby, *Otieno* recognized Mark and jabbed *Najaro* to get his attention. They watched as an American shook their hands. The American held them in conversation for a few minutes. They walked out of the lobby as *Otieno* and *Najaro* followed them and watched them get into a Land Rover and drive off. After Jim and Mark had left, the *Kikuyus* walked back to the hotel and found the American giving orders to the crew.

"*Bwana,* tell us where the film is making today?" asked *Najaro.*

"*Sani Maui* prison. You boys get in line for your costumes or you'll miss the bus."

"Yes, Bwana." They exchanged looks and joined the line for the German costumes. Outside they changed behind a truck, so no one could see them hide their .45 caliber pistols in the baggy walking shorts. The men checked each other's appearance and smiled. They hurried to the waiting bus and got on.

Sixty Four

The room had been a linen closet for the infirmary. Now it was Astrid's prison cell. A tiny window with bars were near the ceiling. If she stood on a wooden table, the only furniture in the room besides a cot, she could look out onto the prison yard.

She had not slept. Rats kept her awake, squeaking as they climbed the walls to go in and out through the window. They were so brazen they would drop on her cot and remain there until she pushed them off.

She heard a sound at the window, looked up and saw a black face staring down at her though the bars. She picked up a tin cup by her cot and hurled it at him. He yelled some dirty words at her and left. Through the night she heard the cries, moans, and yells of the prisoners. They called out her name and made sexual remarks about what they would do to her if they could get to her. She felt terrified. She worried that she could be flogged in the morning. She expected any minute for the door to fly open and the commandant would enter and asked her to disrobe again and submit to him.

After the slow hours passed, she heard the early morning crowing of a rooster somewhere in the distance. She hadn't taken off her prison issue, which hung from her like a flour sack. They were all one size, made large for men.

She pounded on the door. It opened a crack. She could see the guard peering in. She told him she needed to go to the toilet. He came into the room and smiled at her. She looked at him closely. He was tall and rather attractive, but his speech was sing-song and he had an effeminate manner. The commandant had given her this guard because he wasn't interested in women, she thought. That amused her and she thought she would try to make him her confidant. Maybe he might help her.

"What is you name?" The guard looked at her suspiciously and said, "Robert *Sundouki*."

She put out her hand and said, "*Jambo*, Robert."

Robert almost smiled and said, "*Jambo, Memsahib*. Come with me." Astrid followed him into the infirmary. The beds were full of sick men. Some had open sores. Others lay in dirty beds full of feces. An African male nurse was administering an IV to a prisoner who looked almost gone.

"Robert, these men are dying. Why is there no care for them?" "They die every day."

"Your commandant is a monster. He should be removed from his position."

"I make mistake. Talk too much. You no get Robert in trouble with commandant?"

"No, but do this. Tell the commandant I'd like to help out here. With you to protect me, I'd feel safe."

"You *oky doky, Memsahib*. Hollywood, she come to prison today. I be in film," he said as he smiled proudly. "Do you think I handsome?" he asked as he put out his chin and made an exaggerated smile.

Astrid flattered him. "Yes, Robert. One of the most handsome men I have ever met."

Her remark pleased him, his self-conscious grin changed into a real full smile and he began looking at her differently. She remembered a movie company had planned to use the prison for location. A ray of hope hit her. Maybe, she thought, there will be some way of escaping.

"Robert, what are you doing in the film?"

"Be a actor, *Memsahib*. The commandant told me I would. He said film use infirmary. I tell to nurse to get man out, but I think that man," Robert pointed to the sick man, "He die today. Commandant he want him gone."

Robert opened the door to the washroom and motioned Astrid to enter. She walked inside and Robert closed the door and went to a small hole in the wall and peered in.

Astrid inspected the row of toilets. They were filthy. She tried not to think about them. She didn't sit, she half stood over the bowl. As she looked ahead she saw the hole in the wall and could make out a movement behind. She was being spied on, she thought. She felt violated. It gave her a sick feeling. How awful. Maybe Robert is not what I think he is, she thought. She'd have to be careful.

When she finished she turned on a dripping water faucet over a long tin trough. She let the water run. She saw how dirty it ran and was disgusted. When it appeared to be cleaner she splashed it on her face. Her mind started to race with anticipation of how to escape. She had a chance, she thought. There would be confusion having the film company in the prison. It would change everything. She already saw how it had affected Robert. She was sure the commandant and the other guards were as excited. There must be some way out of there.

Back in her cell she heard a commotion coming from the prison yard. She stood on the small table, looked out through the barred window and saw a formation of prisoners lined up at the whipping post. Two guards brought *Molo* into the yard. His upper body was bare. Two guards dragged him to the stone post and tied his hands to an iron ring. A muscular guard with a bull whip came forward and whipped *Molo*'s back as the prisoners counted off "One, two, three, four, five," and on.

Astrid could no longer look and fell back from the window.

Sixty Five

The fortified double doors of *Sana Maui* prison opened as Mark, Jim and Chuck the assistant film director drove through and stopped at the main prison building. The guards acted impressed, smiling as they greeted them. Jim got out of the Jeep and looked though his lens finder up on the wall and then turned to the prison yard to check out some camera shots he had planned. One of the guards waited for him, then led them inside to the commandant's office. He rose to greet them. "Welcome gentlemen," he said, bowing.

"Thank you, Commandant. I'm Jim Fielding, I'm taking over for Tony Morse. He came down with a bad dysentery. This is Mark Livingston, my assistant," said Jim. Mark acknowledged him, but said nothing. "And Chuck, my assistant director."

"How unfortunate for *Bwana* Tony. Will be return?"

"The doctors will be the judge, Commandant. We have two scenes today. We'll start with an exterior. The English soldiers attack the fort. Then we'll come inside and get some shots up on the wall showing the Germans struggle to defend the fort. If we have time I'll try to get to the infirmary, where one of the leads is dying from a gunshot wound," said Jim.

"Very good. I see no problem, *Bwana* Jim. Will you be needing any of my men in the film?'

"I'd like to use you to play a German officer directing the troops. Costumes will be here soon. As for others, I'll know better when I see how the battle scenes go," answered Jim.

By the expression on the commandant's face he seemed pleased.

"I have one request," he said.

"Yes."

"One of my guards thinks he's an actor. Would you be so kind as to give him something to do in the film?"

"Of course, Commandant. I'd like to walk around the prison to see where I'll position my cameras before my crew gets here."

"I'll personally escort you."

"That won't be necessary, Commandant. My assistants will."

"Then I insist that one of my guards escort you. He's the one who wants to be an actor. He can see how films are made," said the commandant.

"Have him meet me here now," said Jim as he looked at Mark and Chuck. The commandant spoke rapidly to an attending guard, who saluted and ran off.

Astrid saw Mark and Jim arrive in the prison yard from her small window. She wanted to call out Mark's name, but thought it would bring too much attention to her. Anticipation raced through her mind.

Robert *Sundouki* stood in the commandant's office some minutes later with his wide perfect smile. The commandant introduced him to the film makers.

"Robert, escort the Hollywood gentlemen around the prison, but keep out of the prison wards, that could be dangerous. The prisoners have been acting up. I'm holding them in their cells for punishment. *Bwana* Jim has an acting part for you. Don't be surly now," said the commandant. Robert looked pleased and he thanked the film-makers bowing and smiling as they left the commandant's office.

When they came into the prison yard, Mark drew Robert aside. "A white woman was brought here yesterday. Have you seen her?"

Robert looked at him suspiciously and turned to Jim.

"Where does *Bwana* wish to go?"

"The infirmary."

"Yes, Bwana. Follow me."

Jim was ahead with Robert. Mark followed them along the side of the building toward an entrance that led back to the prison.

Astrid remained at her small window. This was her chance. "Mark, look down. I'm in the infirmary," she called out as Mark walked by.

Mark heard her and stopped. He looked down into the window and saw Astrid's face looking up at him.

Robert turned around up ahead. "This way *Bwana*," he said.

Mark caught up with Jim and followed them into the building.

They stepped into the infirmary. Mark noticed a guard sitting in front of a door at the end of the room. He took Jim aside. He made a motion with his head toward the door and whispered to Jim, "She's in there."

Jim nodded, and looked around inspecting the room and said to Robert, "I'll put actors in these empty beds." He looked at a bed and saw *Molo* on his stomach. The wounds from the lashes were open. When he recognized Jim, he tried to smile, but Jim gave him a sign.

"This prisoner needs attention. Have someone dress his wounds. I'll use him in a shot," said Jim looking at Robert.

"Yes, Bwana." Robert motioned for an African attendant to attend *Molo*. "Put bandages on this man."

As they came out into the prison yard a bus full of costumed extras drove into the yard and unloaded the passengers.

A young English actor dressed in a British uniform caught Jim as he passed by. "Jim, Tony said I'd be in the first shot. Where do you want me?"

"Outside the fort. Get out of the sun. I'll call you when we're ready for you."

"Right-O," said the actor and walked over to makeup, which had been set up in the shade next to the wall.

Mark needed the makeup man and asked him. "Do you have some chalky gray and black or dark brown makeup?"

The makeup man looked through his case and gave Mark a plastic jar marked "native". He opened it and looked. The color was almost black. "Mix this white with it." He handed Mark the jar of white. "What do you need it for, governor? We got the real thing everywhere you look." Mark smiled and thanked him and went on his way. He wrote a message on a piece of paper with two one-thousand-shilling notes. He tied them with the note to the jars and went by the window where he had heard and seen Astrid. He dropped the jars through the opening and walked on.

"Robert, open up," yelled Astrid through the door. The door opened a crack and a African guard looked in. "Robert no here."

She pushed a one thousand shilling note at the guard. "Here you can have this if you let me see my servant, *Molo*."

The guard looked to see if anyone was looking, grabbed the note and opened the door. Astrid pushed him aside and ran through the infirmary. She found *Molo* on his cot, his back covered with fresh bandages. "It's Mama. Do as Mama says. Mama is going to get us out of here." *Molo* gave her a big grin.

From her prison uniform she took out the jars of makeup and applied it to *Molo*'s face. The gray made *Molo* look near death.

Sixty Six

The uniformed film extras sat in the stone prison yard and lounged around waiting to be called. Jim, with his African interpreter, *Milma*, stood before them giving them instructions.

"You men in the English uniforms, go outside the fort and join Chuck, my assistant director. He'll give you positions for the shot. I'll be up on the wall with the cameras. When I yell "action", you men charge the fort. Chuck will give you a number. When he calls it, fall to the ground as if you've been shot or wounded. Make it look natural. Don't do any over-acting."

Milma, Jim's interpreter, repeated in *Chagga* dialect. The extras got to their feet and left the courtyard for the outside, laughing and joking among themselves.

Mark heard some ruckus from above, looked up and saw the prisoners peering down at them through the iron barred windows, watching.

The commandant entered the infirmary. He went directly to the linen closet where the guard stood. When the guard saw him he sprang to attention.

"Open the door," the commandant demanded. The nervous guard fumbled with the key trying to get it into the lock. "Give me the key," he demanded. The guard handed him the key and the commandant opened the door and closed it behind him.

Astrid lay on her cot her back to the commandant. He moved slowly toward her taking out of his pocket a scarf and a black cord. Astrid didn't move. He sat down next to her and put his hand on her hip.

"I don't have much time. I've come to play a game with you, *Memsahib*," said the commandant in low whisper.

Astrid turned toward him. The commandant jumped from the bed and gasped. Astrid had done a magnificent makeup job on herself. Her eyes looked sunken, her skin grey. Her tongue looked almost black. Saliva ran from the corner of her mouth. In a husky low whisper she said, "I have cholera, Commandant. Let me die in peace. He backed away, his hand to his mouth. "Cholera." He rushed to the door to leave.

Astrid lifted her head. "My servant. . . he. . . has. . . it too." She fell back on the cot.

The commandant exited the room and slammed the door behind him, taking a breath. He said to the guard, "Show me the white woman's servant." The guard ushered him to *Molo*'s bed. *Molo lay* on the cot, face up. His skin grey-black. His eyes were red and sunken.

"Where is the nurse?" asked the commandant with alarm. The guard shook his head. "Cover him up–Let no one see this man," he said as he rushed from the infirmary.

Otieno and *Najaro* sat in the shade with the rest of the German costumed extras as Jim approached.

"You men in the German costumes come with me. I'll show you your positions on the wall." Jim had spotted the two *Kikuyus*. "You two big men. I like your faces. I'll use you for close-ups. Stick close to me so I can give you prominent position in the shot."

The *Kikuyus* followed *Milima*, Jim's interpreter, who told the extras to go up on the wall. He ushered them up the stone staircase to the top of the prison wall.

Jim approached Mark, who was standing in the prison yard with Robert. He said to Robert, "Get the commandant. I want him in this shot." Robert ran off to locate the commandant.

"Robert's our man. You bribe him. He's star-struck and wants to be in the movies. Tell him if he can get to London, I'll give him a part in my picture. Give him enough money so he can get there."

"I'll give him a thousand dollars and tell him there's another thousand when he deliverers Astrid to us outside the prison walls," said Mark as he went off to find Robert.

Sixty Seven

A crowd had gathered in front of the district commissioner building in Moshi. Some were carrying signs that said, OUTRAGEOUS UNFAIR RELEASE ASTRID. A white lady, middle-aged, carried a double sign in big red letters, FLOGGING SHOULD BE REPEALED. Another white man had a sign that said, RACISTS LIVE IN TANZANIA.

Inside, in a meeting room, Charles *Nandanga* sat in front of three African officials, one of them is Malcolm, the local magistrate.

"I demand you release Astrid Dryden from *Sana Maui*. I want an investigation into why she was sent there. Prisoners of war are treated better." A stern-looking official wearing an English suit and tie said, "The woman committed a crime and was given a reasonable sentence."

"Why is she confined to a prison with no facilities for women? If this gets out to a human rights tribunal they'll hit on us like a plague. Is this what you want for our country? Shame?" asked Charles, rising from his chair advancing to the table with a raised voice.

"We're looking into it. The judge, I believe made a mistake, and we will try to rectify it. I'm taking the case to my superiors in Dar. I'll notify you of their decision," said the official.

"God help us. I hope it's not too late," said Charles as he left the room.

Sixty Eight

Jim came down from the wall, joined Mark and said, "I need another white face in my shot. Would you get in a German officer's uniform?"

"Glad to, mate," said Mark.

"Action," yelled Jim from the prison wall.

The British Army, with the English actor in front of his troops positioned behind rocks, made their advance toward the fort.

The cameras were set up in four positions, two down on the ground with the advancing extras and the other two on the wall, getting shots from that angle. Gunfire filled the air as the blank cartridges fired from the extras rifles. Chuck, the assistant director, called out numbers. The extras dropped to the ground simulating being wounded or killed. The scene went on for a few minutes. "Cut!" Stay in those positions. I'll be right down. Cameramen, get your cameras in position for close-ups." yelled Jim from the wall into his bullhorn.

In the prison yard, Mark had taken Robert aside. The expression on Robert's face was to be serious. He looked up at the commandant in German costume. Jim was telling him what to do in the next scene.

Otieno and *Najaro* spotted Mark, dressed as a German lieutenant as he came up the stairway to join the other actors in the scene. They watched him walk to the edge of the wall and look down on the scene below from behind a parapet. They kept their eyes on him, waiting for their chance.

Shouts and yelling came out of the prison as the prisoners pounded on the bars of their cells with tin plates and cups. Pandemonium spread through the prison and brought the filming to a stop.

The commandant raced to the side of the wall and yelled down to the guards. "Tell those hyenas to stop acting up or there'll be no rations tonight."

"Yes, Commandant," said the guards as they went back into the prison. More boos and yelling and racket came out of the wards. "Commandant, they say the white woman has cholera."

The commandant looked stunned. "It's a lie. Tell them if they don't stop, no recreation for a week."

The guard went back into the building and more commotion was heard as the prisoners continued to protest. "CHOLERA—CHOLERA—CHOLERA." The word ran through the wards like a dam had broken loose. First in *Swahili*, then in English and the other dialects of the prisoners.

The commandant rushed to Jim. "I'm sorry, *Bwana* Jim, these animals have caused you a delay. I'll have their ring-leaders flogged. I don't tolerate insubordination. I'm leaving to take charge. It's this white woman. She caused this outbreak," said the flustered commandant as he left Jim's side and went down the staircase to the yard below.

Jim looked for Mark to tell him the plan was working. Astrid had pulled it off. Jim saw Mark on the wall looking out toward the stone quarry. As he went to join him he saw one of the German extras lunge toward Mark in an attempt to push him off the wall.

"Jim yelled, "Mark! Behind you!"

Mark turned toward Jim and saw a man coming at him. He stepped aside as *Najaro* rushed past and fell to the stones below with a bone- breaking thud. *Otieno* looked over the wall's edge and saw *Najaro*'s body on the rocks. He moved back and looked for a way to escape. Mark saw him coming. Otieno took off running. Mark chased after him. Jim followed. *Otieno* ran into a guard and pushed him out of the way. He ran on, Mark following close behind. *Otieno* turned to fire his .45 hand-gun, but missed. He stumbled over the camera cables running along the stone floor. Mark caught up and tackled him, bringing him down. Jim was behind him and helped hold *Otieno* down.

Mark turned him over and looked into his face. "This bloody *Wog* killed Helmut."

Sixty Nine

The guards put *Otieno* in irons in a prison cell. The rioting had gotten worse. The commandant had taken over. He ordered the guards to bring out the water hoses. The guards rushed back and forth pulling hoses from the wall and carrying them into the prison. When they got inside they yelled to turn on the water. They waited but no water came through the hose. The commandant ran out and turned on the water. He hit the guard with his whip, calling him stupid. He and the guard with the spurting hose went through the wards hosing the prisoners in their cells. When one section quieted down another section started up.

During the rioting, Mark and Jim had raced to the infirmary. It was deserted.

Molo waited for them. "Mama in there." He pointed to the linen room door.

Jim helped *Molo* off his cot. He was weak from the flogging.

Mark was at the linen room door. He tried to open it, but it was locked. He gave it a hard shove. It wouldn't give. He yelled. "Jim, give a hand with this door."

Outside the prison a Land Rover stopped at the front gates. Seated in the front seat sat Charles *Nandanga* and Malcolm. A prison guard intercepted them.

Charles showed the guard a paper. "I have a signed release for Astrid Dryden and *Molo Kampi*. I demand to see the commandant."

"I can't let you in. The prisoners are rioting. Much too dangerous, sir."

Charles waved the papers at the guard. "If you refuse me, I'll tell them of your insubordination. You'll have no job, man."

The guard looked reluctant, but opened the double door and let the Land Rover drive through.

Mark and Jim made a rush at the door. It broke loose and Astrid stood in the center of the room, her face and arms covered in gray makeup.

Mark rushed to her and threw his arms around her.

"Don't kiss her, Mark! She'll give you a disease."

Astrid looked at Jim. "I will not."

"Come, let's get out of here. Robert's waiting for us outside," said Jim.

They made their way up the stairway and into the prison yard and Robert's waiting vehicle. Astrid and *Molo* got on the floor in the back. Robert drove. Jim and Mark sat with him in the front seats. They drove to the front gates.

"Put a handkerchief over your face when we get to the entrance," said Jim. "It will scare the shit out of this guy."

Robert spoke to the guards in *Swahili*. "Don't get close to us. Open the gates. The men in the back have cholera. The commandant has ordered me to take them to the hospital in *Arusha*. Let us pass, man," said Robert.

The guard backed away. "Yes, Sergeant *Sundouki*. Go!" said the guard as he went into the guard shack and opened the gates. They drove through.

Anne stood waiting at the *Moshi* airstrip when they drove up. The plane was to take them to *Entebbe* in *Uganda* where they could get a flight to London. Anne had packed Astrid some clothes and she had Jim's luggage loaded on the plane. Astrid hugged Anne. *Molo* stood next to Astrid. "Get aboard, *Molo*," she said.

"No, Mama, I stay. I take care of orphans."

"When they find out you've escaped from prison, they'll put you back. Please *Molo*, come with us," pleaded Astrid.

"I take chance, Mama."

Astrid looked at Mark and Jim. "I'm not going. I'm staying too. *Molo* is right. I can't leave my babies."

Mark took Astrid in his arms and looked into her eyes.

"Astrid, you always said you wanted to go to England to school. This is your chance. I've got enough money to support us. You can come back later when all this trouble blows over. Surely we can ask for a new trial. There should be no question you did nothing to receive the sentence you got," Jim interrupted.

"Mark has a point, Astrid. Give yourself some time. Time heals all. Come on. Do yourself a favor, get on the plane."

Astrid looked at *Molo*. "Go, Mama. I run hotel for you. Never worry. *Molo* in charge." Astrid hugged him. "Molo, you've always been in charge."

She turned to Jim and Mark. "Let's get going, gentleman." She turned to Anne. "Can I stay with you for awhile, till we get settled?"

"Of course, darling, I insist."

Astrid climbed on followed by and Anne and Mark. Jim took Robert aside. "Here's your money, Robert." He handed Robert five hundred dollar bills. "If I were you, I'd get on the plane. Your life won't be worth ten shillings if you stay."

Robert smiled and said, "Yes Bwana, you oky doky."

Seventy

When Anne arrived back in London at her flat in Cadogan Place, there was an urgent message from Alex, her husband. She had tried not to think about Alex in Africa. Her heart was still there, she loved it so. She kept thinking about Astrid's wildlife orphanage and hotel. She had been happy there and wanted to go back. She put Alex's call off. She had to think about their relationship a little longer before she would see him. She had to see if Jim had some plans for their future before she saw Alex.

The next day Anne had gotten up early. She was still on African time. Mark and Astrid stayed with her as house guests. She sent them off to see some of the sights of London: the National Gallery, the Victoria and Albert Museum. She told them she would meet them for lunch at a restaurant she liked off Pont Street.

Jim called from Shepperton Studios outside of London, to tell her he would be by in the evening.

Astrid kept talking about going to Cambridge, but she felt she should wait until Mark found something to do.

Anne had heard that one of her father's old friends, Lord Comstock, who owned a seventeenth-century country manor house in Norfolk on three thousand acres, had decided to turn it into a preserve for wild African animals. It would help him and his family hold onto their ancestral heritage by charging the public to view the wildlife roaming around his land. He had been looking for someone to manage the operation. He seemed delighted when Anne called him and told him about Mark and Astrid's background. They took a train up to see him. After their interview, he put them to work getting the stock he needed to open his park. Along with the position, they were given a stone cottage.

Astrid had the bungalow looking charming and quaint in a matter of weeks. She used lots of English chintz for curtains, chairs and sofas. She had always wanted an English garden and started planting immediately, going through garden books to get ideas of what to put in the ground.

But she missed *Molo* and East Africa. She wished he would be with her, but he was looking after the hotel and orphanage. She trusted him to take care of her animals. She knew he wouldn't be happy in England. The climate would be hard on him and would be homesick if he came. There were a few inquiries on buying the hotel, but she had a terrible time in making a decision. She wanted to make sure the orphans would be well taken care of.

Mark initiated a wild-animal-capture program in Rhodesia to supply the estate with the animals he thought the public would want to see. The animals had to be quarantined for months to enter the country and that made for a few problems.

Astrid set up a veterinary clinic. She knew the animals would need attention and could be susceptible to new diseases in England, but was told not to worry. England made it almost impossible, because of the long quarantine rules.

Anne was sick in the morning and became suspicious of her condition. She called her doctor and at nine o clock the next morning she walked into his office. She was his first patient of the day and his nurse greeted her.

"Good morning, your Ladyship, the doctor will see you now. She followed the nurse into the examination room and the nurse gave Anne a gown. "When you're ready, get on the table and Doctor Ryan will be in," said the nurse and left.

After she removed her clothes and put on the gown, she stepped onto the scales, and stared at the number. She'd put on ten pounds. She never weighed so much. It's that Kenyan food, she thought. Jim was right, everyone eats too much there.

The doctor, a middle aged Irishman, came in. By the look of the bright blood vessels on his face, Anne knew he liked his whiskey. "Good to see you again, your Ladyship. What seems to be your trouble?"

"I think I'm pregnant. I have all the symptoms. Sick in the morning. I feel bloated. I hope it's true. I want a baby."

"Well, let's find out," he said and started the examination.

When she came out of the doctor's office she wanted to yell to everyone. I'm pregnant! The doctor said her condition seemed to be normal, but to stay away from alcohol. Today, she thought nothing could upset her.

She finally called Alex at his studio. "Hello, I'm back."

"I want to see you. Can you come by my studio?"

"When?" she asked.

"Make it eleven, love, Ciao."

Anne took a cab over London Bridge to Billingsgate where Alex had his studio in the old marketplace. He had fixed up an old warehouse that he used to live and paint in. Anne hated the location because of the fish smell coming from the market, but Alex liked it; he said it gave him a creative place to work, and the rent was cheap.

The cab dropped her off in front of the warehouse. The streets teamed with the morning market activity. She rang a bell at the door and a buzzer sounded. The door opened enough for her to push to enter. She took an open elevator to the third floor and got off.

Alex waited for her in the doorway. He had the look of a rock star. He wore his long dark hair in a ponytail. His loose shirt and jeans hung from his lean frame.

"Good day, love, you ate well in Kenya, it shows. Come in," he said. Anne frowned at his remark and walked into a large high ceiling room. Giant surreal canvases, painted in blazing colors, were scattered around in various areas.

"I've got the water on. Will you have some tea?"

Anne nodded.

"Have a seat, love."

Anne sat on a sofa covered with a white sheet. He came from the back of a large screen, one of his paintings, and handed her a mug filled with steaming tea.

"You missed all the bad weather, love. It hasn't stopped raining since you left," he said as he looked out his studio skylight window. "And today, the sun is out. You brought it, how nice of you."

Anne gave him a pleasing smile. "Alex, you didn't get me here to discuss the weather. What is this urgency?"

"I'm hoping you will give me a divorce."

Anne's heart leaped. She almost yelled Yes! "What did you say?"

"I want a divorce. There is no sense in this charade of ours. You don't love me, and I've found someone that does."

"What do you mean I don't love you? I fell in love with you the first time I saw you. How could you say that to me?" Anne caught herself. What am I doing, she thought, I can't believe this. I'm getting off the hook and acting like I still love him.

"I'm sorry, love. I hate to be so blunt, but it's over, you know. You wanted to marry me, you knew I wasn't ready for marriage. I became part of your rebellion. You don't need a man like me. You need a chap that can give you some attention. I'm not that sort."

"The girl you're in love with, she doesn't need attention?"

"It's not the same with her. She knows me, and knows I'm impossible. She's an artist herself. There's not this social distance between us. I'm on the wrong side of the Thames for you, love. Your crowd is Mayfair, I don't fit there and never will. I haven't been fair with you. You should have those children you want, before you can't have them."

"You've been reading my mind." Anne got up from the sofa. "You can have your divorce." She extended her hand. "I've been mulling over the idea of moving to Tanzania. You have made the decision for me. Thank you, darling. Goodbye."

London wasn't the same for her, Anne thought. Her work no longer interested her, and she felt her life incomplete. She saw Jim almost every day since they returned to London. He remained busy finishing up his film. She hadn't told him she was pregnant. She kept it a secret from everyone. She looked forward to being with Jim, but she didn't want her pregnancy to make that decision for them.

Seventy One

Astrid did the cooking and she had no idea what she was doing. She had seldom gone near a kitchen in Tanzania. Africans did all the cooking in her life and she missed that. They took to the European way of cooking, and did it well. *Molo* was the chef at Astrid's house and the hotel, and he trained others to cook. Astrid had never learned. Mark ate what she gave him and never complained.

They had just finished up a steak and kidney pie in the cottage oak beamed dining room. Astrid thought the meal had turned out better than expected.

"Did you like dinner, Mark?" she asked, being rather pleased.

"It tasted jolly good. You're improving. Now that you have our household all done up, we should be thinking about getting married. There'll be a scandal if it gets out we weren't."

"If we look and act married, why don't we leave it that way?"

"Astrid, I don't understand you. Don't you want a family? The way you love animals you'd think that you would want a baby or two. I can't bloody figure you. What do you want? If it's not marriage what is it? It's this bloody vagueness of yours, it drives me crazy. I said this before and I'm saying it again. I love you. Will you marry me?"

"Yes, Mark I'll marry you."

Mark jumped up from the table and took Astrid in his arms and kissed her. He pushed her back to look at her and gaze into her soft blue eyes.

"Astrid, everything is going to be wonderful from now on. You'll see. We have each other and this marvelous opportunity to make this place into the best wildlife park in the world. It's not East Africa, but it's the next best thing."

"Anne and Jim will be here this weekend. We'll ask them to stand up for us and have the wedding on the estate.

Astrid invited Anne into her garden. They walked through the paths of bright yellow, red, violet and pink perennials. "Look Anne, at the rhododendrons, they're growing like weeds. I'm so happy with my garden. I've always wanted an English garden."

"I see you have the touch. It looks lovely. I've had no luck gardening. I hate to get my hands dirty. I'd rather buy my flowers from the florist, but I do admire someone who does. It must be rewarding when you see them bloom."

"When I think of what happened to my garden in Tanzania, I get sick. My orphans would destroy the flowers overnight. But, Dad had said: Astrid, either you're going to have your orphan animals or a garden, you can't have both."

"Do you think I would make a good hotel operator?" asked Anne with a smile.

"What do you mean?"

"Would you sell me *Kilimanjaro* Lodge?"

Astrid rushed to hug her. "You mean it?"

"I certainly do. I can't wait. That is, if we can come to together on a price."

"Don't worry, we will. You'll keep *Molo*, won't you?"

"I wouldn't buy without him. Can you see me out in the kitchen getting a luncheon together for a large group? I'd die first. But that doesn't mean I can't learn, darling."

"I've been so worried. I prayed every night someone would come along I liked and would like my orphans and want the hotel. What about Jim? Will he be joining you?"

"I haven't discussed my plans with him. You know he has his own agenda. I'm hoping he will, but he works in America. It's a long way from *Moshi*. I don't think I could live in America. I fell in love with Africa all over again. I've discovered I need a change."

"Anne, I need your advice. I told Mark I'd marry him. We've known each other since we were students in *Nairobi*. He's been my only lover. Mark says he's always loved me. But I don't think I'm in love with him. How are you supposed to feel when you're in love? Don't you think love is where you can't live without that person?"

"I do. I felt that way about Alex. I thought I couldn't live without him. I'd have done anything to marry him. I was so in love. But he never loved me. He always said he was a part of my rebellion. That I never knew what love was because I felt my parents never loved me. That remark has been hard on my ego. We started to drift apart and now it's over. Astrid, you're still young, do what you have to do first. You can't marry someone you don't love. Trust your feelings, don't rush them."

Mark and Jim drove up in a Land Rover.

"Mark!" yelled Astrid. "Guess what? Anne is buying the hotel and orphanage."

"Congratulations, old girl," Mark yelled back.

Astrid looked at Jim. He looked troubled. "Jim, aren't you going to congratulate me?"

"Sure. Congratulations."

After dinner, Astrid was in tears. It hadn't turned out well. Mark had Anne in conversation about the wildlife of East Africa. Jim came into the kitchen while Astrid was tidying up.

"Jim, I'm sorry about dinner. I tried my damnedest, but I don't seem to do well in a kitchen. I wish *Molo* were here. I miss him so much."

"I was too busy looking at you to know what I ate. I'm going to say what's bothering me. You don't love Mark."

"Where do you get off telling me that?"

"It's your eyes, there's no smile in them when you look at him. I don't see love. You love him, but more like a brother. Not a lover." Why is he saying this, she thought. He's being American. They're always telling everyone what they should do, but he's right, I could be making a mistake and Anne thinks so too.

"Jim, I'm coming in to London to do some shopping next week. Give me a number to reach you," she said.

Seventy Two

Jim had booked a flight to Los Angeles in the morning. He had finished his photography and was taking the film to his distributors.

When Astrid got to London she called Jim. He told her to meet him at the Clermont for dinner, and then called Rene to have champagne iced at the table when Astrid arrived.

At the Clermont Anthony Roseli sat in the dining room, with his back to the wall with a group at a corner table, where he could see everyone coming and going. Jim came into the dining room. Anthony's cold blue eyes followed him to the table where he saw Astrid seated.

"Have you been waiting long?" asked Jim. "You look lovely."

"I just got here. I don't have the clothes to come to a place like this. Everyone is so dressed. I feel out of place."

Rene poured the cold champagne. "I'll be back to take your order." he said.

"I'm sorry, I don't drink champagne, remember," said Astrid.

Jim smiled. "Yeah, I remember, I'm sorry."

"I'm very upset. You said I shouldn't marry Mark, I do feel like he's my brother, but what am I going to do? I can't leave him. He depends on me. Tell me what to do, Jim."

"It's easy. Come to Hollywood with me."

"You're making it worse. You've got Anne. She's in love with you and getting divorced to be with you."

"Anne has her own agenda. She bought your hotel. She has a new life for herself. I can't live in Tanzania. I have my work. She'll get over me. You and I have the same problem. I thought I was in love with Anne, but I kept having these dreams about you. If you're in love with someone that person should be on your mind around the clock. Right?"

"I suppose so."

"That's the point. I'm not in love with her, I love you." "Jim, I don't know how I feel about you. You're certainly different. I just know I'm not in love with Mark."

"Why don't you do this? Leave with me. We'll buy a place in the San Fernando Valley. Our animal shelters are full of orphans. We can have our own Tanzania. See if you can love me, and live my kind of life. Give it a try. I know you'll be happy with me."

"Mark may be dull, but he would be faithful. What about you?" "Of course I would. I've matured. I grew up on this trip. You're too important to me for me to screw up. You've got to trust me." Astrid looked at Jim and felt his sincerity. The way he looked at her she could tell he did love her. Mark in time will get over me, she thought. He has a good position and money to fall back on. Anne will hate me, taking her man, but Jim said she does have her own agenda. She'll find someone. Jim certainly is sexy. I like that part of him. I know him pretty well, and have seen how he operates under pressure. He's kind and Dad liked him. Life is meant to be lived. I'm going to take that chance with him, she thought. "When I think back on what my parents taught me about honor, they would have stuck it out with a mate, regardless. I feel I'm of weak character. Running off. I read love stories where it would happen, but I never thought I would ever be in that position. I have no clothes. Nothing. You're getting an orphan. I hope you know what to do with her," she smiled.

"My heart's pounding and look!" Jim showed his palms. "They're sweating. I feel brand new again. If we hear Africa calling us we'll go back." Jim took Astrid's hand. Did you bring your passport?"

"It's in my bag."

"Let's have dinner. I don't think I can eat a thing," said Jim as he looked for Rene and motioned for him to come to the table.

Anthony Roseli kept an eye on their table. When he saw Rene taking their order, he got up from his table and slipped out of the dining room.

Astrid and Jim finished dinner. They were outside waiting for the doorman to get them a cab, when a lone man wearing a long coat and a dark hat concealing his face walked towards them. Astrid saw him and realized it was Anthony from the way he walked, and she panicked. She left Jim's side and ran toward Anthony who she caught off guard. "Anthony! Are you hiding from us?"

Anthony seemed startled when he heard his name. He pulled a gun with a silencer out of his overcoat and took aim at Jim.

"Jim! It's Anthony! He has a gun!" she yelled and pushed Anthony's arm into the air as the gun fired. The muffled pings pierced the air as Jim ran toward Anthony throwing him to the concrete. The gun fell to the sidewalk.

Astrid ran after it and picked it up while Jim struggled with Anthony. Some other patrons came out of the Clermont at the same time. The women screamed as their men shoved them back from the entrance. The doorman blew his whistle and yelled, "Police! Police!"

Anthony got loose from Jim's grip and started to run across the street as an Aston-Martin coupe made a fast U-turn in front of the Clermont. You could hear the thud and screaming of the car brakes as it ran Anthony down. The driver hadn't seen him until it was too late. Jim and Astrid ran to the car. Anthony was pinned under the Aston. The driver jumped out. He looked young, in dinner clothes. A woman sat in the passenger seat not moving, in shock. The driver ran to Anthony, who lay in a pool of blood. "I didn't see him. He came out of nowhere," said the driver frantically to Jim .

"He's unconscious, but breathing", said Jim as he stood up from examining Anthony. Astrid came to his side. He looked at her and said, "You saved my life. She looked up at him and nodded.

"You know something, Astrid. I felt a lot safer in Tanzania." Astrid looked at him, and said, "So did I, Jim, so did I."

Seventy Three

O ver a year later a Jeep stopped on the road leading into the Mount *Kilimanjaro* Lodge and Camp. Astrid Dryden stepped from the vehicle as the morning light broke through, casting a brilliant beam and a long shadow over the animal compound. Her hair looked shorter with a little curl and she seemed to have a look of sophistication she hadn't had before.

The animals were awakened by the shrill cry of a male peacock who announced her presence. The orphans came to the fences of their compounds and wire cages to see what stranger was in their midst. When they saw Astrid, they became wild with excitement.

Astrid spotted Ingrid, who jumped up and down screaming with delight. The two lion cubs, who had grown into adults, raced back and forth behind their wire cage bellowing a playful sound. Astrid was thrilled they recognized her. It brought tears to her eyes. I'm home again, she thought. Back where I belong with my orphans.

She ran to the lionesses' cage where Lucy was purring, rubbing herself against the wire screen, her sister doing the same. Astrid put her hand through the wire and scratched her furry back. "You've missed me, Lucy. I missed you too," she said.

She looked at Ingrid who was making such a fuss she had to go and open her cage. The chimp jumped up on her and wrapped her arms around Astrid's neck. She kissed and hugged her making her sneeze. "Ingrid, you got Mama sneezing and my eyes are running. Mama's home, darling face, she's home."

Inside the hotel, guests milled around the lobby. Some went into the dining room where breakfast was being served. Two waiters dressed in *kanzus* and red *fezes* chased after the green monkeys who came every morning to steal edibles from the buffet table. Fruits, rolls, French breads, jams, jellies, cheeses, cereals, scrambled eggs, ham, bangers, bacon and juices were displayed in quanties. The guests stood in line loading their plates, helping themselves to vast amounts of food, amused by the monkeys. The fresh smell of coffee, picked and roasted near Kilimanjaro penetrated the busy atmosphere.

Tour busses and mini-vans lined up outside the lodge waiting to pick up the tourists and take them to view the wild animals or on to a new destination. They seemed to talk to one another in different languages. Another tour bus arrived discharging its passengers.

Anne stood behind the front desk looking flustered, but remained cool, checking out some guests. *Molo* stood near her giving orders to a porter in Swahili. In a high-chair behind her sat a small boy playing with a toy.

A middle-aged Englishman and his wife ran to Anne as they entered the lobby.

"I say, miss. We have a cobra in our tent," said the Englishman, rather coolly. His wife, who seemed panicked, said, "Dear girl, I can't go back there. I just can't. Oh, it was awful, that horrible thing. It stood up and hissed at me."

Anne turned to *Molo*, "Get the mongoose. When you finish with the cobra, check on the animal compound. Some strange noises are coming from there. Must be a wild animal come to visit." Anne turned back to the Englishwoman. "I'm terribly sorry, madam.

Contretemps such as this can arise in the bush. What's your tent number?" The Englishman answered. "Seventeen. How does one get the bugger out of there?"

Anne called after *Molo.* "It's seventeen."

Molo ran off.

The Englishwoman said to a flustered Anne, "I will not stay in that tent one more night. I must have a room in the lodge. This morning a herd of wild buffalos stampeded by our tent. I thought we'd be trampled to death, and now a cobra in my bed. I must say, this trip has exasperated me." The lady looked at her husband and sobbed, "Nigel, I'm getting on a plane tomorrow. I want to get back to my rose garden."

A middle-aged American woman, wearing glasses, dressed in khakis and a droopy cotton hat with two cameras draped around her neck, moved up to get Anne's attention.

"Can I help you?" asked Anne, hoping the woman had no complaint.

"I'd like to tell you how much we've enjoyed staying here. Your guides are just wonderful. They drove us near a lion pride yesterday." She lifted one of the cameras. "And I took so many wonderful pictures. I'm thrilled. I'm having the most wonderful time. It's the best vacation I've ever had."

"Thank you." said Anne, relieved. "It's so kind of you. I do enjoy hearing from my guests. Good or bad." She looked at the English lady and then back at the American. "It makes for better service."

From the highchair the baby started to cry. Anne turned and picked him up. "Josh, you precious sweetheart. Mommy's busy, she'll feed you in a minute."

Seventy Four

*M*olo ran to the animal compound and went directly to the cage where they kept the mongoose.

Astrid saw him coming and disappeared behind a wide-standing acacia tree. *Molo* opened the cage and took out the little mongoose.

As he left, Astrid jumped in front of him and said, "BOO." She startled him he almost dropped the mongoose. "Mama! Mama!"

Astrid hugged him and gave him a kiss. Tears appear in his soft black eyes. "I missed you so much, *Molo*. Almost every day I thought about you, the orphans, and this place. I'm so happy to be back in Tanzania. It's my home, *Molo*. I can't live anywhere else. I tried, but I've been miserable."

"Now happy. Mama home."

"You always knew I'd come back. Didn't you? You knew this place is in my blood." *Molo* nodded.

"Oh, yes, Mama. *Molo* know."

"I haven't changed. I still have a mission to save elephants. I thought about it a lot and about going to jail, and you being flogged for our beliefs."

"Oh, yes Mama, *Molo* never forget."

"Americans have an expression, they say, 'I'm gonna kick ass,' Poachers, beware, Astrid is back. We'll organize and stop the poaching here. I plan on making life so miserable for those bastards, they'll wish they never heard our names. Are you with me?"

Molo looked skeptical. "No want to go back to jail."

"You won't. Charles, my lawyer, warned me to be careful. I could be sent back. I'm on probation. We'll be careful. *Molo*, you'll be our symbol, an African, who's been put in prison and flogged for his beliefs. You can tell other Africans it's wrong to poach. We'll educate these Africans. Let them know they're destroying the future of East Africa. We've got to get them to learn to appreciate the wild animals, and only then, will we be able to save the elephants and rhinos from extinction."

"Who listen? *Molo* simple man. No have education to make talk."

"Speak in *Swahili*, you speak it beautifully. They'll listen." *Molo* thought for a moment and smiled. "If you say, Mama. *Molo* can do."

"Good man," said Astrid, pleased she had made him understand.

The mongoose, *Molo* had been holding tried to get out his hands. It squirmed and tried to bite him.

"What are you doing with the mongoose?"

"Need take to tent to kill cobra."

"Why don't you shoot it?"

"Oh, no Mama. No gun. Missie, she no like gun."

"How do you like Missie? Has she been good to you."

"Oh, yes, Mama. Missie nice lady. Be very busy with baby and run hotel. She tired. Much work now business get big."

"Baby!" Anne has a baby? Who's baby?" It must be Jim's, she thought. "What's the baby's name?"

"She call, Josh."

"Humm, Josh. Will Missie want to see me?"

Molo searched Astrid eyes and said. "*Molo* no say, *Molo* no know."

"Has she ever mentioned me?" *Molo* shook his head.

"Come, I'll help you get rid of that cobra."

Astrid and *Molo* stood outside tent number seventeen. She looked around and saw two rows of new green safari tents that hadn't been there before. African boys dressed in *kansus* and red *fezs* were taking out linens, making up beds and cleaning and sweeping the tents getting them ready for the new guests. She looked at *Molo*. "I see new changes. Anne must be a good businesswoman, it looks to me she's doubled the occupancy."

"Oh yes, Mama. She work hard make place popular," replied *Molo*.

Astrid lifted the canvas flap and peeked in. In the corner of the tent she spotted the cobra curled up. It looked like a six-footer, she guessed. She turned to *Molo*. "Let me have the mongoose." *Molo* handed her the little animal. She pushed it into the tent. The mongoose knew what his mission was and immediately attacked the cobra, which rose to challenge. Astrid was amazed to see how fast the mongoose could avoid the lightning strike of the cobra. She turned to *Molo*. "We'll let them fight it out. That little fellow is fierce." She dropped the flap and they waited outside the tent listening to the fight to the death inside.

Astrid looked up into *Molo*'s expressive face and smiled. "*Molo*, I missed this kind of action so much. You have no idea how bored I've been in America. Much too civilized. They have so many stupid laws. What really shocked me was their pet cemeteries. I saw a granite mausoleum where someone had buried a cat. Americans take their animals too seriously. And their zoos made me cry. I would have done anything to have heard the roar of a lion and trumpeting of an elephant in the bush. I longed to be back here. *Molo*, you have to help me. I want so to come back, but I don't know if Anne will have me."

"Missie need Mama help. Missie work hard. No time off. Go talk to Missie."

"You're sure? She won't ask me to leave? I did take her man."

"Is Mama still with Bwana?"

Astrid shook her head.

"Then, Mama have no worry," said *Molo* to reassure her. "Go to lodge. Much happen there now. Guest check-out, guest check-in. You show Missie how good Mama is. How Mama make everything go good. When Missie see how fast Mama get job done, how could she be mad at Mama?" Astrid smiled and gave Molo a kiss on the cheek. "Molo, you're a genius."

Astrid entered the lobby of the lodge, *Molo* behind her. Anne stood at the desk. A line of tourists stood waited to check in. The baby was crying. Anne gave him a pacifier and then back to the front desk to check in the arrivals, who looked excited about being there, but remained patient. Anne looked flustered. Her long black hair fell in her eyes.

Astrid had never seen her before without makeup and she thought Anne looked older and tired. She straightened up, took a deep breath and went behind the front desk and said, "*Jambo*, Anne, you look like you need help. Take the baby. I'll look after the guests."

Anne looked shocked and stood back when she recognized Astrid. Astrid announced to the line of new arrivals, "Would you have your passports ready. I'll need them to check you in." They opened their bags and packs and took out their passports.

"Which one of you is the tour guide?"

A middle aged American man stepped forward. "I am," he said. "Can I have your manifest? How many are in your group?" asked Astrid.

The tour guide handed Astrid a sheet of paper. "Eighteen," he said. She looked to the group. "Leave your passports with me. There's coffee and food in the dining room. Go in and help yourselves. I'll be in a few minutes to give out your room and tent numbers.

The group looked happy and relieved and left for the dining room. Astrid looked to *Molo* in the background and caught him smiling at her, giving his approval. So far so good, she thought.

Anne stepped up to the desk with the baby in her arms. "When you're through, come to my cabin. It's next door. I believe it was yours. We'll have a little talk," she said giving no sign as to how she felt as she left the lobby.

Seventy Five

Twenty minutes later Astrid walked into Anne's cabin, Josh in her arms. How different it looked now, Astrid thought. Anne had it decorated with great style in an African motif. Zebra skin lamps and coffee tables. A large screen painted with a herd of wildebeest pursued by a pride of lions on the *Serengeti* plains behind a suede skin sofa. Suede covered chairs. Ostrich skin lamp shades, animal horn lamps that stood on a hardwood table. Soft suede curtains hung on the windows.

"I knew you'd be back, darling. This is Josh, my son."

Astrid went to Josh and put her finger out to him. Josh took it and giggled. "He's adorable. How lucky you are to have the baby you always wanted. I'm so happy for you."

"How sweet of you to say so, darling. I'm not a bit surprised to see you here. How's Jim? Did you marry him?"

Astrid shook her head. "No. I lived with him, but we never married. He wanted to but I resisted. I love Tanzania. I couldn't live in America. It's a great country, but I belong here. There's no other place for me."

"Did you ever love him?" asked Anne searching Astrid's eyes.

"No. I don't think I've been in love yet. I've never found that kind of deepness that must be love."

"Where is Mark? Do you hear from him?"

"Mark is still in England, I guess. I don't hear from him. I broke his heart. But what was I to do? I didn't love him."

"What did you do in California? How did you spend your time?"

"I worked for a veterinarian. It made the time go fast. Have you forgiven me for running off with Jim?"

"I have. Remember, I knew Jim first and know what he's like. He was fun and likeable, but we both realized he'd make a terrible husband. I have his baby. I thank him for that. He doesn't know, and we'll keep it that way. Agreed, darling?" Astrid nodded. "Josh is my life. And with the lodge I've never been happier, but it's been a terrible amount of work. I haven't been able to give the animals the attention they should have. Business has been so good the Aga Khan Hotel Group has made me an offer to buy the lodge, but they don't want the animals. I've been contemplating their offer."

"Don't sell, Anne. I still have the money you paid me for the lodge in the bank. I'll give it back to you for a half interest." Astrid could see Anne perk up at what she had said. "We could be a good team. You won't need to work so hard. You can have more time for Josh with me here, and I'll be back with my animals. I'm sure I could get back the film business we had. What do you say?" asked Astrid with a pleading look.

Josh said. "*Jambo* Mama." Anne looked astonished. Josh was smiling and giggling.

"He's never said words before," she said laughing.

"He's telling you to make me your partner," said Astrid.

"I think he is. Well, don't stand there, get back to the lodge. You need to get the menu together for dinner. We're full up."

The End